THE POPE'S BUTCHER

Based on the True Story of a Serial
Killer in the Medieval Vatican

JOSEPH C. GIOCONDA

"Where God builds a Church, the Devil builds a chapel."
Martin Luther, 1640

THE POPE'S BUTCHER

Based on the True Story of a Serial Killer in the Medieval Vatican

This book is a work of historical fiction. Many names, characters, places, and incidents are the product of the author's imagination or are used fictitiously to build a believable historical world. For story purposes, the author altered the timeline of historical events but attempted to stay as close to the truth as possible.

ISBN: 978-1-7372860-0-4 (Paperback)

ISBN: 978-1-7372860-1-1 (Hardcover)

Library of Congress Cataloguing-in-Publication Data

Front cover image by C5 Designs II

Printed by IngramSpark and Amazon

First printed edition June 2021

Published by Newtown IP Holdings LLC
301 South State Street, Suite 102S
Newtown PA 18940

www.ThePopesButcher.com

Contents

Foreword

The *Pope's Butcher* contains descriptions of cruelty and torture, as well as imagery and occult text that many will consider offensive and blasphemous. The author did not include such material gratuitously, but rather to impress upon the reader how heinous these events were.

ACKNOWLEDGEMENTS

I want to thank Professor Christopher S. Mackay, Ph.D. (Classics, Harvard) for his painstaking and helpful translations of newly discovered original source materials from Latin and German.

I also want to thank fellow author Jonathan Putnam for his encouragement and Martin Biro for his assistance with editing and character development.

Finally, I want to thank another fellow author, my wife Alison, for keeping an eye on our children Luke and Morgan while I disappeared for hours and hours each night to complete this book.

BRIXEN

E ager to find a prostitute after a long trip from Rome, Father Heinrich Institoris walked into a beer hall in Brixen called Agnello Macellato—the Slaughtered Lamb. Brixen was only a seven-day ride from Rome in good weather with a convenient stopover in Florence. However, after heavy rains, the town was a mess of mud, and it had taken the priest over two weeks to arrive. Brixen was also the first territory within his jurisdiction where he could enjoy hunting witches.

Fattened cows and bleating pigs vied for street space with villagers. Barefoot peasants hawked fabrics stolen from merchants on their way from Burgundy. Blacksmith apprentices watched their lessons in shacks which gave off black smoke as the clanking of iron against iron could be heard echoing. Streets were nothing more than roughhewn planks thrown down over open sewer ditches stinking of wet dung.

Brixen was in the County of Tyrol well north of Venice, but south of Salzburg. It bore the hallmarks of Bavaria with a slightly milder climate. Villagers looked more Swiss than German, but being at the crossroads of Europe, it was not uncommon for foreign travelers to stop on their way to locations as far as Munich, Milan, or Florence. Nonetheless, Heinrich stood out both for his striking clerical garb and his severe countenance.

Once inside the rowdy beer hall, Heinrich walked directly up to a chubby barmaid with enormous breasts cinched tightly in her blouse, her arms holding a number of dripping steins.

"Would you like some wine, Father? Third one is on the house at the

Slaughtered Lamb. Always is! Spiced and sweetened with odds and ends, perhaps? You won't like our beer though. Tastes like piss, if you ask me."

"I do not wish to partake in these . . . frolics," he replied, teeth clenched. "I am looking for a harlot."

The chesty woman laughed. "What man isn't? Talk to Frau Keffer." While clutching the steins, she tried to point to a seated woman who was cackling at minstrels' bawdy songs. Dressed in baggy garb, they stood beside the tables, regaling the guests with song for a small donation. The lyrics were inside jokes to the townsfolk, who laughed uproariously. Refrains were repeated as a chorus by the inebriated guests.

Heinrich walked straight over to the matron, who looked up at him but continued laughing. She shouted over the din, "Don't look so glum, Father Sourpuss—join us for a drink and a laugh!"

His crystal blue eyes glinted. He never seemed to blink.

"Find me a girl."

"Hah! Men so rarely get right to the point! I can't say I don't find that attractive! Will cost you six gulden."

"You will receive a gold florin and not one more," he said.

She paused, considering the offer, then nodded her acquiescence. The flint-haired priest reached into his black robe and yanked out a leather pouch containing a substantial number of freshly struck gold coins. He plucked one out and handed it to the woman, who inspected it and buried it snugly in her purse.

"I prefer florins anyway, the gulden's gone all to hell." She pointed at a girl on the far side of the room. "Girl's name is Flores. She's seated near the fire. Beautiful, wouldn't you say?"

The priest glanced over at the girl, a painfully thin woman half his height who was sprawled across the gray slate of the hearth. She was covered in sores and bruises, and lesions oozed on her skin.

"Perfect. Direct us to a private chamber."

"She'll bring you up herself." The woman looked him up and down again and then went back to laughing at the minstrels mocking the townsfolk.

Heinrich walked over to the stone hearth. Other young girls lay around. They reeked of perfume.

The waif looked up at him. "I am Flores, the little flower. Shall we go upstairs?"

"Immediately."

"Ooooh, a man eager to be pleased." She took his hand. "Follow me."

Flores was the least desirable prostitute in the hall. But for his purposes, she was perfect.

Drunkards, misfits, and grimy old men huddled around barrelheads in the corners of the room, playing games of chance. Dice was never a fair game here since the poor light in the tavern facilitated trickery by professional cheaters.

The grim priest and prostitute walked up to the second floor and into a room. He closed and barred the door behind them. They could still hear the singing and yelling downstairs as well as the sounds of drunks arguing and roughhousing. Tobacco smoke wafted into the rafters. The room was dimly lit and stank of alcohol, vomit and urine.

"All right then, Father. Out of them saintly robes," she said wistfully. She started to untie her blouse. Her breasts were ample for such a pitiful waif.

"No." He stood at some distance with the closed door behind him. "We are not going to engage in any perverse or illicit pleasures. Do you know who I am?" The priest's icy eyes flickered in the candlelight. He slowly approached her.

"No, sir . . . but please do not hurt me." She re-tied her top and inched away towards the open window.

"I could not possibly do to you the violence you have already done to your immortal soul. You are Christian?" His gaze never left her eyes.

"Yes, Father. Before she died, my mother raised me to follow the Lord Jesus and the Blessed Virgin."

"Wouldn't your own mother want to save your soul from the fires of hell? Would she not want your virtue to shine, rather than for you to die a godless harlot in this pit?"

"My mother never wanted this life for me, Father. But not even God can save me from my sins." The girl sat down on the floor and began to weep into her hands.

"Flores, have you heard of Magdalene?"

The girl looked up and shook her head.

"Well," he explained, "she was a filthy siren just like you. She was almost destroyed for her sins, and she would have rightly deserved it. But Jesus forgave all her sins, as terrible as they were."

She sniffled and wiped her nose, her tears subsiding.

"How did she get forgaved?"

"Well, He absolved her because she changed what she was. But it takes more than that. It takes a *sacrifice*."

"A what?" she asked.

"An angel spoke to me last night about you in a dream. That is why I came here to see you. The angel told me that you need to do something to become a good Christian again and for God to forgive your terrible sins."

"He did?" Flores' eyes widened. "What did the angel say I have to do?"

"The angel told me that you have to hide in an oven."

There was a long pause.

"An angel told you that?" she asked skeptically.

"The angel said that you and I must combat the powers of the Devil here in Brixen. Lucifer himself has taken control of the hearts and minds of many people in this town and God wants to put a stop to his power here. You surely want to combat evil, do you not?"

"How does me climbing into an oven do that?" Years of prostitution had made her defensive, even toward priests.

"The people in this town have lost all their fear of God," he explained. "What you will do is restore their grace, because only you know the villagers' secret sins. Many of the Devil's followers in this town have hurt and abused you for years, have they not?"

"It is true." She began to cry again. "They done terrible things to me and the other girls. You have no idea how awful they have been to us. Even the mayor."

"And I think you know which are the thieves, liars and hypocrites."
She sniffled again. "What does that mean?"

"It means that the same men who pollute you on a Saturday evening here are praying Sunday morning at Mass."

"I know which men are thieves and liars, but . . . I am scared of them."

"If you pretend to be Satan speaking from inside that oven, you can accuse the evil people in this town of their own secret sins. I will take care of the rest."

He knelt beside her and put his hand on her bony shoulder.

"You will be safe; no one will know it is you. Together we can put a stop to their sins and save their souls from hell. They must be led back to the Lord's flock. And if you do that, if you save a single soul in this town from hellfire, then all your sins will be forgiven and forgotten. The angel of the Lord told me that this is your sacrifice."

He stood up, his tone turning from warmly persuasive to cold. "And if you do not do it, you will be discarded by God and burn in hell forever."

She kissed his outstretched hands. "I will do what the angel said. I do want to be God's helper. I don't want to go to hell."

"Excellent. Meet me at the friary tomorrow at daybreak. I will show you the oven. You will see—God will be pleased."

SUMMONED

Sebastian's fingernails imprinted crescent moons on his knuckles. He had remained in the chapel after matin prayers had ended and the other seminarians had gone off to the day's labors and their studies.

The sun's morning rays streamed in through arched windows, each pane telling a Biblical story. Air bubbles hung frozen in the wavy stained glass, gleaming ochre or scarlet. The windows projected a kaleidoscope onto Sebastian's chocolate-brown burlap robes as he kneeled on the hard, cold marble floor. The sweet smell of leftover copal incense wafted throughout the church.

Sebastian Alberti was muscular, broad shouldered with green eyes and chestnut brown hair. Because of his strong build, he did not look like his classmates, who would shortly be ordained priests. And he certainly did not look like a man who would be happy about the lifelong vow of celibacy expected of him.

While he absentmindedly recited the Lord's Prayer, Sebastian's mind wandered. He was again bouncing around on the platform of a dirty oxcart, his mother weeping as he slowly drifted away, bumping over rocks in the road.

In his mind, he was instantly transported to La Spezia, near Riomaggiore where he had been born. He recalled his mother Aradia only vaguely now. A man should be able to clearly evoke his mother's face from memory, he thought as he prayed. He did remember her smile though.

He was only six when she had slipped him onto a caravan, to be sent off to faraway Bretagne to be raised by strangers. After an interminable overland trek of which he could not remember any details, he had been left at the doorstep of Saint Malo Cathedral on a freezing November night. He was found shivering and wet in the morning by Father Francois De La Choüe de La Mettrie, the pastor and a benefactor of the Cathedral.

Francois was a sweet man and would have gladly taken him in as his own son. But the Cathedral already had a chaplain, a curate, a clerk and two pages on its payroll. He also considered celibacy a quaint notion, an ideal more expressed than honored. In fact, all four of the priest's illegitimate sons were living in the parish, three of whom themselves had become priests and a fourth who became a scholar. His mistress lived across the street. So, he had many mouths to feed, not counting his demanding parishioners.

Sea captains from town knew Sebastian was an orphan and so they let him bring some of the leftover catch each day back to the many hungry mouths in his parish. Sebastian stood outside the outer doors after Mass and sold oysters, mussels and an occasional sea bass. Those were somewhat happy memories.

But he gritted his teeth as bitter memories also crept into his wandering thoughts. Father Francois had died of the Black Death, and a large effigy was erected in the Cathedral in his honor. The priest's sons kept on with their mother elsewhere.

The new rector of the Cathedral was not enamored with the idea of a sea orphan perpetually living in the basement of the rectory's Saint Julien wing, selling leftover fish to survive. So, once Sebastian had reached the age of majority, the priest petitioned the Bishop of Rennes to allow him to receive a formal education at a seminary.

This the Bishop was more than happy to recommend, as the boy could be sent off as far away as Rome for the remainder of his years, even if he had no idea if Sebastian would make a good candidate for the priesthood. In fact, he had his doubts, as the boy was rough around the edges and was apparently satisfied sleeping in a basement after working long days on fishing boats.

But Sebastian had surprised everyone by excelling at his classes in Rome. He found that his peers were far less worldly, as most of them had been sent there to study by wealthy parents who were nobility or even royalty. However, his experiences were still limited. When it came to the Church, it was his entire life. He could not remember a time when he did not eat, sleep, or live within Church walls. He just always assumed that he would become a priest.

Now, deep in thought, he didn't notice a shadow that emerged from behind the altar. The silhouette floated past the gilded communion rail, its drawn hood hiding a gaunt, pale face. The phantom slipped a yellowed scroll into Sebastian's hands then quickly turned, vanishing through the heavy wooden chapel doors before Sebastian could even look up.

He rubbed his bleary eyes and reoriented himself. Seeing no one, he stared down at the roll of starchy parchment that had been shoved in his hand. Blood red wax sealed it at the seam, an ornate coat of arms stamped upon it. He cracked the thin wax button in half, unfurling the yellow vellum and reading the Latin quickly and silently under his breath.

He scanned the exquisitely penned calligraphy that inscribed his own name in deep black octopus ink. He had just been served with a formal summons from the Inquisition.

Based on the inscription on the writ, Father Heinrich Institoris had commanded him to appear at a nearby church tomorrow. Notably absent from the inscription was *why* the Grand Inquisitor had ordered him there. He had heard rumors that someone powerful had been probing into his life, asking his teachers and friends peculiar questions. He had also heard that this Inquisitor was a zealot, a skilled interrogator who had risen through the ranks by virtue of his skill as a political operative.

But he also knew that receiving a summons was a dangerous sign. It was rumored that when the Inquisition was seeking its next round of victims, strange men were seen lurking beforehand. It was also whispered that Inquisitors had enjoyed torturing and setting their victims—particularly women and children—on fire.

His stomach knotted. He had questions; he had to discover the truth about who was stalking him—and why. Sebastian rushed out of the chapel and raced out of the church complex, into the bustling streets of Rome.

Even at this early hour, it seemed like the sun shone directly overhead, leaving no shadows on the ground. The smell of the city filled his nose; burning wood fires roasted fish and meat on street corners and vendors barked their offers at traveling pilgrims. Children in torn tunics dueled with pointed sticks, becoming gladiators.

Sebastian climbed up dusty Palatine Hill. One of the seven original hills of Rome, Palatine attracted far fewer pilgrims than the grand Coliseum or Christian churches. It attracted only the studious who desired to see the crumbling vestiges of the pagan Roman Empire.

Once he reached the top of the hill of the ancient city, he called out "Brother?" and searched the surroundings.

"Sebastiano!"

Sebastian saw his favorite professor and mentor digging in the sandy dirt with a trowel. Cracking his back, the squatting plump monk stood up, his robes covered in fine brown silt. He walked over and hugged Sebastian with gusto.

"I may have found remnants of the houses of Livia and Augustus." Fra Giovanni was a tonsured Franciscan monk who had instructed Sebastian on numerous subjects. He had taught him how to sketch Rome's buildings and explained the strange stories behind its archaic pagan monuments.

The school for men studying to enter the priesthood was still being established under the official authority of the Papal States. Consequently, a variety of monks, bishops, and priests from differing religious orders agreed to assist with teaching duties. Dominicans mingled with Franciscans, Benedictines and even Cistercians. Members of each group tried to convince the men to join their own ranks. The rivalries were largely friendly.

"I came to ask your advice," said Sebastian, dusting off his sandals.

"Is that so?" the brother asked, looking intrigued.

Sebastian unfurled the summons and showed it to the monk. His heart palpitated as he looked at it again. Giovanni wiped his hands on his robes and leaned in to scan the ornate Latin calligraphy.

"Heinrich…" he exhaled.

"You know him?"

"Yes." Giovanni turned away. "We used to call him the Peddler, because that is what his family name means, although he despised it. He preferred to be called the Pope's Butcher."

"But what could he want of me?" Sebastian asked.

Fra Giovanni turned back toward him, his face paler. "I do not know, but he repeatedly asked me about you."

Sebastian had hoped to find solace in Giovanni's guidance. Instead, he was only becoming more alarmed by his words.

Giovanni paced over to a petrified log lying on the ground. He sat and opened a flask that, from the way the monk swallowed and grimaced, Sebastian assumed contained more than water.

"Heinrich," the monk said, wiping his mouth with the back of his hand, "was appointed the collector of funds for a crusade against the Turks. His superiors commanded him to explain major financial discrepancies. Pope Sixtus' letter to the Bishop of Augsburg required him to restore money, silver and jewelry that he had stolen from a widow named Stefani, a relative of the Pope himself."

Sebastian was dumbfounded. "And now he is the Grand Inquisitor?"

"Not only," the monk said, shaking his head. "After Sixtus died and the new Pope was elected, Heinrich even received *The Witch Bull*. Do you know what that is?"

"No," Sebastian said.

"It is a document that gives him unchecked power to hunt and kill anyone," answered the monk. "The rumor is that he wrote it out and the Pope signed it, without even reading it. Now Heinrich believes that he has the authority of God Himself.

"He has expressed desire to destroy heresies, but not the traditional ones. He uses methods that the Church deems questionable, to say the least. When he arrives in a Diocese, he is not welcomed, for when leaves, there are far fewer souls left alive," said the monk. "But I still do not know what he wants of you…" He trailed off.

"What must I do?" asked Sebastian, biting his fingernail.

Giovanni looked him in the eye. "Never for a moment forget you are being questioned by a zealot. Inquisitors like him do not perceive the color gray, only black and white. Mostly black, I'm afraid. We cannot begin to understand their true motives. They can take a hundred lives and sleep well after what they would consider nothing more than a hard day's work."

Sebastian had hoped to develop a rational and calm strategy for approaching the Inquisitor. Now, he had no choice but to face his questioning with total ignorance of the reason the man was stalking him. His visit with the monk had served only to make him more nervous.

"Has he asked about anyone else?" asked Sebastian.

"No, I am afraid not. Only you."

"Pray for me," Sebastian requested, his voice cracking.

"I will." Lost in his thoughts, the monk jostled his rosary beads in his sweaty hand as Sebastian retreated down to the hill to an uncertain fate.

PANTHEON

Sebastian could not sleep. He dreaded where he would be in twelve hours. Would the Grand Inquisitor accuse him of an imagined crime and torture him until he confessed? Why would a man of such prominence interrogate a lowly seminarian? There must be a mistake, Sebastian thought, as he flipped from one side to the other on his straw bed. He got up and stared at the summons again, rubbing his bleary eyes. His full name was perfectly inscribed, it could not be a mistake, he thought.

He craved being in his mother Aradia's arms again and nearly cried. He hadn't thought of his mother often, but today, he could not stop thinking about her. He had never found that peace in his heart that she once gave him when she stroked his boyish hair. She was crippled for as long as he could remember her. She said that she had gotten hurt, but she always found the strength to hold him close to her heart. Someday, he dreamed, he would find the will to go back to La Spezia and uncover the truth about what happened when was six. Maybe there was some explanation to why Aradia sent him off.

After she abandoned him, he wanted to dedicate his life to learning and helping others, but he didn't know how. Why would anyone forsake a child, he often wondered? He spent endless hours studying languages, philosophy, theology, and the classics, looking for the answers to life's great questions. Certainly, there must be some purpose to his suffering. He wasn't alone in that regard. Everywhere, he saw widows, orphans and the poor struggling to stay alive. The plagues decimated families and left entire villages empty.

God must have some great purpose to all of life. When he rose in the ranks of the Church to become a prelate, a bishop, or maybe even a cardinal someday, he could find out the truth. Certainly, men with titles have access to the truth. The secrets must be hidden away in sacred books. The Church and its teachings handed down through the centuries from the Saints would give him peace. But tonight, he just wanted to sleep. He missed his mother more now than ever.

The next morning, it did not take long for Sebastian to arrive at the nearby Church of Mary and the Martyrs, where he had been summoned to appear. He knew exactly where it was, since he had often wandered past it after spending his free time reading in Campo di Fiore while crossbow makers and tailors plied their wares nearby.

The Pope had promoted the piazza's recent cleaning and redesign and it was usually bustling with commerce. But when Sebastian arrived at the piazza, he found it empty. He saw only one man.

Standing in the center of the piazza, gripping a faded brown leather breviary and dressed in black and white Dominican garb, was the Grand Inquisitor. His looked Germanic, with a tense, chiseled jawbone, a prominent nose, and thinning gray hair. As Sebastian approached him, he could see that the Inquisitor's eyes were crystal blue, reminding him of wintry ice. The deep crevices in his face made him look much older than he probably was.

He wore the standard black Dominican cloak over a white habit, but unlike the cappas worn by his brethren in the Order, his had a long black hood that hung to his lower back. Sebastian had never seen this hood on clerical vestments before.

Heinrich Institoris the Grand Inquisitor stood tall and erect; a towering man too comfortable with his responsibilities. Sebastian now realized why the piazza was so empty today. Merchants and villagers dare not cross his gaze.

"Inquisitor?" said Sebastian.

"You are late." His intense eyes didn't seem to blink.

Sebastian knew that he was early but apologized anyway with a lie.

"I hope I have not detained you. I am honored to be summoned by you," he said with a lie. He delivered a slight bow of his head, but not before he perceived how the Inquisitor's gaze felt like it was reaching through his ribcage and feeling around for his heart.

"You did well on your examinations," said the Inquisitor, turning to walk away. "You have already taken five passes and have attained notable distinctions." He strolled across the cobblestones. His tall frame marched more than walked, with an awkward stride that left Sebastian scurrying after him.

"Do you know why I commanded you to appear?" the Inquisitor asked. Sebastian was now sure that this was a man who relished power and status, even if his superiority was only the luxury of knowing particular facts that others did not.

"No," he replied.

The Inquisitor continued walking with his hands behind his back, still clutching his leather breviary behind himself. "I have spoken at great length to your instructors. Your final examinations in theology and the classics were superb. Fra Giovanni speaks highly of you."

"I enjoy learning from him," Sebastian replied.

Heinrich smirked. "He was once a tough and wise Dominican before he succumbed to frailty and joined the fat Franciscans. Now he placates the Medici and tutors their children like a dutiful monk. Yet, he extolled you with praise he reserves for the rich contessas he courts as lovers. I know his praise did not spring from his usual greed or lust, so I tended to give it more weight."

Sebastian was not sure if this was an attempt at wry humor, or if the priest meant the insults he was hurling. That Giovanni had spoken highly of him made him feel a deep sense of gratitude and even more respect for his friend and mentor. In contrast, he was rankled by the indignities being uttered in his presence but thought it wise to ignore them.

Institoris abruptly changed the subject anyway. "I have been working on a project, and it must be consummated by exactly this time next year. In due time, Professor Sprenger will be involved in the editing process. Do you know him?" He halted and glared at Sebastian again.

Sebastian shook his head.

"Well, do not dare let him know of your ignorance!" he scoffed in feigned indignation. "Sprenger is now the Dean at the University in Cologne. More importantly, he was appointed as the Inquisitor Extraordinary for Mainz, Trèves and Cologne. His activities in this post demand constant teaching and travelling through that very extensive district. His contribution will be limited to reviewing the entire project later. His name will add tremendous credence to this endeavor."

The two men walked through the empty square past several pilgrims scampering away from them. To facilitate the flow of pilgrims between the two sides of the Tiber River in the recent Jubilee, Pope Sixtus had built a new bridge on the ruins of the Ponte Sisto. The renovation had increased the piazza's significance.

Quaint taverns that fed weary travelers and faithful pilgrims had popped up around the church like mushrooms after a rainstorm. But when proprietors saw the Inquisitor, they shuttered their establishments hurriedly. Sebastian heard muted conversations inside the buildings, the inhabitants nervously discussing the unwelcome visitors to their piazza.

They arrived at the entrance of the church and stopped. The round building had always intrigued Sebastian. It was a remarkable ancient Roman structure which had somehow survived over a dozen centuries intact. It had a massive portico of three ranks of granite Corinthian columns under a pediment opening into the rotunda, above it a coffered concrete dome.

The most notable aspect of the dome was a round central hole called the Great Eye, open to the sky above. On stormy days, rainwater would run down a large grate in the center of the marble floor into the sewers underneath the city. Niches filled with alabaster statues of saints and martyrs were carved into the walls at the rear of the portico. The hefty bronze doors to the cella, formerly plated with gold, remained, but the looted gold had long since vanished. The pediment was once decorated with a sculpture in bronze showing the Roman epic, *Battle of the Titans*. Now only holes could be seen where the clamps had held the sculpture in place.

The interior of the edifice was illuminated by sparse torches and tapers. Even at midday, only oblique rays of sunlight shone in from the Great Eye in the dome. The building was suddenly silent, devoid of pilgrims who scurried out of the doors when they saw the Inquisitor.

"You are wondering what this has to do with you, and why I ordered you to meet me in this musty old shrine," said Institoris, gliding more than walking into the church. He dipped two fingers into a small receptacle filled with holy water and made the sign of the cross on his head, chest and shoulders while muttering a prayer in a strange language with which Sebastian was unfamiliar. It certainly was not Latin but did not sound like any language Sebastian had ever heard.

"I confess that I have been curious," said Sebastian. He also crossed himself with the holy water and entered the church. *"In nomine Patri, et Filio et Spiritu Sancti,"* he whispered, following the Inquisitor more closely.

"Tell me what you know about this place," demanded the Inquisitor.

"Well, an ancient temple once stood here, but it was later consecrated."

"What do the Romans call it?"

"Rotunda, because its height and diameter are equal. However, to this day, they still refer to it as the Pantheon."

"Why?" the Inquisitor asked, clearly knowing the answer.

"It was originally built as a temple to the deities of the seven planets in the state religion."

Institoris now stood in the center of the church and looked up at the sky through the eye in the Great Dome above. "What we have done here is magnificent. We have taken the heathen world and recreated it. Do you see that image over there?" He pointed to an oil painting of the Archangel Gabriel speaking to the Virgin Mary, who was kneeling with head bowed.

"Yes, *Annunciazione* by Melozzo da Forlì," replied Sebastian.

The Inquisitor paused. "Giovanni was right to laud you," he said with the first slight hint of praise, before continuing. "Once, these walls were adorned with graven images of the heathen gods, and the filthy Caesars were honored here as if they were saints. Now, the Church announces the Gospel in the same place where women sacrificed their children to idols. Is that not glorious?"

"Yes, Father, it is." He had no idea what the Inquisitor was talking about.

"It is our duty as disciples of the Lord to promote faith throughout the world, especially to pagans—and *women*. You see, all wickedness is but little to the wickedness of a woman. A woman is a wheedling and secret enemy—did you know that?"

Sebastian was confused by the bizarre turn in the conversation.

"Which brings us to my project, which, please God, will become *our* project," stressed the Inquisitor, still standing directly beneath the ocular opening in the ceiling and staring up at the clear blue sky visible through it.

He lowered his gaze dramatically toward Sebastian and whispered, "There are heresies afoot. The Cathars and Albigensians present serious challenges to my authority. Despite what you hear, the Knights Templar remain a threat. I, though unworthy, have been designated to eradicate heresy in Tyrol, Salzburg, Bohemia and Moravia." He did not sound for a moment like he believed himself to be unworthy of his titles.

He walked towards the sanctuary, continuing his sermon. "Heresy is evil fomented by a huge revolutionary body, exploiting its forces through many channels, and having as its sole aim chaos and corruption in the Holy Church. However, a very old heresy is regaining intensity and spreading. Worship of the Great Beast is spreading throughout Christendom—"

"The Devil?" interrupted Sebastian, puzzled.

The Inquisitor ignored the interruption and continued his soliloquy. "In France, Gilles de Rais was recently tried on charges of sorcery and was executed. He confessed to kidnapping, torturing, and murdering over two hundred children. Sometimes they were decapitated and dismembered, or their necks were broken. The children's remains were found heaped in rotting piles throughout his chateau. He practiced the evocation of devils and concluded pacts with them. The children were offerings to the demons, do you see?" He seemed bemused by the abject horrors he was recounting.

"In Scotland, the Earl of Mar was convicted of treason and charged with employing witchcraft against the king. He was put to death by having his artery opened. In other principalities as well, there are allegations, often involving charges of high treason. As Inquisitors, we must investigate the Pope's concerns."

Institoris finally genuflected toward the altar, bending his right knee to the marble floor. He then sat down in a wooden pew near the front row. Sebastian sat next to him, listening intently.

"The best research we have on hand is from Johannes Nider, but unfortunately it is outdated. There is growing concern among certain church members over the increasing power of the Devil to endanger Christian society. We want to understand the magnitude and nature of these unholy practices. For instance, what do these witches believe? What do they do in their ungodly rituals? The sole purpose of this project is to report on the extent of the problem to the Pope."

Still seated, he turned and faced Sebastian, who continued to stare at the ornate crucifix hanging above the altar, mostly to avoid looking directly into his superior's eyes.

"Our objective as Inquisitors is to *enquire*. This is a preliminary investigation. And that is what your role will be. You would be . . . a field researcher. You would be given my complete authority to travel and would find safety and rest at monasteries, abbeys and manors that remain faithful to the Pope and my Inquisition."

"And what of arms?" asked Sebastian. "Would I have a guard? Pardon my frankness, but the Church's Holy Inquisition is not welcome everywhere."

"You would be armed...by your intellect. But your mission will be peaceful. You are gathering facts. There are several dangerous books that have been lost to us. We are seeking to return them to our safe care in Rome. We suspect that witches have catalogued their wicked practices into these hazardous books. They should be secure in our care, here.

"If you return these to us, we will also gain insight into the nature of the dark heresies waging war upon our Holy Mother the Church. Upon your return, which would be no more than twelve months from now, you would present your research materials and conclusions in the form of a written journal. This text would incorporate all your findings. Professor Sprenger and I will review and edit it, presenting the final version to the faculty of our universities for academic review and approval. Do not mislead yourself, young man. This is a tremendous opportunity. The Pope himself will review and approve the final product."

The Inquisitor's last sentence hung in the air. Upon hearing him describe the mission, it did seem like it could be the opportunity of a lifetime. But the chance that Sebastian's work could end up before the Pope ended any of his uncertainty.

"With all respect, Inquisitor, you are requiring me to set all my studies aside for over a year, risking my life to research a dangerous topic in the remotest parts of the world. I am a poor orphan of the Black Death and I owe everything I have to the Church, but this mission you are requesting that I undertake is serious. I must have an assurance that my sacrifices and labors will be rewarded."

Heinrich stood up abruptly and responded in German. "You dare to try and *negotiate*? Archbishops have been burned at the stake for uttering less."

Sebastian froze, his heart skipping a beat.

However, the Inquisitor slowly sat back down.

"A seminarian posing a question to the Grand Inquisitor takes *bravado*. Giovanni spoke the truth about you. It is actually one of the reasons I chose you."

Sebastian exhaled. Blood returned to his ashen face.

"But to answer your impetuous question, I will explain why you are perfect for this task, *Sebastiano*." The Inquisitor then began to speak in numerous languages.

"Your language skills are exceptional," he began in French. "Consequently, you will have no problem traveling throughout Christendom," he continued in German. "Your intellectual reputation has preceded you," he pronounced in the King's English. "Out of all the scholars we investigated, you were the only man who possessed both the sharp intellect and strength of character needed for this noble task," he concluded in Gaelic.

Sebastian had learned Gaelic while living in Bretagne, an area in France known for a culture heavily influenced by Hibernia. The Breton fishermen he knew had taught him various colorful Gaelic phrases about women, most of which could not be repeated in a church.

However, while he had excelled in formal language examinations of Latin and Greek in seminary, he had never had his abilities in Latin, German, French, English and Gaelic tested in such rapid sequence. His head was spinning.

"I personally assure you that success in this important task will guarantee you a very prestigious post after your graduation. And I am not asking. I am commanding."

The Inquisitor suddenly put his arm on Sebastian's shoulder. "When I was a young man, I was appointed to the position of Prior of the Dominican House in my native town, Schlestatt. It was from this post that I continued my ascent to my current position. You too can follow such a path. Perhaps someday you can even return to your hometown as a dignified man. I would imagine that you want to be remembered as a noble emissary of the Church rather than as a poor boy, abandoned by his heartless parents and left to die."

Sebastian's face flushed, but he remained composed. His arm still on Sebastian's shoulder, the Inquisitor skillfully noted his involuntary reaction to the insult.

"Perhaps most importantly," he concluded, "you will be helping those who are lost. As a result of your successful efforts, we will save poor souls from the fires of hell. You know that that is our highest calling as shepherds of Our Lord's wayward flock."

Sebastian looked the Inquisitor squarely in the eye for the first time. "When can I depart?"

DEPARTING

"Y"ou are leaving?" asked Amancio, his mouth falling open. Amancio was younger than Sebastian by two years, shorter and olive-skinned.

The school that they attended was in Vatican City next to the original Saint Peter's Basilica, west of the Tiber River. There had been some discussion about razing the old church and rebuilding it, as it had fallen into disrepair. Sebastian had heard rumors that brilliant men had begun discussing a design, but when the previous Pope died, the plans had been shelved.

"Yes, I am going to Hibernia," said Sebastian. The students stood in his cell, in the dormitory attached to their seminary. Sebastian stood next to his straw bed, packing his meager belongings into a leather satchel he had fashioned out of thick, tanned horse leather purchased in the nearby Trastevere neighborhood.

"You should use one of my brother's ships!" offered Amancio.

Amancio had been a reliable friend to Sebastian ever since both men had begun studying for the priesthood four years earlier. His father was a well-established merchant in Spain who owned a fleet of medium-sized ships that were used for commercial hauling and other commodity trading across the Mediterranean. Amancio had agreed to join the Franciscan friars only under protest, as his father had insisted that at least one boy in the family must become a priest for good luck.

Because he was the youngest, he became the family's only choice, as his brothers became sea captains early in life. He and Sebastian had developed a keen friendship, despite their great differences in upbringing.

Sebastian smiled as he continued packing. "I am sure the mercenaries that the Inquisition pays will keep me well-fed and warm on their ships."

"Fine, but my brother would do much more than that. He would bring you to the finest taverns and introduce you to the finest women, and he has the best wine on board. Everyone says so."

"I do not need that type of service, but thank you." They both laughed.

"Do you remember telling me about Jeanette?"

"Of course," said Sebastian, stopping to stare out the window for a moment. "Do I remember? I never forget her."

"Do you think you will take the vows when you return?"

"Poverty will not be much of a challenge," chuckled Sebastian, pointing at his meager belongings.

Amancio laughed. "True enough, but I meant the other one."

"Celibacy?"

"Is there anything harder than that?" asked Amancio.

"I do not think so, honestly," said Sebastian. "Not having a family of my own makes my heart ache. But as a priest, I can help more people."

"Trust me," Amancio said. "My brother will take good care of you. He will keep you safe and warm on the *Perestrella*. She is a strong carrack that laughs at rough seas, and she traveled with Colombo. His convoy was attacked by the French and they took refuge in Lagos with the other Genoese. You are going to need a good ship and a captain like Valentino to get you across the channels. They can be rough in the winter, trust me. If I were not to be a priest myself, that is how I would earn my living," he said with a hint of remorse.

There was a pounding on the door to Sebastian's cell, and the heavy wooden door swung open to reveal Fra Giovanni standing in the doorway.

"You were not at Vespers. Well, what did Heinrich want with you?" Giovanni asked, in equal measure puzzled and annoyed.

Amancio grimaced at the monk's entry and quickly excused himself from the room.

"I am sorry," replied Sebastian. "When I returned, I had so many matters to resolve, to prepare for my departure," he apologized while folding a brown tunic and pressing it deep into the satchel.

The monk closed the door behind him. The cell had only a small window, a single shelf which held a standing metal crucifix, and a straw mat. Sebastian's few garments were piled neatly on the mat. A book with blank parchment pages was resting on top of the satchel.

"I can see that you are still in one piece, which is a good sign, but you are apparently leaving, which is not so good."

"I was expecting to be jailed, or worse... instead, the Inquisitor assigned me a task," Sebastian enthused.

"A task?" The monk looked incredulous.

"Research," replied Sebastian.

"You are a stone's throw from the greatest collection of books and art since the Library of Alexandria, and you are packing your belongings to travel?"

"Travel so that I may research heresy," replied Sebastian. "The Inquisition has directed me to research satanic practices, but not in a library. They have ordered me to discover true facts in the countryside." Sebastian went back to packing. "He informed me that it was a preliminary investigation into the nature of the problem."

"That assumes there is a problem," the monk said.

"There is a growing dread of the power of witches in our midst. . . and he said that the Pope himself may review my work."

"Evil is everywhere, Sebastian, in the hearts of men. Did he tell you what the exact purpose of this research is?" asked Giovanni.

"No, he just said that I must inquire."

"Do you know what Inquisitors do?" asked the monk.

"They ask questions?" Sebastian joked.

"They *inquire* into who they are going to massacre. And Institoris is known for love of women, but not in the normal way..."

Sebastian now felt guilty for his flippant remark.

"Did he offer you any more specific details about what or who he wants to research?" asked Giovanni.

"I was ordered to seek out certain treacherous books and collect information about the unholy practices of witches, so that the Holy Father can ferret out what evils they are plotting against the Church."

"Books? Witches?" The monk sounded even more aghast. "So you have already been assigned?"

"I am still in one piece, as you said."

"Yes, but for how long? And where are you going exactly?" asked the monk.

"Barcelona in Aragon. He has suggested several locations. I have heard that there are many witches in Hibernia. Is that true?"

Giovanni sat down on the harsh straw bed. "It would not surprise me if the practices of some pagans are tolerated there. But if you leave now, you will be gone for ages. You will not graduate or be ordained! Hibernia is months away, especially at this time of year."

"I expect to be gone for at least a year. Father Institoris and Professor Sprenger need the manuscript draft by then."

"Sprenger is involved?"

"He will be editing it," said Sebastian. "Do you know him?"

"Sharp as a tack, and a good Dean in Cologne. But Institoris takes advantage of his intellect. What of your studies toward ordination?" asked Giovanni, interrupting himself. "You have spent years; your success is on the horizon. The Franciscans are terribly excited to have you join the order."

"I must postpone my graduation until after I return."

"Sebastian, I will speak to Heinrich and disabuse him of this notion of sending you out into the wild. Complete your coursework, graduate on time, and we can even work on excavating a Roman building together. That is the wiser course." The monk stood up to leave, believing the matter settled.

Sebastian placed his hand on the monk's shoulder. "Thank you, Brother. It means a great deal that you would do that for me. But this is a mission that I welcome."

"Did he entice you with promises of a prestigious post when you return… *if* you return?" Giovanni asked.

Sebastian pulled back his arm.

"There is an old saying: 'Ambition is the ecclesiastical lust,' and it is true for rising stars as well as old men," said Giovanni.

"The Inquisitor said that out of all the students, I am the best suited, and I believe him," said Sebastian indignantly.

"Just because the Church raised you, that doesn't mean you owe it your whole life."

Sebastian became angry. "I do owe the Church. The plague should have killed me. I could have died starving on the street."

"You only owe it to God to be happy. Only when a man is truly happy is God happy with him," said Giovanni.

"It will make God happy for me to do my duty," said Sebastian. "I must complete packing now. I leave tomorrow, after matin prayers."

"Sebastian, look at me. I have always seen you as a son. I want nothing more than for you to be safe. So, please, in God's holy name, stay safe. And *when* you return safely, I will be waiting for you."

"Thank you. But I will be fine. I now have the Inquisition protecting me."

GOLSER

"You have not been diligent, Georg. Satan's power has gained a foothold in your city. There are many bitter, betrayed women here." Heinrich Institoris spoke condescendingly to Georg Golser, the Bishop of Brixen, as the two clerics ambled through the warm streets of Innsbruck in mid-July.

Sandwiched between alpine mountain ranges, Innsbruck was a prosperous, if not unspectacular, south Austrian city. It was notable primarily for its proximity to other places that most travelers would rather be during the summertime.

In July, when the Inquisitor arrived, the town center was relatively quiet amid unusually hot weather. Unlike most European cities, Innsbruck attracted more travelers during the winter, as the peaks of the nearby alps presented a strikingly beautiful location for wealthy nobles to bring their families for Christmastime. The city had also developed diverse cuisine, as migrants settled here from as far south as Palermo and as far north as Munich.

But the Inquisitor had not come here this summer for the city's food or trifles. Rather, he was here to permanently remedy their witch problem. Tyrol was a hotbed of the occult, he had heard, and like Brixen, Innsbruck was squarely under his jurisdiction. So, when he first met with Bishop Georg Golser to present him with the authority of his *Witch Bull* that the Pope had issued, he was more authoritative than usual.

"Where there are many women, there are many witches," declared the Inquisitor. "Circulate written notices throughout your Diocese," he instructed, as the two men walked along the cobblestoned streets together. "The Pope instructed me to tell you that you must also dispatch a letter to all ecclesiastical personnel, commanding them to assist me. Offer a plenary indulgence of forty days to anyone who will step forward to denounce and accuse witches."

The Bishop walked alongside him and continued to listen. Golser was tall and heavily built with fair skin, a long face with a softly shaped jaw and a hooked nose. His blue eyes were angular and thoughtful and his jet-black hair was short and straight.

Instead of the traditional Bishop's garments, when he was walking around in public he dressed like an ordinary priest, except he wore a gold cross on a long chain. All around the men was the squeal of cart-wheels, ringing of church bells, and the barking of dogs.

"Also," Institoris continued, "I published advertisements, and prominently positioned announcements on the walls of your parish churches, and in the town hall. I ordered anyone with any knowledge of witchcraft whatsoever to promptly come forward and testify under penalty."

He gestured toward billboards in different languages that had been plastered all over nearby stone edifices. They were engraved in large typeface and townspeople were gathered around them, asking one other what they meant.

"You should not have done such a thing without my approval," Golser replied, perturbed by Heinrich's impetuousness.

Institoris ignored his criticism and continued. "I have begun a vigorous schedule of preaching to instruct the faithful of the telltale signs that their family members are witches. I have only been in Innsbruck for a few weeks, and I indicted over fifty witches so far."

The Bishop scoffed. "These people cannot read or write. They cannot tell the difference between a sickly dog and a cursed pig. You will only create disturbances."

Stopping in front of one of the announcements posted on a wall, Institoris asked him bluntly, "Shall I tell the new Pope that you are not cooperating with my Inquisition?"

Georg Golser was not easily threatened. He had been appointed Bishop three years earlier after a bruising political battle. The son of a farmer from Werfen, he was enrolled at the University of Vienna and acquired the academic degree of Doctor of Canon Law. Based on his sophistication and achievements both academical and political, he was unanimously elected to the bishopric according to an old tradition. But there was a serious dispute over his legitimacy and the previous Pope did not want to recognize his authority. Both the Pope and the Emperor had wanted to push through their own candidates and the wrangling was only settled years later because of the successive renunciation of all his opponents. Golser was finally confirmed by Pope Sixtus in 1471. He had become affected but savvier as a result.

"Of course I am cooperating with the Inquisition, he said. "But these announcements will only inflame the town. Many will come forward with vendettas and accuse their enemies without any basis. Also, the blind, the lame, the withered, those with infirmities will swear that their maladies were caused by witches—"

"And how do you know that is not the case?" Institoris interrupted. I have seen a dozen lepers wandering the streets today. That is not unusual when witches are about."

"I do not know," he said emphatically. "But it stands to reason that illness occurs with or without witches. Are you suggesting the Black Death came from witches?"

"Your own failure is not a unique situation," said Institoris, ignoring the question. "In Brescia, their problem was worse, and I was able to stamp it out entirely. No less than six thousand utterly destroyed," Institoris bragged. "I personally burned over two hundred. The flames lit the sky, could be seen from twenty miles away. It was glorious."

The Bishop was disgusted, but recognized the limits of his power, at least right now. "You can tell the Pope that I will give you my full episcopal jurisdiction to conduct necessary trials in my name," said Golser. "But you need to install proper *procedures*. You cannot come here and execute faithful citizens based on rumor, legends, accusations, and snippets. That is not evidence, that is nonsense, despite whatever horrors you committed in Brescia. I suspect that out of the fifty here that you have already indicted, not more than one or two *might* be worthy of a proper trial. I even have my doubts about that."

"Have you spoken with them? An especially large number of the vicious women here are suspected of love magic," said Institoris.

The Bishop stifled a laugh. "Love magic? Their poor husbands."

Institoris did not find it amusing. "You will see yourself. As these trials go forward, you will see."

"Yes, well, in any event, you cannot begin this charade before October. It will take that long to assemble the witnesses, pastors, notaries, and commissioners to conduct proper proceedings. Use the time wisely between now and then and please reconsider. We cannot have errors, dissension or scandal in my beautiful city."

"It is not your city, Georg. This is not your playground," said the Inquisitor.

"Nor is it yours, Heinrich. Mind yourself." The Bishop said sternly as the two men arrived at the door to the Bishop's Chancery. He turned his back on Institoris and entered the building, closing the door behind him abruptly.

Just as he did so, a well-dressed middle-aged woman walked past and spit upon the hem of Institoris's black and white robes. She had a very aggressive look and triangular face with a sharp jaw, a pointed nose, full lips, and her dark green eyes were narrow. Her brown hair was short, uncommon for a woman of her age.

"Shame on you, you bad monk, may the falling evil take you," the woman said angrily, wiping spittle from her lips.

Institoris was astonished. He had not encountered such hubris from a layperson in ages, much less a woman with apparent financial means. This woman's behavior certainly proved the rumors true. The wickedness in this city knew no limits. He must learn more about her.

Institoris called over a young page who was sweeping the steps of the Chancery.

"Come here, I say."

The page shuffled over dutifully. "Yes, Father?"

Institoris craned over and asked him, "Who is that woman, who just passed?"

"Helena Scheuberin, Father."

"I see. And who is her husband?"

The page whispered into the priest's ear, "She has a rich burgher, Father, but she poison'd a great Knight called Jörg Speiss. *Mala fama*, me mother told me about'er. Speiss was sick they say, and his doctor told him not to keep seein'her. The Knight died in her bed, they say, because of 'er evil spells."

Institoris stood back up. "Thank you, my son," he said, giving the boy a small silver coin out of his pouch, as a token of appreciation. "If you can find out more about the Scheuberins, I will be at the friary. Please find me."

"Yes, Father!" said the page, enthusiastically holding the bent coin up to the sunlight to watch it glint. He ran off to show his friends his newfound treasure.

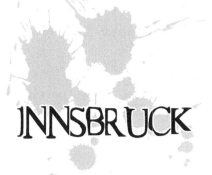

INNSBRUCK

Two months passed, and Heinrich had indeed spent his time wisely in Innsbruck—at least he thought so. He invested a significant amount of time and treasure threatening as well as paying townspeople to collect and report the most valuable rumors and innuendoes they could muster. He always believed that there was much more truth in rumor than in hard evidence. Much more. So, he spent week after week walking around Innsbruck, preaching, collecting evidence, and harassing unwilling witnesses.

On the first brisk Sunday in early October, he was delivering a loud sermon on a tree stump outside the Cathedral about the mortal dangers of witchcraft and its many female minions. Suddenly, Helena appeared and disrupted his sermon by loudly proclaiming that the Inquisitor was in league with the Devil himself.

"He says we are witches, but why is he so proud, I say? Why is he telling us so much about these here Black Arts? And how does he know so much about them? Maybe he is a sorcerer himself, I say! Let us all question *him*!" yelled Helena at the top of her lungs, her shrill voice echoing in the square outside the Cathedral. "These sermons are rubbish. Just like this evil monk. Off with him, I say! I have found the Devil, and he is the Inquisitor!"

"What else say you, Helena—are you guilty of diverse acts of witchcraft and heresy, of which you are suspected, or not?" asked Institoris.

The crowd murmured. As she laughed and strolled away, the Inquisitor handed a scroll to a hooded monk, who scurried through the crowd after her. The rolled scroll was thrust into her hand.

"What is this?" she exclaimed. "You are serving *me* with a summons?! Now that is a rich one!"

She gleefully tore up the summons into several fragments and dropped them onto the ground, where a light breeze blew them across the cobblestones.

"Arrest her!" shouted an armed Knight, who had accompanied the Inquisitor. Three more armed knights took hold of Helena's arms behind her back.

"Don't you dare touch me, grimy bastards!" she screamed. "Do you know who I am?"

The Inquisitor said loudly, "Helena Scheuberin, I know exactly what you are. I hereby accuse you of the heresy of witchcraft by Order of His Eminence Bishop Georg Golser. You are to be tried before God within the fortnight. May God have mercy on your soul," he said, dramatically making the sign of the cross over her and gesturing to the knights, who dragged her, flailing, into an armory to be held until they could take her to the dungeons underneath the Chancery.

When her public trial began on Saturday, October 29 at 9 a.m. sharp, Heinrich Institoris stood at a lectern that was somewhat shorter and less impressive than he preferred. At a nearby table sat Bishop Golser. Seated next to the Bishop was Master Christianus Turner, licentiate in decretals and Commissary General, who was delegated by the Bishop to deal with spiritual matters, as well as Master Paulus Wann and Sigismundus Samer, two defense lawyers.

The Inquisitor was unhappy with this arrangement of lawyers and furniture. It placed him on eye level with witnesses and defense counsel. He preferred to be in an exalted position to match the nature of his role in these proceedings. He began anyway.

"I hereby call to testify one Ingfried Beutelg. Announce your presence and title."

"I am she. I am legally married to one of the household of the Archduke." The woman was tall and plump with reddened skin.

"And what is your true testimony under oath in the presence of God and His Saints?" asked Institoris.

Ingfriend stood in the center of the room and explained. "Well, in my maidenhood, I had been in the service of one of Innsbruck's citizens, whose wife became afflicted with grievous pains in the head. I was working in her home, and a woman came there who said she could cure her.

"This woman began strange incantations and rites which she said would assuage my mistress' pains. And I carefully watched what she did and saw that she poured water into a vase. But the pains in my mistress' head were not assuaged by these means.

"I addressed this evil witch with indignation. I said to her: 'I do not know what you are doing, but whatever it is, it is witchcraft, and you are doing it for your own profit!'"

"Then the witch at once replied: 'You will know in three days whether I am a witch or not.' And so, it proved; for on the third day when I sat down and took up a spindle, I suddenly felt a terrible pain in my own body. First it was inside me, so that it seemed that there was no part of my body in which I did not feel horrible shooting pains; then it seemed to me just as if burning coals were being continually heaped upon my head; third, from the crown of my head to the soles of my feet there was no place large enough for a pinprick that was not covered with a rash of white pustules; and so, I remained in these pains, crying out and wishing only for death, until the fourth day. At last, my mistress' husband told me to go to a certain tavern; and with great difficulty I went, whilst he walked before, until we were in front of the tavern. 'See!' he said to me; 'there is a loaf of rye bread over the tavern door.' 'I see,' said I.

"Then he said: 'Take it down, if you possibly can, for it may do you good.' And I, holding on to the door with one hand as much as I could, got hold of the loaf with the other. 'Open it' said my master, 'and look carefully at what is inside.' Then, when I had broken open the loaf, I found many things inside it, especially some white grains very like the pustules on my body; and I saw also some seeds and herbs such as I could not eat or even look at, with the bones of serpents and other animals. In my astonishment I asked my master what was to be done, and he told me to throw it all into the fire. I did so; and behold! Suddenly, not in an hour or even a few minutes, but when that matter was thrown into the fire, I regained all my former health."

Bishop Golser chuckled and whispered to the Commissary General seated next to him. "The pox. She blames her pox on a rotten rye." The General stifled a laugh.

Institoris declared: "Madam Beutelg, I find your testimony true and compelling. I ask you now, in the eyes of God and His Holy Church, who cast these evil spells upon you?"

"I am afraid to speak her name, Father, as she is a witch who will use black magic on me and my household the way she used it on the Knight," said Ingfried.

"I order you to declare her name, so that her beguiling spells may be broken at once," ordered the Inquisitor.

"Her Christian name is Helena. Helena Scheuberin," she said. The visitors in the courtroom gasped.

Just as Helena's name was pronounced, two knights dragged her into the center of the courtroom. She was barely recognizable in a torn tunic.

Seated at counsel's table, the defendant's lawyer raised a protest to the Commissary General.

"I must interpose an objection," he said. "The sworn witness has declared that Ms. Scheuberin is guilty of witchcraft. But the second part of the witness' story does not compel the first. The witness first swore that Scheuberin did nothing more than pour some water into a vase. Then, the witness swore that within the week, she herself grew ill. Finally, she alleged that she found a loaf of bread over some unnamed tavern. Even assuming, *arguendo*, that this loaf played some part in the witness' illness, the witness has not borne true testimony accusing Helena Scheuberin of anything apart from watering some flowers. I hereby move to dismiss the complaint against her with prejudice."

"Your point is well-taken," said the Commissary General. "I have carefully examined the Articles that you professed are the formal accusations against these defendants. They are insufficient as a matter of law. Inquisitor, I trust that you have more compelling evidence against the defendant than this…story," he scoffed.

The Inquisitor was not prepared for this obstruction of his authority and sneered. "Fine, we shall continue this trial until October 31."

On Tuesday morning of All Hallow's Eve, the trial resumed.

"I hereby call as sworn witnesses Cynebald Braddocke and Eysteinn Durrg," declared the Inquisitor.

Two scruffy vagrants emerged from the shadows in the rear of the room. They reeked of liquor, even though it was only 9 a.m.

"Announce your presence and title," demanded the Inquisitor.

"Uh, I am Cynebald," said the taller one with red hair, removing his cap. "No titles here," he said.

"And I am known as Durgg," said the shorter, stout one with black hair. "I never had a title either, I suppose."

"What say you about this Defendant under oath?"

Cynebald began. "Helena is a good one," he smirked. "When we drink with her, we found that she is a good one. What more you need me to say?"

Durgg snickered.

"What say you about her morals and good character?" demanded the Inquisitor.

"She's a character for sure," laughed Durgg with a sly smile. Several townspeople in the rear of the Church laughed loudly.

"Be specific in your testimony," demanded Institoris forcefully.

Cynebald cleared his throat and stood more erect. "Yes, well, she lusted after me, Your Honors. She's had many lovers, so I didn't partake in her, me good Fathers. I am a married man, after all. She cursed me wife so I got no love for her anymore! Plus, she killed Speiss in bed, I heard!"

"Sworn witnesses Cynebald and Durgg. Is it not true that a man's member can be seen as separated from his body?"

The men grew silent. They had no idea what he was talking about.

"Answer me," the Inquisitor demanded.

The two men looked at each other, thoroughly confused.

"Uh, I don't know, Father," said Durgg, shrugging. "Maybe sometimes?"

"Helena Scheuberin," the Inquisitor turned to the defendant, changing the subject entirely. "Do you fornicate with men aside from your husband?"

"I object!" shouted Samer the defense lawyer, standing up excitedly.

"I withdraw the question," said the Inquisitor.

"Can your husband maintain an erection when he copulates with you?" continued Institoris.

"I object again!" proclaimed the defense lawyer, banging on the table.

"Your Eminence," the Inquisitor explained, turning toward the seated Bishop, "a witches' obstruction occurs in the matter of inhibiting a penis' erection, which can more easily happen to men. And therefore, more men than women are bewitched. Most witches being women, they lust more for men than for women. Also, they act in spite of married women, finding every opportunity for adultery when the husband is able to copulate with other women but not with his own wife, and similarly, the wife also has to seek other lovers."

"The objection is sustained," said the Commissary General. "Madame Helena is married to Sebastianus Scheuber, and she has a good way of life. There is no basis whatsoever to this absurd questioning."

"It is simple, Your Excellency," Institoris continued, speaking to the Bishop. "Witches obstruct the genital power, not intrinsically by harming the penis, but extrinsically by rendering it useless. A witch can make a man impotent towards one woman but not toward others. But no such bewitchment can be permanent, it never annuls a marriage that has already been consummated. Therein we have evidence that Helena Scheuberin is a witch."

"Objection!" shouted the angry defense lawyer, again slamming his hand on the table. "What is this nonsense?"

"Helena Scheuberin, are you a virgin?" asked the Inquisitor.

The Commissary General banged his gavel so hard it might split.

The Bishop exchanged a frustrated glance with the Commissary General and they conferred in a whispered tone. The Bishop then stood up, cleared his throat and spoke commandingly.

"The accused must be released after putting up a reasonable bond to appear should this case be resumed. Helena Scheuberin and all other six defendants are all freed and shall do a mild penance." He signaled to the guards to immediately release the prisoners from custody.

The Inquisitor was incensed, and demanded to know from the Bishop, "What, then, is to be thought of those witches who collect male organs in great numbers, as many as twenty or thirty together, and put them in a bird's nest, or shut them up in a box, where they move themselves like living creatures, and eat oats and corn?"

"Inquisitor, whatever are you going on about?" asked the exasperated Bishop, putting his face in his hands. "Your questions are sheer madness. Male members eating corn and moving about? Virginity, impotence? What in God's holy name does any of this have to do with the charges of witchcraft you have brought against these good women?"

Institoris went silent.

The Bishop then solemnly pointed at the Inquisitor.

"I have found the Devil in Innsbruck," the Bishop declared, echoing Helena's earlier pronouncement. "He is in the Inquisitor himself. Now you must leave, Institoris! Withdraw with all speed. More than enough scandals have arisen because of this bad trial. You should not remain in this place, lest anything worse should follow from this…or happen to you!" he screamed.

LEARNINGS

"We leavin' for Corsica," said Mudazzo, the *Daniella's* first mate. He leaned on the wooden post of a dock in Civitavecchia near the highly maneuverable sailing caravel. The port had recently become free and was now the main entryway to Rome. Seamen stood on the pier, hunting for work from captains traveling to Sardinia, Sicily, Malta, Tunis, or Barcelona. These relatively nearby destinations had become popular quick trading routes for excess wool, hides, silk from Genoa, wine, salt fish and grain, easily exchanged for gold and silver in these ports.

Sebastian stepped on the gangway and boarded the square-rigged ship, thew his heavy satchel onto the deck, and sat down. Much larger galleons and carracks were docked nearby, preparing for long voyages across the seas.

While most captains had steady crews, a few barked offers seeking extra men willing and able to board for weeks at a time. Experienced mariners preferred to hire only one or two men for longer treks to Lisbon, Brest, or Plymouth, as too many unknown men aboard at once could lead to a mutiny from a disloyal crew.

"Must be nice, sittin' 'round while we do the heavy lifting 'round 'ere," said a newly-hired deckhand, wiping sweat off his brow. Sebastian ignored his comment and looked out at the sea. A dozen sailors stomped past him, working on the outrigging and preparing for the short voyage.

Mudazzo walked over and slapped Sebastian's back. "Welcome aboard, Father," he said warmly.

"Oh, I am not a priest. Please call me Sebastian."

"Aye, but don't tell the men you aren't," he jokingly warned. "They'll have ya' scoopin' fish entrails off the deck all day."

The Grand Inquisitor maintained a steady payroll of reliable mercenaries and seamen, among other necessary evils. Mudazzo had owed a substantial gambling debt that led to a bitter vendetta with a rival. Their bad blood led to him committing murder, but the Inquisition spared his life in exchange for lifelong fealty. "You make sure that Father Institoris knows that I am takin' good care of ya'," said the first mate, who offered him some spiced wine.

"I will, thank you," said Sebastian, taking the flask.

"We set sail for Corsica. Only a few days' trip across calm waters," said the first mate. "We'll unload our cargo of rock salt for some silver. We'll then cross to Sardinia, a stone's throw away. There, we'll reload with sugar to trade for some gold in Barcelona." Sebastian would disembark to travel overland once they arrived there.

As they set sail, a cool breeze swept over them. Once at sea, Mudazzo sat down with Sebastian under the mizzen mast, offering him a piece of fresh bread and some cheese while the sails flapped gently above them. On long voyages, for food to last at sea, it needed to be dry. Staples included dried and salted anchovies and cod, pickled or salted beef and pork, dried grains like chickpeas, lentils and beans, and hardtack biscuits. But on shorter trips such as this, the food was fresh and included salted vegetables, fresh fish and even cheese. Sebastian enjoyed the brief trip.

"What does Father have ya' doin'?" he asked curiously, gnawing on the end of the bread.

"Research," said Sebastian, taking a piece of bread from him. "Thank you."

"Researchin', all the way from Rome to Barcelona? Sounds like a good time to me," the first mate chuckled.

"I am studying witchcraft," whispered Sebastian.

Mudazzo's face grew ashen, and he crossed himself, spitting out the bread. "You don't have no spells or black magic in those books now, do ya?" he asked fearfully, pointing at Sebastian's satchel.

"No, not yet anyway."

"Aye, well when you return, take a different boat, by God. We are all Christians on the *Daniella*; we don't need no trouble with the likes of that piss," said the obviously frightened first mate.

Sebastian had spent a lot of time on fishing boats as a boy in Saint Malo. He was not surprised at Mudazzo's reaction, as he knew that mariners were a superstitious lot. But he began to understand that gleaning any information about witchcraft was going to be challenging, as the mere mention of the topic seemed to have quite an effect on some people.

"Did I hear you're studyin' witchcraft?" asked Ferrando, one of the hired deckhands. He had just finished dragging a net and was climbing down the main mast to adjust the swifting tackle when he overheard the conversation. Mudazzo got up and walked away quickly. He wanted no part of this.

"Yes," Sebastian replied.

"If you're looking for it, give me a gulden, and I'll tell ya everything I know."

Sebastian reached into his pouch, pinched a gulden and gave it to the man, who hid it in his vest pocket. Ferrando looked around furtively and whispered, "you'll want to go to Paris."

"Paris? Why, what is there?" asked Sebastian, confused as to why Paris would be a better locale for gathering information about witchcraft than Rome, Aragon or the countryside.

"A book, I think it's called *The Great Grimoire*, or *Big Grand Grimoire*, or something like that. My brother Aldonza told me that men killed for that book when he was in Paris. And when he was sailing from Athens, Greek sailors told him that some book called the *Ars* was in London, I think."

"Thank you, that is helpful. What else do you know about the subject?" asked Sebastian.

"The story goes," the man whispered, "there are certain tricks, things you can say and do, that will give you *powers*."

"Powers?" asked Sebastian.

"You can go invisible, I think. Maybe not; I don't really know. But my brother said that these books can make you rich. Powerful too. With whatever's in 'em, you could have any woman you want. Not sure if that's helpful, but that's what I know." Sebastian wasn't sure if this muddled information was worth a gulden, but he had to start somewhere.

The rest of the trip was uneventful, save for a broken outrigger. Four days later, when the *Daniella* docked at Port Vell, the weather was still glorious. Barcelona found itself on the frontier between Islam to the south and Christianity to the north. Its strategic location was decisive in the city's growth, establishing it as a trading point between the two worlds and, eventually, the greatest maritime power in the Mediterranean, despite not possessing a port worthy of its name. The ships that anchored between the Royal Shipyards and the city were badly exposed to the great storms that often affected the coast, and which caused many shipwrecks.

Nearby the harbor, Sebastian spotted a recently launched caravel he had heard about: the *Niña*. The sailors on the *Niña* were engaged with adjusting the rigging, trimming the sails, and inspecting for leaks, plugging them with spongy scraps of old rope.

After he disembarked the *Daniella*, Sebastian saw Mudazzo standing at the edge of the pier, holding the reins of a gorgeous black mare. "Her name is Epona," said the mate. "Best Spanish mare that gold can buy. Here—she is yours now."

"A beauty," said Sebastian, taking her reins and patting her long neck. Mudazzo then pointed to a large brown leather pouch hanging off the saddle. "A hundred ninety-two gold florins and a few extra gulden thrown in there. Fifty-five silver, as well. Compliments of Father Institoris." Sebastian looked shocked. He assumed that the few coins given to him in Rome would be enough for necessities. But Mudazzo was handing him a small fortune in heavy coinage.

The first thought that went through Sebastian's mind was how he was going to avoid being robbed. His second thought was how was he going to spend it. All necessary transportation, lodging and provisions were already being provided courtesy of the Inquisition's minions. Unless he needed to purchase a small chateau, this much gold and silver carried by a cleric would only arouse suspicion and invite bandits. Nonetheless, he accepted it, as he wasn't sure if he might need it for some unexpected purpose, such as buying cooperation from those unwilling or unable to speak about witchcraft.

"Thank you; this is generous," said Sebastian.

"Take it and guard it well. And let Father Institoris know how good I was to you," replied Mudazzo, reemphasizing the point. "Where you headed first?"

"Well," answered Sebastian, "I planned on starting here in Barcelona, but eventually making my way all the way through the countryside to Paris, possibly."

"Here is a map." The mate handed Sebastian a tightly rolled scroll. "This should give you enough detail for most of your journey. Once you get to Hibernia, you are on your own. And as I said, find another ship back home, 'ey?"

Sebastian acknowledged the request, thanked the first mate again, and climbed onto Epona's saddle. His first stop was to learn more about how Spaniards had uncovered information for their own successful Inquisition, although it sounded like Paris was a good long-term destination.

He rode until he reached a stable, tied off the horse there, and first felt the stirrings of hope. He would finally be able to start his research in earnest. He walked the rest of the way and stopped and partook in a delicious drink called sangria on his way to the newly built Church of Santa Maria del Pi. He thought it was funny that the drink was named after blood.

At the church, he would meet with Father Angelo. He had heard that the Spanish Inquisition did not see eye to eye with the Roman Inquisition controlled by Heinrich Institoris, and he wanted to learn more.

"Welcome," a round-shaped tonsured Franciscan priest said cheerfully at the door to the church.

"Thank you for welcoming me," said Sebastian, smiling at him. "This is a beautiful city."

"Indeed it is! Come, let us walk outside and enjoy the warm weather a bit." The priest and Sebastian walked through the city streets next to the church to the town center. Young boys played in the shadow of the spire, and vendors offered fruit to the clerics without charge. From the buildings, the pavement, the trees, even the sky and the people, the city gave off a rainbow of hues at every turn.

"Peter the Ceremonius' generosity built this church," Father Angelo said, pointing at the steeple. "But he had conflicts with Nicolas Eymerich, the Inquisitor General of Aragon. Nicolas published books about Jews that irritated him. The Inquisition here was focused on converting Jews. Nicolas had had many *auto-da-fé*. He was brutal to them. Terrible."

"I am only here to learn about witchcraft," said Sebastian.

"We do not see the same evils here that Rome does about that subject, either," Angelo continued. Sebastian followed closely as they walked the streets.

"What Institoris calls witchcraft is not witchcraft in all eyes, you see," said the priest. "Some merely follow old traditions. They believe in God; but they follow their own customs. Many of our holy days were absorbed from theirs."

"What do you mean? And may I write this down, Father?"

"Of course. Let us sit awhile." They sat on a stone bench. The sun overhead was strong at noonday and Sebastian wished he had more of that sangria.

"When I first came here as a young missionary, I discovered that the people had strong beliefs," the priest said, gesturing at several young women walking by who were wearing colorful clothing.

"They were not opposed to the Church's teachings or the Bible. But they were also not prepared to give up habits that their families had kept for centuries, sometimes longer than that," he continued. "So rather than fight these poor people or worse, kill them, we believed it was better to adapt our celebrations to theirs."

"The Church adopted witchcraft?" asked Sebastian, confused and looking up from his scribbling.

"Let me give you an example," Father Angelo said, turning toward him. "The fourteenth of February was a pagan holiday. I believe it was called Lupercalia. The Pope abolished it and renamed it Saint Valentine's Day. The people barely noticed any difference, but we used it to teach them about Saint Valentine."

"So, when there is a pagan tradition, the Church adopts it?"

Father Angelo nodded. "Their most important one of the pagan year was the first of November, when they honored their dead. That day is now known to us as All Saints' Day. Yule on December 21 is now Christmas. Our Lord was born in October, after all." He smiled.

"The Church adopts pagan customs but condemns those who follow them. I will include this in my manuscript."

Sebastian put his journal away and thanked Father Angelo, who walked back to his church. Rather than stay in the rectory, Sebastian retired to an inn where he had rented a room. He was learning to enjoy staying at inns that were not churches. The people he encountered were far more interesting, and the rooms were much nicer than the sparsely furnished church rooms in the cloisters.

Over the next three weeks, Sebastian rode Epona north and briefly stopped in several towns and villages along the way. At each, he would make it a habit to visit the friary, convent or church and display his scroll of introduction to the local Ordinary. He would usually purchase a room at a nearby inn, but other times, the priests would offer him a modest room.

The parish priests informed him over and over that not only did they not perceive any serious threats from witches in their midst, but the villagers also merely seemed to embrace folklore and harmless remedies that only the Inquisition was calling malicious witchcraft.

Most of the priests explained that the women in their towns and villagers occasionally accused of witchcraft were also often looked to as midwives, as well as advisers on matters relating to health and well-being. These towns lacked sophisticated apothecaries such as might be found in Rome or Paris. In these places, these women grew and dispensed medicinal herbs and roots.

Sebastian kept copious notes in his journal listing the names and locations of each of these sources of valuable information. Certainly, Fathers Institoris and Sprenger would be interested to follow up by meeting with particularly helpful sources.

SAGE

"Richard the Lionhearted built this road," said Beatrix, the young blonde girl Sebastian was chatting with as they passed Chateau de Val on a rural road in Limousin in central France.

The girl's mother, Cecile, smiled at the precocious little girl talking with the robed man.

"Oh, is that so?" Sebastian smiled.

A group of villagers had been walking down the road when Sebastian had caught up with them.

"I like your horse," Beatrix said to Sebastian, smiling.

"She likes you too. Would you like to ride her?" he asked her playfully.

"Oh, mama, may I?" The girl turned and pleaded with her mother.

"Of course, but please be careful," Cecile said.

Sebastian carefully placed the girl on Epona's saddle. The horse was trotting and enjoying this quiet stretch of road.

"See, I told you, she likes you," he said sweetly to the girl as he held the reins carefully and patted Epona.

Limoges was Sebastian's latest stop on a long overland journey from Barcelona to Paris. The predominant population here was cattle. Yet, despite its lack of density of people, it was bitterly contested between the British and French kings.

Sebastian had chosen to travel through this region precisely because it was so rural, and he suspected that witchcraft might more likely take root in a distant community like this than in the larger cities. They passed the castle's six towers which were perfectly reflected in the lake surrounding it.

"Father, what brings you to Limousin? I detect Bretagne on your tongue," asked Cecile, who walked next to her daughter astride the horse.

"Oh, I am not a priest. But I did grow up in Bretagne. I was sent by Rome to do research here. Well, not just here. I am gathering information about witchcraft throughout this beautiful countryside," he said.

"Magic?" she asked inquisitively.

"I suppose. I don't really know exactly." He smiled. "I have spent months traveling but I have not uncovered very much yet. The more I ask, the more difficult it seems to learn the truth about the topic."

They continued to walk under the trees, which had started to turn gold in late summer.

"My husband is away fighting the British," Cecilia said.

"I am sorry to hear that," replied Sebastian. "Hopefully he will return safely soon."

"Since you are studying magic," she said, "there was once a woman near here, named Annick. She lived outside of Limoges; she was a midwife and a sage. I am not sure if that is what you are seeking."

"A sage? Is that a witch? I do not know exactly what a witch is either, to be honest," confessed Sebastian, a bit embarrassed. "I am just starting to gather information and I am still learning."

"She helped those in need," Cecile continued. "She never had any children of her own, but when I was with child, I gave birth in her home." She twirled Beatrix's flaxen hair as the girl smiled and rubbed Epona's mane. "She offered helpful advice."

"Did you not speak to the priests or brothers here for help? Perhaps a doctor or a barber?"

"Those men are not interested in helping us. They frowned on her, and some even called her a witch, but she helped me. She also helped my sister Valerie after our mother died," she continued. "The Church does not help those in need. They will gladly take our money to build big cathedrals and wear silk clothes, but they do not teach us, and they do not give us advice. Sometimes, a young mother may need to learn how to heal a child's wound. Annick once taught a young farmer how to save an animal that had become gravely ill. But the Church has never helped us with such things."

"I find that unfortunate," said Sebastian sadly. "Did she worship the Devil?"

"Of course not." Cecile laughed. "Her practices had nothing to do with religion. But when a farmer's field went bad, or cattle died, the priests were quick to suggest that she was to blame. Perhaps because she could heal, they assumed she could also strike men down."

Beatrix looked at Sebastian. "Sir, do you have any cakes?" she asked.

"I do not. I am sorry," Sebastian confessed. She frowned.

"Here, I do." Cecile offered her a small piece of cake out of her purse. The girl ate it and smiled.

"When I began my journey," Sebastian said, "I was told that witches were assaulting the Church. I was taught that they are at war with Christ. So far, at least, I have seen nothing to suggest that is true."

"The Church is at war with itself, Annick used to say. She would say she was giving advice and healing, and she would forever do so, but the Church still persecuted her. When she died in her old age, the Church refused to let her be buried in the cemetery," Cecile said.

"Why was that?" Sebastian asked.

"They never formally accused her of being a witch, but the Church still saw her as a threat, I suppose, even after she died."

Sebastian frowned. "I greatly appreciate your time," he said. "May I pay you for your trouble? He reached in the pouch on Epona's saddle and offered Cecile a handful of freshly struck gold coins. They would allow her to live rather comfortably for quite a long time.

"Pay me? For what?"

"For your time and this helpful information," Sebastian said.

She looked at the handful of gold. "Thank you, but I have no need for your money. The people here take care of my needs. Give it to the widows and orphans. They are the ones who your Church should be serving.

WELL

"Carla, it is good to see you again," the handsome Count Walter Bergstrom said to the long-haired blonde maiden who had been in his concubine years earlier. Walter, the high-born count of Westrich, had frequently enjoyed carnal relations with the girl when they were younger. He noticed that Carla looked well and not a day older than when they were last together only a few years ago.

When Walter was a young count, his parents encouraged him to marry within other high-born families in Westrich. His mother had advocated for Amelinda Fiddlere, whose family was also wealthy. Their families would do well together.

But Amelinda was short, dowdy and boring. She was nowhere near as fetching as the tall, beautiful, and well-endowed Carla, who was the daughter of a cobbler but had inherited stunning looks and a healthy figure. And so the young count had spent all his time with Carla, creating a willing concubine that could serve his every desire.

Virtually each night during the summers, the mustached count would invite Carla and all her girlfriends to a nearby tavern, where he would engage in every form of debauchery imaginable. His father's extensive land holdings gave him an ample allowance to invest in excess. And invest he did.

He drank several bottles of fine wine every night and devoured more rare mutton than the butcher could account for. Carla was always his favorite. She had kept him more than satisfied and content. But eventually, he relented to his mother's wishes when his father refused to continue to finance his lifestyle. He dutifully married Amelinda three years ago. But life was never the same after that.

When he suddenly came upon Carla while walking the streets and lanes of Metz on a warm late Autumn day, surrounded by his servants and family, he was forced to address her unexpectedly and politely. He asked her how she was, while Amelinda looked on suspiciously from a distance.

"I am doing quite well, thank you," Carla said. "But more importantly, how are you? How is your health and your situation?" She leaned in closely toward him, seeming more interested in his well-being than should be expected under the awkward circumstances. He suddenly remembered how good she smelled.

"I am doing very well. Um, thank you very much for asking," he continued matter-of-factly. "Everything is turning out quite prosperously for me and my kin."

Carla just stood there, looking him up and down silently.

"So…would you enjoy attending a dinner party that my wife Amelinda is hosting at our castle next week? It would be very nice to have you present," he asked insincerely.

"Thank you, but no. And how is your wife?" she asked, glancing over at her.

"She is quite well in all regards," said the Count, "thank you for asking."

"And your children? Have you fathered any children?" she asked.

The Count was becoming increasingly uncomfortable with Carla's aggressive questioning and responded with a lie. "I have three sons. My wife has given birth to one each year."

Carla went silent again.

The Count whispered to her, "I don't doubt that you are glad for me on account of my good fortune, but I am surprised at your insistent questioning."

"Truly, I am happy for you," she leaned forward and whispered in return. "But I have missed you terribly. I am shocked that you have been able to perform the carnal act with…her," she said, again glancing over at the dowdy matron down the street.

"Whatever do you mean?" he whispered angrily.

"After the pleasures I provided? I cannot believe that you were able to sire sons with her," she confessed in a breathy voice.

The Count finally admitted the truth. "I was lying about my sons. I have not been able to sire any children with her at all."

"I can change that," she whispered in a sultry tone. "After one night with me, you will feel like young Count Walter again." She reached over and touched his hairy chest lightly through his silk shirt quickly so that his wife could not see it.

"Amelinda will find us out," he whispered back even more quietly.

"I know exactly what you can tell her…"

"What did that girl want?" asked the Count's anxious wife once he had rejoined her. "Do you know her?"

"Damn that old woman," he muttered angrily.

"Old woman? What do you mean? She is a maiden."

"No, not Carla. Curse that old woman who offered to affect my body with sorcery," he replied. "A witch told her that I would be hardly able to perform the carnal act with you."

"What do you mean?" the Countess asked, growing disturbed.

"The well in the middle of our courtyard has at its bottom a jar that contains certain objects for sorcery. Out of revenge and spite, Carla confessed that she paid an evil witch handsomely to place it there long ago so that I would have impotence in copulating with you for as long as the jar remained there. And it did so."

"Whatever are you talking about?" she asked.

"I…must depart, Amelinda. I will return home immediately. Please excuse me, dear." He abruptly turned to walk away, as Carla looked on.

"But continue your trip," he said, calling to two of his servants to accompany Amelinda, who was growing ever more suspicious.

The Count did not waste a minute. He walked away quickly and met Carla at a nearby tavern. He drank a bottle of wine with her and then retired upstairs to a private chamber.

Afterward, he snuck home and took his shirt, which smelled like Carla, and placed it in an open jar full of pins and needles and tossed it into his well. After reentering his home, he directed his servants to empty the well.

"We must reinvite all the nobles to a new wedding, Amelinda!" he declared, walking into her bedchamber. "You are now the mistress of this castle and the entire territory after remaining a maiden for so long!"

"Why such exuberance?" asked Amelinda. She knew that after their opulent wedding three years ago, the Count was unable to consummate their marriage. Each time they had tried, he was unable to even begin to perform the expected role of her husband.

Amelinda had tried everything. She had worn thin frocks, she had offered him the finest meats and wines, but nothing had ever worked.

"The jar, once it was removed, I will feel like a man again," he said.

"Jar? What jar?" she asked.

"Come downstairs. Ask the servants what they found at the bottom of our well tonight!" he exclaimed.

"We found a jar full o'needles and pins, and your husband's favorite silk shirt." said a maidservant.

Amelinda was astonished. But now she desired revenge. That Carla had invited a sorceress, a witch, to destroy their marriage with black magic—and she had almost done so.

But now that she had the jar as evidence, she would go to a man she heard about in Metz. The tall Inquisitor, they had called him. He was apparently looking for information about this very type of thing. He would know what to do about that witch—and that damned Carla.

PARIS

Over the course of the next two months, after Limoges, Sebastian stopped in Toulouse and Saint Etienne. He heard the same refrain over and over. Those women who were suspected of witchcraft posed little—if any—real threat to anyone, much less the established Church. When he finally arrived in Paris, he was forced to stable Epona at the city's outer limits and enter the town center by foot as the city streets were too narrow to permit individual horses. It was autumn but the city was still warm.

While it did not have the same ancient history, Paris was similar to Rome in its size and sophistication. The city still had the feel of a village in parts. Hens scratched among the cobblestones along the river looking for feed, sheep somehow found their way from pens into the streets, and squealing hogs wandered by every so often, nosing into garbage heaps. Church bells frequently pealed and peddlers crowed about their wares on every corner. The visit made Sebastian miss being in sunny Rome.

He was not sure what information about witches he might be able to gather in the city since he learned in the countryside that it would provide more fertile ground for his field research. It seemed that the parish priests and those who dwelled here were perpetually busy and not very approachable. Nonetheless, he thought he would at least try to learn what he could, as well as to investigate whether the alleged *Grand Grimoire* was still in Paris, as he had heard from Ferrando on the *Daniella*.

He stopped in a few taverns that offered outdoor seating on street corners overlooking the Seine River and chose one. In French, though still with his Breton accent, he ordered some crusty bread, warm brie and red wine, and tried to figure out how to best approach his unorthodox research here.

"Food is good? More wine?" asked the bearded waiter, who was trying to speak Bretagne for Sebastian.

"Yes, thank you. Best I have enjoyed since Rome."

"You from there?" the waiter asked.

"Yes."

"Remarkable! A priest?"

"No… Well, not yet. I am studying to become one."

"World needs good priests. We have bad ones," the waiter said, shaking his head dramatically while pouring more red wine.

"Oh?"

"Priests here are bad."

"Bad?"

"Terrible things they done."

"May I ask what things?" asked Sebastian.

The waiter leaned over quietly. "Go to Montrouge. See the mines."

"The mines?"

"Inside the red mountain."

"Uh, thank you." The man refilled Sebastian's cup with red wine until it overflowed onto the table and stained the cheap tablecloth. He did not charge Sebastian for the meal.

Sebastian had no idea what the waiter was talking about. There was a good chance that it was going to be a waste of his time to find out. Nonetheless, he had not gathered that much information about witchcraft up until now and any leads that he could get in Paris were worth investigating.

He thought about the conversation he had with Cecile in Limoges. What the Church was calling witchcraft did not seem to be the threat they had suggested. Maybe I'm not looking in the best places for information, Sebastian thought to himself.

He walked back to his room and washed up. It was nearly 4 p.m. already. It would not be dark for a few more hours, so that left time for him to travel to Montrouge, which he discovered was only about two and a half miles away. He was planning on speaking to the Cardinal at Notre Dame first thing tomorrow, so if he was going to investigate the mines, now was going to be the time.

Asking directions several more times from clearly annoyed Parisians, he found his way to Montrouge on foot. It consisted of a red hill of dirt, few shacks, a tiny monastery, and a meat market that had flies surrounding it. He approached the monastery and oddly found it completely empty.

He walked up to a vendor selling freshly cut beef and asked about the mines. The villager crossed himself and pointed to an older man on the other side of the town square, who was sitting on a stool. Sebastian walked up to the old man and again asked about the mines. He nodded, stood up and led Sebastian to an open pit in a field nearby. The dirt surrounding the pit was red.

He asked for a pittance in exchange for giving Sebastian what he hoped would be safe passage down into the pit. They climbed down a ladder whose rungs ended in a dark flat void. The man brought down a lit torch that was their only illumination once the sunlight from above ceased to reach the depths.

The mines were apparently a poorly designed underground quarry from which a substantial amount of rock was being removed, creating the red hill. The guide explained that this quarry had opened to permit the removal of red stones that could be used to construct churches and cathedrals throughout Paris, and even beyond the city. Because of the haphazard mining technique of digging wells down to the deposit and extracting it horizontally along the vein until depletion, many of these illicit mines were uncharted, and when depleted, abandoned and forgotten.

The guide explained that these tunnels went on for miles underneath the whole city of Paris, and that countless lives had already been lost down here. Miners were often just boys who worked to earn a few extra coins chipping away and dragging heavy rocks to the surface. Other times, the allure of the darkness beckoned children who played pranks and dangerous games in these tunnels. Once the light—or air—ran out, their bodies were never found. Sinkholes on the surface also occasionally occurred, as supports below collapsed.

But why was an old underground tunnel system relevant to his investigation of witchcraft? Why had the waiter suggested this place was worth a visit? Sebastian thought to himself.

He asked the guide if there was anything else worth knowing about the tunnels. The guide said for a silver, he would divulge it. Sebastian handed one to him.

The guide then led Sebastian down a narrow corridor that veered off to the left. After a trek on a downward sloped path, the air became colder and stale. The distance between the walls was becoming so narrow that Sebastian was finding it difficult to breathe and shimmy along them. He started to wonder if the guide had made a practice of luring men down here to rob them and leave them to die.

However, they soon reached an opening to the mouth of a large cavern. The guide walked around it and lit several dry torches that had been crudely mounted on the rock walls. Once Sebastian could see the whole area in the cave lit up, he saw exactly what it was.

Unlike the Roman catacombs under the Appian Way that Sebastian had once visited, which housed early Christians' underground ceremonies, it appeared that this was the site of ungodly rituals.

A flat stone table rested in the center of the dirt floor. Brown stains of blood were visible on it, and in the dirt around it. A strange symbol that looked like a five-pointed star with circles was crudely marked on its top surface. Letters surrounded the star.

This was the first time that Sebastian had encountered something tangible and maleficent related to witchcraft. It was unclear if someone had killed an animal on this altar or a human being. There was no fur or feathers in the blood or on the ground, so it was unlikely that the offering had been a chicken or a dog.

It could have been a hog, he thought, but a large animal would not have been able to squeeze along the narrow corridor that led down into this room. He shuddered at the prospect that a human being was convinced—or coerced—to come down here only to be ritualistically slaughtered on the table. He also noticed that there were no bones on the ground or anywhere in the room. Whatever was killed down here was fully removed afterward.

After spending enough time eyeing the room and inspecting the altar closely to memorize the sight, he thanked the guide and desired to leave that accursed mine as soon as possible.

They quickly made their way back out and up the ladder. Sebastian had not realized that they were down in the mines so long that daylight had already turned to dusk. He again thanked the guide and walked back in the growing darkness to his room at the inn. He made notes in his journal, including a rough sketch of the cave and the strange symbol he had seen in the underground quarry.

That night, as Sebastian tried to sleep, he kept going over in his mind why there was a blood altar in a cave deep within the earth. Why would someone slaughter a living thing in such dank conditions? Certainly, there was no explanation other than witchcraft. Perhaps the Grand Inquisitor was right. Maybe there really was some strange threat under the surface of the world.

CATHEDRAL

T he next day, Sebastian woke up and prepared to visit the grand Cathedral of Notre Dame. As he approached it, he was taken by the remarkably symmetrical archways and the buttresses along the Seine river. He walked into the nave of the basilica and presented his scroll of introduction to the sacristan, who offered Sebastian only a few minutes with the Cardinal. He was apparently busy attending to serious financial matters.

"Your Eminence," said Sebastian, bowing and kissing the Cardinal's gold ring. The Cardinal was a striking figure, tall and lithe. His red silk cassock and white lace surplice were exquisitely sewn, even by Rome's elevated standards.

"I have been researching and studying the practices of witchcraft, for the Inquisition," he told the Cardinal.

"Yes, I read your scroll. Have you discovered interesting information during your travels?"

"No, I am afraid not. So far, all I have learned is that many who are often called witches do nothing of the sort. They seem to mostly practice innocent customs and midwifery. But Father Institoris also asked me to inquire about esoteric texts relating to witchcraft. One may be called *The Grand Grimoire*. I was led to believe that it might be located near here," said Sebastian to the prelate, who was now sitting behind the largest wooden desk Sebastian had ever seen, ornately carved on all sides with cherubs and figures of saints.

"That accursed book was spirited away from Paris years ago," said the Cardinal. "We did not want that foulness in our city. It was hauled off to the fortress at Mont-St-Michel, where it is secure deep in the crypt. Now, it will never fall into the wrong hands. It contains information that no man should know. Other copies are safely in Hibernia, at Clonmacnoise."

"Your Eminence, I was also told that there may be priests or monks who may be involved in witchcraft? I visited an abandoned mine last night in Montrouge. There was signs and strange symbols of a ritual sacrifice there. Do you know about it?"

"Men of God can easily be tempted to fall away from the faith by Lucifer." The Cardinal became rankled. "Please destroy those books if you find them." He stood up and offered Sebastian his ring to kiss again, abruptly ending their meeting.

Sebastian thanked him. He knew that he would need to travel due west to Mont-St-Michel to investigate further. As much as he understood and respected the Cardinal's warnings and recommendation that he destroy infernal books if he found them, he knew that he could not. He was duty-bound to locate them, as well as study them and return them to Rome for safekeeping.

BAY

"The tide, she come in like a galloping steed," the grizzled guide murmured. He spoke in French garbled with Breton. "Flat's not easy to cross in winter." He stared off into the distant night sky and scratched pensively at his scruffy beard, as though he were a scholar. After a weeklong trip on horseback from Paris, Sebastian had finally arrived at the northern tip of Bretagne, near Rennes. While it was late Autumn, the weather was already showing signs of winter ahead. Several crows circled overhead in the overcast sky.

Sebastian was not far from Saint Malo, where he had spent the remainder of his youth, but bittersweet memories of that time of his life kept him from visiting. He did not want to see what remained of the Saint Malo Cathedral where he lived or view the statue of the priest who'd given him shelter as an orphan. Besides, he had a schedule to keep, and visiting quaint old towns out of a desire for nostalgia only made sense if he could also gather information that was relevant to his mission.

Seeking a guide to assist him in crossing the harrowing bay between the coastline and the islet, he now peered across the pier. At the mouth of the Coueson River, shrouded by virtually impenetrable mists and engulfed by stormy seas in the distance, was the island of Mont Tombe—the Tomb on the Hill. And soaring proudly above the glistening gray sands of the island stood the mystical fortress and Abbey of Mont-St-Michel, Sebastian's intended destination.

He had never been to the fortified Abbey before. It had always intrigued him as a reputedly influential center of monastic learning, but it was still caught in the middle of a century-long war between the French and English when he was a boy. It was also the subject of a bitter and occasionally violent property dispute between Normandy and Bretagne for as long as anyone could recall. Because of the dangers of travelling there, only the most devoted pilgrims, called *miquelots*, dared to brave the trip.

Violent waves slapped the skiff that the guide was precariously balanced upon, somehow emphasizing his point. "A new moon too," the guide pronounced, pointing his calloused index finger upward at the moonless sky. Rough, weatherworn skin stretched over tough bones, telling of countless trips across the bay.

Sebastian knew this guide's routine well. He himself had even practiced this method of negotiation in Bretagne as a fisherman. The guide would emphatically express his concern about the particularly difficult nature of the request, and in doing so, would negotiate a higher price. Sebastian also understood that, while the guide most certainly had made an art form of exaggerating the difficulty of paid travel, this time, he didn't have to stretch the truth.

The bay was churning angrily, and the howling winds didn't look like they'd be dying down any time soon. Beyond the bay, in the disorienting mists, marshy flats extended for several miles, and would be filled with treacherous traps of quicksand. Worse still, the high tide would cover the tidal flats suddenly and, without warning, drowning all in its path without mercy. Sebastian had heard that countless pilgrims to the Abbey had met their mortal end this way, never reaching the fortressed monastery that had been their aim.

He also knew that these tidal flats were far more dangerous—and inviting—than the churning bay itself. When the tide was low, one could comfortably walk across the bay and arrive at the shore of the island on which the Abbey stood. However, only a few short hours bridged the gap between high and low tides, and a weary traveler lost in the mists would not reach his destination alive. Not, that is, without a sure and steady guide beside him.

"Sir, I realize that the trip is very dangerous, but I still must reach the monastery. Winter is coming and I must cross now. So how much will it cost me?" he asked.

"Hmmmm..." The guide stroked his matted beard again and stared into the dark distance as if pondering the meaning of life itself. Salty water slapped the docks.

"Fine, I will find another way across." Sebastian, bluffing, turned to walk away, even knowing there was no way to safely reach the Abbey across the tidal flats without a guide and a skiff.

"Well, how much you got?" the guide yelled.

Sebastian reached into his leather pouch and plucked out a silver florin. He turned around to face the guide, displaying his offer.

The guide grunted, stepped onto the dock, and grabbed the coin out of his hand, waving at the small boat being tossed in the foamy waves.

Sebastian climbed unsteadily into the lurching skiff, falling onto the soaked wooden slat that traversed the center of it. Despite the turbulence of the choppy waters, he found himself relaxed. Until now, he hadn't realized how much he'd missed the excitement of working on fishing boats. In fact, he didn't mind this relatively brief trip at all.

Once they left firm ground, the guide grabbed the rope and untied the noose from the pier, pushing off with a long wooden paddle. The boat rocked as the guide paddled first port side, then starboard, drifting them across the bay into the inky darkness.

As their boat continued rocking, the only light emanated from a small oil lantern dangling aloft on a tilted shepherd's hook. Now and again, soundless flashes of lighting would light up the moonless sky, illuminating undulating whitecaps in the distance.

"Why you goin' there?" the guide inquired, paddling the skiff slowly but confidently with huge arms, the muscles formed by countless journeys across this stretch of sea.

"I am seeking something," Sebastian replied, squinting into the mists.

"Who isn't? Hah!" The ferryman seemed to understand and said no more.

As they approached the point at which the bay turned into a silty marsh, stronger waves punched the hollow hull of the skiff.

After about an hour, they arrived at a crooked wooden pole anchored into the ground where the tide reached its low point. The guide tossed a noose over the pole and heaved a leather traveling pack over the side of the boat, slopping it into the watery marsh. The pack sank into the light gray muck underfoot.

Sebastian slowly stepped out, sinking into the silt past his ankles. The earth tugged at his legs heavily, holding him in place. With each step, his sandals were swallowed by the greedy mud.

The guide jumped out of the boat, yanked his heavy pack out of the silt with one hand, and hastened away with sure footing. He appeared to float over top of the silt with ease.

The guide turned his head and shouted gruffly. "Little time—hurry!"

"Sir, I am trying, but the ground is too muddy!" shouted Sebastian.

"Don't stop! Earth and sea might eat ya up!" The guide laughed. From his tone, Sebastian was certain he had mocked many travelers before in this exact location.

Sebastian tried to follow his lead. As he grew angrier and more frustrated with each step, his footfalls grew more deliberate. After a while, he realized the guide's method was the right one—by taking high strides and avoiding the temptation to remain in one spot for more than a fleeting moment, one could practically glide on the surface of the marsh.

After another hour of such grueling hiking, however, Sebastian's knees were screaming with pain. Thunderless flashes of lightning flickered across the barren gray landscape more frequently now. The momentary illuminations enabled Sebastian to take his mind off the pain in his knees by focusing on the growing outline against the far horizon.

"City of the dead," muttered the guide, who had noticed him staring intently into the distance. "She belong to Bretagne, not Normandy."

As they progressed closer to the shape in the distance, Sebastian saw more details emerge. He could make out several vaulted towers, round turrets and two tall spires. A wide road seemed to snake up a rocky hill toward the gated entrance. The guide pointed. "Pilgrims' path. It leads to God." The guide crossed himself and kissed his thumb.

Sebastian was growing weary and wanted to rest his legs, but the guide only seemed to increase the length and frequency of his strides.

"Slow down, I cannot maintain this pace!" he yelled ahead. The guide ignored him, the man practically running.

Suddenly, the sound of rushing water emanated from all sides.

"The steed! She gallops!" the guide screamed in Breton, hysterically. "Saint Michael, protect us!"

Sebastian didn't need to ask what the guide meant. He felt the cold foam of salty water rising around his shins. He ran as quickly as his legs would carry him, but the foam surged from all directions. He made it to the coastline as the waters lapped at his chest.

The guide laughed and walked off up the hill.

They had reached the edge of the Abbey. But Sebastian realized that his scroll of introduction from Father Institoris wasn't going to protect him from the harsh elements in days ahead.

Sebastian and his guide walked up the rocky shore towards the road. He shook himself off and approached the Arcade's Tower to the left of the main gate.

The two men saw a mustached soldier, decked out in heavy plate armor. The soldier neared Sebastian warily, his right hand perched on the handle of his longsword.

"Approach and announce yourself!"

"Yes, sir." Prepared, Sebastian presented his soggy scroll of introduction. The soldier unfurled it and stared at its smudged Latin words. Sebastian looked up and thought he could see the three fleurs-de-lis on the flag of Normandy in the darkness, whipping above in the sea breeze.

"Stay here," the guard ordered sternly, pointing his index finger at Sebastian. He walked away to the post window to confer with another soldier. Before long, five of them were trying to decipher the Latin words on the scroll.

Sebastian approached, employing his best French with the senior officer. "It says I was sent by Rome, by the Inquisition, sir." The soldiers looked at him skeptically. Sebastian realized that they probably detected his slight Breton accent, only adding to their suspicions.

"How'd you get here?" one of the soldiers asked him.

"I paid the guide," Sebastian said, pointing back toward the coastline. The guide had vanished off into the mists.

"What you want?" asked another.

"I respectfully request to meet the Abbot. I have much to discuss with him. I was sent by the Pope."

"Stay here!" The officer pointed at him and turned towards the gates of the monastery. Despite the gravity of the situation, Sebastian found these continued warnings and questions somehow amusing, considering he was stranded on an island surrounded by seawater on all sides, and he certainly couldn't get very far even if he wanted to.

He heard the grating of metal against metal as an ancient pulley system lifted the iron portcullis. A hooded Benedictine monk, hands folded, emerged from the shadows within.

"Weary pilgrim may the peace of Christ be upon you," he said, flipping his long hood back. "I detected an air of concern from our guards. What brings you to us?" He took the scroll from the senior guard.

"My name is Sebastian, Brother. I am a researcher, sent by Rome."

"Yes, I can see that much," said the monk, scanning the scroll. "But what does your research have to do with us here?" he asked.

"Well, I had prayed that I might find shelter, rest, and perhaps conduct my work here. You see, I report to the Grand Inquisitor Father Heinrich Institoris . . ."

The monk looked up from the scroll, terrified by the utterance of the Inquisitor's formal name.

"Will you be staying here long then?" he asked. His expression indicated that he would follow the command of Institoris.

"No, Brother. I was planning on staying no more than a few days."

"Then you are welcome to stay with us to pray and conduct your research for as long as you desire. The Rule of Saint Benedict prescribes that all guests that come be received as Christ, for He will say: I was a stranger and you took me in."

The monk rolled up the scroll carefully and handed it back to Sebastian.

"I am Brother Aubert. I took my Christian name in honor of the saintly man who sanctified this mountain in God's name after pagans had dirtied it with their filthy rituals." Sebastian swallowed hard, wondering how Brother Aubert would react to the specific nature of his research. "Normally, we would welcome a weary pilgrim in the almonry, but allow us to receive you in our special room, reserved for guests of honor. Come with me."

The monk waved his arm to the soldiers to signal that everything was fine. They trudged back to their posts. Sebastian suspected that this was the most peaceful and least interesting event that had happened on the island in quite some time.

Brother Aubert lowered his voice apologetically as they began the long walk up the steep road up into the heart of the hill.

"The Duke of Normandy means well. He assigned these guards to protect us."

"From whom, may I ask?"

"The British Crown spent almost an entire century trying to overtake this mount. They never succeeded, praise God and Saint Michael. This Abbey has been a source of controversy, and the addition we call 'The Miracle' has only made matters worse, I'm afraid." He pointed to the three-story monastic complex rising on the hill high above them.

"Yes, our shining city on a hill has become the envy of many, for good and ill," said Brother Aubert as they reached yet another fortified entrance.

"I understand, Brother," said Sebastian, following the monk. "It is magnificent. Aptly named."

"When the weather is clear, I will show you our gardens and cloister on the mount. They are sublime. They grow roses for the soul," said Aubert.

"That sounds wonderful, thank you."

The monk swung open a heavy, arched door which led to a steep staircase.

"We choose to live on the highest level. We choose a life of poverty, chastity and obedience here as far removed from the rest of the world as possible. We entertain honored guests, such as yourself, on the second level."

They rounded the second level of the wide, steep staircase and entered the interior of a spacious room filled with tapestries and icons. The vaulted ceilings were made of wooden beams. Flickering torches were mounted aside every other doorway.

He invited Sebastian to sit on a velvet-draped chair that Sebastian figured must be the only comfortable furniture in the Abbey, given the sparse and austere surroundings.

"I will call upon the Abbot to greet you. May the Peace of Christ find you and stay upon you." The brother gave Sebastian a kiss on each cheek, and then vanished into the dark shadowy hallways of the byzantine labyrinth.

Sebastian, seated, did not see abbot enter the room.

"Now, tell me of this research you seek here," asked the overweight Abbot, rolling in more than walking, dispensing with any introduction whatsoever.

"Oh hello, Abbot. Greetings from the Holy Father," said Sebastian, startled. "My research relates to heresy," he said vaguely.

"Heresy? How fascinating. You must tell me more," said the Abbot. He sat down across from Sebastian.

"Well, it has come to the attention of the Inquisition that old heresies are again spreading. My task is to explore how true that may be."

"How intriguing a topic, but what does it have to do with us? We are cloistered, far removed from the world. You won't find any heretics here. What heresy troubles us these days? Knights Templar?"

"No, I am not aware of the Knights Templar posing a threat. Do they even still exist?" asked Sebastian.

"I do not know," said the Abbot. "The Knights once defended this rock," said the Abbot. "They were godly soldiers for the Church. I do not know what happened. There are rumors that the Pope was abusing them. Using them to steal the money they had amassed. He ended up owing them a fortune. Killing them was his way of paying off his debt, I suppose."

"I do not know much about them," said Sebastian. "I am only seeking to locate a book," said Sebastian, unsure how much detail to reveal. The Abbot didn't probe further.

"Well, this place has been called the City of Books. Over centuries, we have collected within these walls some of the great treasures of the past. Through time, we defended ourselves from constant attack, and matters of academics were sometimes left ignored, I am afraid. Whatever is left is crumbling from rot."

"That is unfortunate," replied Sebastian.

"However, we have rebuilt the Scriptorium in the new hall that we have added. It is my goal to return this Abbey to its former place as a beacon of learning. I have told the Dukes of Normandy as much, and they approve.

"But if it is research you seek, our cache of learning is kept deep in the mountain. Speak to Father Macron, the sacristan of Our Lady Underground on the first level. He will direct you further. I trust you will let me know if you need any further assistance in finding what you seek."

"I shall. Thank you."

"With that, I shall be returning to my duties. But please, keep in mind that most of our brothers have taken vows of silence and prefer to not be disturbed."

"Of course, Abbot."

"When you are ready to retire for the evening, there is a room already prepared for guests near the Knights' Room. Here—the Abbey can be very cold this time of year." He handed Sebastian a small pelt and fingerless leather gloves. With that, the Abbot departed, leaving Sebastian to wander the halls of the mysterious mountain in the sea, halls that few had ever gazed upon in person.

COLOGNE

Nine weeks after leaving Innsbruck humiliated, the Inquisitor now stood in a secular courtroom in Cologne. Bishop Golser had not only physically threatened him in front of the entire town, but he also went so far as to pen letters to the Pope and the Archduke, demanding that he be exiled permanently from Austria. Since then, Heinrich had returned to Cologne, where he had more important matters than bickering with a false Bishop.

In this smaller courtroom at least, the Inquisitor struck a terrifying pose at the lectern, towering at least ten feet over everyone else on an imposing platform that he had designed himself. His bearing in the room was higher than even that of the secular judge, who presided over this tribunal from a modest side bench. He had selected this judge as the perfect jurist to manage these trials, since as a devout Catholic from the diocese of Cologne, he agreed to allow the Inquisitor wider latitude in the prosecution of ecclesiastical heresies than Golser did. Heinrich bellowed his questions so that everyone in the building could hear him.

Eighteen-year-old Abigail Kolich, shackled in chains and manacles at the hands and knees, stood in the well. She whispered in response to the accusations, trembling with fear, her head bowed. Her once pretty dress was shredded from weeks spent in solitude deep in the cold jails below the courthouse and her firm breasts were visible through the torn fabric. Her blonde hair was matted with dried blood and her face lacerated and bruised from where she had been thrown down the stairs and beaten and raped by the guards. She smelled of urine and her face was stained with countless tears. It was nearly Christmastime, and the dungeons below were freezing day and night.

She raised her head as far as she could to look at him. "No sir, I swear before God, before whom I stand innocent, that I know nothing of witchcraft or the Devil. I speak before God and His Saints that I am clear from this accusation."

Onlookers in the gallery guffawed at her protestations. This trial, like all Inquisitorial trials, was supposed to be secret, but today Heinrich waived that rule to make public examples of the guilty. In Innsbruck, he would have preferred a private trial rather than a public spectacle. But in this instance, Heinrich had the matter completely under control.

He was unmoved by Abigail's pleas, and read from a detailed script he had prepared days earlier.

"Abigail Kolich, you will hear several witnesses accuse you. What say you to them?"

Abigail raised her head again and repeated her denial, "I have heard the accusations against me, and they are lies."

He stood coldly. "In the absence of a true confession and acceptance of responsibility before this tribunal, we will try the case as the Bible requires. Let us hear the testimony of the first witness." He had come to anticipate defiance, but he preferred confessions. He discovered more salacious details that way.

A middle-aged woman with straggly gray hair was brought by the guards over to the witness box. She hunched over and took the oath on the Bible by kissing it.

"What is your name, witness?" demanded the Inquisitor.

"Dorothy Proctor, Father," the woman answered.

"What specific accusation do you lay against the Defendant Abigail Kolich?"

The witness was all too eager to begin her testimony. "Oh, I saw her perpetrating the evil witchcraft, purchasing a spell, or a potion or talisman or maybe it was an amulet, Father. But I saw it with my own eyes! She's guilty of the witchcraft!" The woman pointed at the young girl as accusingly as she could muster. "She is guilty of it sure enough!" she shouted.

"But tell me, sworn witness Proctor, in the name of Almighty God and His Saints, from whom did you see her purchase these implements of the Devil?"

"From the witch named Jezebel, Father. She's dead now though. Burned up to ash. But I saw it with my own eyes! She was an enemy of God! Abigail must burn too! Up the chimney with her!"

"Do you know why she bought these diabolical implements from the witch?" he asked the witness.

"I hear she wanted a boy to fall in love with her. That evil witch must have told her that she could make the boy fall ill with love for her . . . you see, I heard Abigail loves this boy, but he doesn't love her back . . . he is strange like that. All the girls love him, but he does not seem to like the girls, he's an odd boy—"

"Thank you, good woman. We have heard enough." He interrupted her rambling. "You may return to your home in peace. Know that God's good justice will be dispensed here. Go in peace and in the name of Christ the Lord." He quickly made the sign of the cross over her and motioned to the guards to quickly remove her from the witness box.

The woman wanted to say more, but Heinrich was intent on keeping strictly to his schedule. He had achieved fourteen confessions this morning alone, and wanted to convict eight more heretics, blasphemers, and witches before the day's end. It had been a good day, so far. His executioners would be busy.

"We will now hear from the next witness. Guards, bring him in." He motioned to the guards at the door.

They brought an elderly man to the witness box, who seemed confused about what he was supposed to do next. "Take the oath," a guard whispered to him.

"How do I do that?" the old man whispered back.

"Kiss the Bible, you old fool," said the other guard to his right.

"Oh. You must raise it up to my lips; my back is bad." The guards were losing patience, but they wanted the day to end early, so they appeased him and held the heavy old Bible up to his lips.

Once he was done taking the oath, Heinrich asked, "What is your name, sworn witness?"

"Me? Oh, Wilhelm. And this girl is clearly very guilty. May I leave now?"

"Tell me, witness Wilhelm, in the name of Almighty God and His Saints, what did this girl do which occasions your testimony here today?"

"What you mean?" The man looked around the courtroom, utterly perplexed.

"What did Abigail do, sir?" The Inquisitor was exasperated. "Did she not she consort with a known witch to purchase implements of sorcery to make a young man love her?"

"What? Yes. No. I think she is a witch. Maybe. That's what I heard, anyway. May I leave now?"

The Inquisitor was not pleased with the testimony. The old man had privately claimed that he saw Abigail in the act of performing a love spell. It was not the first time a witness had crumbled under the pressure of giving sworn testimony before the tribunal in open Court, however. The old man could be arrested on the spot for obstructing the proceedings, but that would only delay matters. The Inquisitor already had sufficient evidence to justify further torturing Abigail Kolich until she confessed.

"Thank you, sir. Leave now." He thumbed through his papers, to see what other evidence he could present against Abigail. Seeing none, he began giving his orders.

"Here it may be asked whether this honorable Court, in the case of such a prisoner much defamed, accused both by sworn witnesses and by proofs, nothing being lacking but her own confession, can properly lead Abigail Kolich to hope that her life can still be spared."

The Inquisitor glanced up at her with icy eyes and continued reading his written speech. "If, neither by threats nor by promises such as these, you can be induced to speak the truth and accept responsibility for your grievous offenses, then the jailers must carry out the sentence.

They will torture you according to the accepted methods, with more or less of severity as your crimes may demand."

He turned and looked at the guards. "If, after this torture, this prisoner will not confess the truth satisfactorily, other sorts of tortures must be placed before her, with her understanding that unless she will confess the truth, she must endure those also."

He turned toward the judge. "I hope that this honorable Court shall see to it, moreover, that throughout this interval guards are constantly with the prisoner, so that she may not be alone; because she will be visited by the Devil and tempted into grievous acts." The feeble jurist yawned and nodded his acquiescence.

A distinguished man about Heinrich's age wearing the robes of an advanced legal practitioner stood to the side of the lectern, looked up at the Inquisitor, and whispered, "Father, may I have a word?"

He looked down at the man with derision and asked, "And who are you?"

"I am Arnold Kolich von Eusskirchen, the Public Notary of this Diocese…I am also Abigail's father."

"Well, Notary Arnold Kolich von Eusskirchen, I am about to sentence your daughter to the tortures. If you had anything to bring before the attention of the Inquisition, it should have been brought in the form of sworn testimony. You know that—you are a Public Notary of the Diocese. How dare you bother me now and interfere with the important work of this Court."

"My words are private, for your own hearing only, Father," the man whispered.

Heinrich would have been enraged by the unparalleled intrusion had he not been intrigued by the man's apparent secret. He announced to the courtroom, "The defendant shall remain under oath and in shackles in the dungeon. We shall reconvene this hearing promptly. May the Lord Jesus Christ bless us until then. Amen." He stepped off the podium and walked into the judge's private chambers with Notary Kolich. Weeping and confused, Abigail watched them both enter the antechamber before she was dragged off.

"This is shockingly irregular, Notary Kolich. You know that I can arrest you right now for obstructing this proceeding. What have you to say?"

"Father, Abigail is my only daughter. My wife and other children long ago died from the plague. I will not try to convince you Abigail is guilty only of being a fool. She was in love with a boy. An old woman whom you yourself have convicted of witchery took advantage of her childish foolishness and sold her silly charms so she could try to woo the boy she loves. But in her heart, she is no witch or devil. She is God's child and knows no malice, only love, Father. Please spare her life." He bowed his head in submission.

"If she is guilty of consorting with a known witch, then she must burn just as if she was a witch herself. She should confess if only to save her soul from Satan's hellfire. You know the law as well as I do, Notary Kolich." Heinrich began to walk away.

"Father, if you let her live, I will be in your debt forever."

He turned back to face Kolich. "Let her live, Notary? Let her live? This is foolishness! Besides, what good is it to me to have a Notary in my debt? Justice must be done here. That is the sacred law of the Holy Bible. You know the passages of which I speak."

"Father, I will be your humble servant, and loyally serve you the remainder of my life without recompense, if you would only spare hers."

For a moment, Heinrich pondered the offer. The girl was, after all, not technically a witch herself. And he had already taken care of that evil witch Jezebel.

After a long silence, he responded. "Suppose I was to acknowledge your debt—your services will be mine without any question until you die. You would accept that, Notary Arnold Kolich von Eusskirchen?"

"I do accept, Father. I do." Kolich kissed the Bible, which Heinrich had been holding.

"And you understand that only her *life* would be spared . . ."

"Yes, Father, she is the only family I have left."

"I will need to still spend some time with her, alone in the dungeon, you understand that, yes?"

"Yes, Father," he sheepishly replied.

"Then, in the sight of God, you are now in my lifelong debt and servitude. Be at my offices at the University promptly at dawn tomorrow morning. I will have much work for you to do, without any recompense of course."

"Thank you, Father. God bless you! I will tell everyone how wonderful you are!"

"No. Our agreement shall remain secret, Notary. I cannot have the faithful think I am weak of heart."

"Yes, Father. As you wish. You will not regret your decision today. I will be a faithful servant, Father, all the days of my life, without question." Arnold Kolich was beside himself with joy and tears welled up in his eyes as Heinrich prepared to go downstairs to visit Abigail, who was still in shackles.

"Are you going to release her now?" asked the Notary.

"Yes, she will live. But I shall spend some time with her first…." said Institoris. He picked up a sharp knife he had brought with him, and watched it glisten in the sunlight. He planned on enjoying his brief visit to Abigail in the dungeon.

CRYPT

"A grimoire?" asked the stout, wrinkled priest, leaning forward in his rickety chair. His squinting eyes strained to see Sebastian's face in the dim candlelight of the shadowy chapel aptly known as Our Lady Underground, nestled deep in the heart of Mont-St-Michel.

"It is a book about witchcraft," Sebastian whispered, unsure of what reaction to expect from the old man.

The man scowled as if physically pained by mention of the topic. He leaned back in his chair, which creaked as he did so. After pondering for a moment, he shook his head vigorously. "No, no! We would not keep a book like that here. This is a house of God!" he exclaimed, waving his bony hands dramatically upward at the coffered ceiling. "We have no filth!"

"Of course, but I had been informed that this one is secured here," said Sebastian, matter-of-factly.

"And from whom did you hear that?" demanded the priest, squinting again as though it would assist his strained hearing.

"From an authority in Paris. May I look for it?" pleaded Sebastian, growing frustrated that his months' long journey was being thwarted by a diminutive and uncooperative priest in a basement.

"Hmph. That is the problem with youth…wastes scarce time that could be spent in sacred contemplation of the divine." The monk looked up at the ceiling again.

"I intend to contemplate the sacred once I find this book," said

Sebastian sarcastically. Fortunately, the old man had grown tired of resisting.

"Around those bends on the left," said the monk, raising his thin arm to point down a gloomy serpentine corridor that was dripping. "Down the stairs, in the Crypt of the Ten Candles. That is where my predecessors sleep, and where we keep books no one needs anymore. If we have that rubbish, it is buried deep in there. But mind yourself; we cannot afford to light all ten candles for very long, so hasten!" He giggled to himself.

"Uh, yes, thank you." Sebastian turned and brusquely walked down the sloping corridor.

I would probably go batty too, living down here alone for forty years, thought Sebastian.

The chapels, guest halls and scriptorium possessed windows open to the sky that allowed cold salty sea breezes to penetrate and circulate through them. However, the acrid smell of mildew formed over centuries of stagnant moistness penetrated every ounce of air that Sebastian inhaled. In the interior, windowless rooms of the Abbey, the air induced constant involuntary coughing. He stumbled several times treading on slippery moss and across uneven ground that slanted sharply downwards every fifteen feet without any visible reason other than the drastically sinking foundation.

The flickering taper he held in his right hand created only a tiny orb of light that could not illuminate much more than a few feet ahead. He was forced to use his left hand to guide himself down the hallway, feeling for a doorway to the crypt. The gray stone walls were slimy and wet with at least an inch of mossy growth. He wiped his hands repeatedly on his robes, but the green slime just returned upon his next contact with the wall.

At the bottom, he spotted a gaping entryway to his left, and entered a room decorated elaborately with frescoes on the walls and round pearl-colored stones spaced all along the ceiling's perimeter. Given the depth and dankness of this room, he presumed that he was nearing, or below, sea level. There were no windows, and the air was rank.

Haphazard stacks of voluminous parchment, very little of it bound but all of it covered in thick layers of dust and lichen, were strewn around the room. Most of the paper was rotten with age or had been partially consumed by rodents and fungus, leaving a patchwork of brown, green and yellow paper everywhere.

He tried lifting a single sheaf off the top of a pile, and it crumbled in his hands as if it were made of powder held together with brown fungus and sticky cobwebs.

How am I going to find The Grand Grimoire *in here? What if I came all this way to find nothing?*

His heart sank like a stone tossed into the stormy bay. Panicked, he feverishly pictured the scene of arriving back in Rome, and meeting Father Institoris with nothing in hand…

My God, I must find this book. Where is it?

He rummaged carelessly through piles of ancient documents, casting them about haplessly and putting them into a shamble. After knocking over and destroying two tall stacks of parchment, he calmed himself down.

I have all the time in the world. I can spend weeks here, looking for this book, he thought to himself. *The Abbot invited me to do that…*

However, the room was bitterly cold. There was simply no source of heat. All the large fireplaces in the Abbey were far upstairs, as no chimneys had ever been built this deeply into the rocky foundation. After an hour spent rifling through papers and books, he caught sight of a few larger books buried deep behind several piles, chained to the rear stone wall.

He waded around the obstacles, trying not to cause more permanent damage when he reached the rear wall. Secured into it at eye level was a gargantuan iron candelabra in the shape of a cross with ten candles. Each candle dripped with greasy wax now dry, frozen in time. He carefully lit each stubby candle with his taper until the room was fully aglow.

In the brighter light, he was now able to view the whole crypt. It was decorated with human remains. Finger bones were arranged to create elaborate mosaics on the walls. The pearly stones he had seen were human jawbones arranged all along the perimeter of the ceiling. Eyeless generations of monks' skulls gazed down at him silently. Humerus and tibia bones were lined up row after row, in bizarre shapes and decorations. A cold chill ran down his back as he beheld the surreal figure of a grim reaper in the center of the ceiling formed out of tiny children's skeletons. As far as he could tell, the bones had all been picked clean by rodents, bugs, and birds who had somehow found their way into the crypt from the outside.

He closed his eyes, tried to breathe deeply but coughed. Forcing the images of the monstrous surroundings from his mind, he turned around and faced the rear wall. Chained to the wall across from him were a few large, thickly bound books. One had *"Le Grand Grimoire"* etched on its spine. The leather binding itself was crimson red, and the title was inscribed in deep black calligraphy on the cover. Symbols that he did not recognize decorated the rest of the rawhide binding.

Excited to have finally found his aim, he picked it up and laid it down on the top of the piles of paper. He opened it to the frontispiece where he saw the strange image of a man with three horns, standing upright, with a tail and cloven hooves, but with a man's torso and hands. The figure had a large hoop of metal wrapped around him, and he was sprinkling coins on the ground. Underneath the figure, *Lucifuge Rofocale* was inscribed. Sebastian did not recognize the name, but it sounded like Lucifer.

Sebastian silently read the title page which was written in French: "Concerning the art of controlling celestial, aerial, terrestrial, and infernal spirits." He continued to read.

> O men! O impotent mortals! Tremble at your own temerity when you blindly aspire to the possession of a science so profound. Arm yourselves, therefore, with intrepidity, prudence, wisdom, and virtue, as qualifications for this grand and illimitable work, in which I have passed sixty-and seven years, toiling night and day for the attainment of success in so sublime an object.

Sebastian was terrified but fascinated with the book he had finally found for Father Institoris. He had never beheld a document containing blasphemous and illicit learned magic like this. He continued to scan its contents in the candlelight.

> O Count ASTAROTH! be propitious to me, and grant that to-night you may appear to me under a human form, free from evil smell, and that you may accord me, in virtue of the pact which I propose to enter into, all the riches that I need. O great ASTAROTH, I pray thee to quit thy dwelling, wheresoever it may be, and come hither to speak with me; otherwise, will I compel thee by the power of the strong living God, His beloved Son and the Holy Spirit. Obey promptly, or thou shalt be eternally tormented by the power of the potent words in the grand Clavicle of Solomon, wherewith he was accustomed to compelling the rebellious spirits to receive his compact. Then straightway appear, or I will persistently torture thee by the virtue of these great words in the Clavicle.

Energized to have found the dark treasure he had sought, Sebastian carefully flipped through its dusty pages to find even more mysterious inscriptions.

In addition to the text regarding conjuration, the book contained a variety of incantations, spells and invocations written in different languages, including some tongues that he did not recognize. The operations that he did comprehend included making formal pacts with demons, performing necromancy to speak with the shades of the dead, preventing the conception of children, making women sexually promiscuous, and even spells to repair porcelain vases that had been shattered.

From what he could also see, the preface claimed that the book was originally written by King Solomon, and, according to handwriting on the first page, this copy was supposedly duplicated by hand in Cairo by a person known as Alibek the Egyptian in the fourth century.

A metal plate was affixed permanently to the inner binding. On it was inscribed "Property of Brother John of Morigny." Next to the name was another odd symbol with letters surrounding it.

Without spending too much time studying the book's contents in detail, it seemed clear from the writing style that this book was written by someone intimately familiar with Catholic rites and some type of magic. But it seemed very different from the folk magic that he had discussed with the priests and laity along the way here.

For one, this book was decidedly masculine in both tone and content. The authors had clear familiarity with Christian prayers and complex rites and rituals, as it contained numerous benedictions and commands using names of God, psalms, prayers and verses from the Bible and the canon of the Mass. This text seemed more like dark sorcery than the mild witchcraft Sebastian had learned about in Aragon and Limoge.

He flipped through the book, and a small piece of lambskin parchment fell out, onto the dirty floor. Sebastian brushed it off and picked it up to examine it. Someone had been using it as a form of bookmark in addition to the silk ribbon that was sewn into the binding. On the bookmark someone had written "John of Morigny." The same name that was inscribed on the metal plate inside the book.

Sebastian closed the book and breathed a sigh of relief. This was exactly the tome he had been seeking. He knew that he would spend many weeks analyzing the book's malefic contents, but now a wholly new concern arose in him.

Up until now, Sebastian had never fully considered the practical reality of this aspect of the task he had accepted. The book was so large, he could never realistically copy all its relevant contents by hand. And even if he could do so, the Scriptorium in the Abbey would never permit him to view such blasphemy in its dignified new hall.

Alternatively, it might be a mortal sin—and crime—to steal this ancient book from the crypt without asking permission of the Abbot, and now that he was considering doing just that, he was more than a little concerned about the practical ramifications of that, as well.

If someone catches me stealing this book, I might end up as another decoration on the ceiling. Should I seek the Abbot's leave to remove the book?

He guessed that if he sought permission from the Abbot to take it with him, it would likely be denied. He would have no way of realistically getting an Order from Institoris overruling the Abbot's refusal. It would take months to even get such an unorthodox request to the Inquisitor. Plus, it would probably take at least another month or two to receive a response, assuming the German Inquisitor could even be located. Not to mention, it would likely infuriate Institoris that Sebastian had blundered so early in his mission. He thought about tearing pages out of it, but that would ruin the book, plus he lacked the knowledge of which pages were relevant.

Instead, he took another deep breath of dank and musty air and leaned all his weight and strength to pull the chain affixed to the wall. It broke away from the rock, and he was left holding the book while the iron chain clattered on the floor. He tucked the book under his arm and wrapped the heavy links of the chain around himself, covered by his cloak. He knew that he had to somehow spirit this book back with him to Rome, regardless of the potential penalty for doing so. If he was caught by the Abbot or the knights, he could explain that he believed he was removing something of great evil from their midst.

He blew out all ten candles almost entirely by coughing, then walked briskly back up the sloping, slippery corridor. As he approached the chapel, the old man looked up and saw Sebastian nervously walking toward him.

"You find what you were looking for?" he asked suspiciously. Or maybe Sebastian just assumed he was leery.

Not wanting to lie, Sebastian ducked the question and changed the topic.

"I found the curious display of bones. Remarkable."

"That is where my withered corpse will be hanging soon, my boy. I will be keeping those books and bones company," he cackled.

"Yes, well, thank you very much for your help," said Sebastian, rushing away as quickly as possible back to his guest room with the stolen book under his cloak.

But he couldn't help picturing the old man's dead body pitched high above the room, gazing down at the Crypt of the Ten Candles, forever.

INCUBUS

"It feels good inside her—that is exactly what she said, Father."

"Go on," said the young, dashing Father John Gremper, sitting in the confessional while conferring the sacrament of reconciliation on Gristelde, a fetching nineteen-year-old blonde girl. In the diocese of Basel, in the village called Buchel, near the town of Gewyll, the handsome Father Gremper heard the bawdiest confessions every Saturday after 5 p.m.

Because Gristelde unfortunately had so few interesting mortal sins of her own to confess, each Saturday evening, she would visit and tell the priest all the filthy things her friends were doing. He would sit back and listen intently. He looked forward to these weekly visits.

She knelt behind a screen with her face pressed up against it. The priest was only inches away from her mouth through the screen.

"You cannot possibly let Horace know what you are doing with Diago, I told Alice," she whispered. "Horace will murder him that same night! And this she does with him three times a week, on Sundays, Tuesdays, and Thursdays, and on some of the other more holy nights."

"What exactly does she do?" he asked.

"I am ashamed to say it aloud." She blushed.

"We are in confession, after all. And you have told me many times before how Alice copulates with him. Tell me again."

"She has relations with Diago in all different manners," she said. "I have told you before."

"Such as?"

"Well," she giggled. "Sometimes she mounts him and takes her breasts out and he suckles them. And sometimes, she lays down on her back and he gets on top of her. And sometimes, she uses her mouth—"

"Her husband does not know?" interrupted Gremper.

"Well, I do not think so. But the homage she has given to the devil is of such a sort that she is bound to dedicate herself body and soul to Diago forever. At least that is what she told me."

"She performed a love spell?" he asked.

"Well, some type of spell. That is how she was able to ensnare him."

"I see," said the priest. "Tell me more."

"Her carnal knowledge is not only with him," the girl whispered.

"Oh? She has others?" asked the priest, curious.

"I have seen her go to her barn with many others. She often takes them there after her husband is asleep."

"I see," said the priest. "And what does she do with them?"

"I don't rightly know exactly. But she tells me that some are much larger than others, and she uses her mouth to pleasure them."

"On their members, you mean?" he asked quietly.

"Yes," she said, putting her hands up to cover her face in embarrassment.

"What else does she say?"

"They spend a long time pleasing her, as well."

"I see," said the priest, leaning back in his chair. "Well, since you yourself did not commit any mortal sins, there is no need for you to be absolved. However, you have committed sins of omission, by failing to warn Alice that she is placing her immortal soul in jeopardy. For that, say one Ave Maria and return in a week to tell me more. I want to know more about what men in the barn do to her."

"Thank you, Father." She bowed her head and scurried out of the booth, looking forward to gathering more secrets to tell him next weekend.

There was a loud knock on the door to the confessional and Gremper opened the door to see who was there. Standing outside the wooden booth was a tall Germanic priest wearing the black and white Dominican garb.

"Gremper, I presume?" asked the Inquisitor.

"Yes?"

"Your Bishop instructed me to speak with you. I am the Inquisitor for your region. You have critical information that will be helpful to me in my task here."

Gremper stepped out and closed the door to the confessional behind him, removed his stole, kissed it and put it away. He informed the line of waiting parishioners that they would have to see Father Giblin to confess on Monday. They groaned.

The two men walked inside the Church to a nearby private alcove, where Gremper lit up a pipe.

"So how may I be of assistance, my good Inquisitor?"

"I hear that you are quite the Confessor. The faithful line up for hours to wait and see you," Institoris said.

"Well, I am always willing to save souls," chuckled Gremper, sucking on his pipe proudly.

"I hear that the girls especially enjoy confessing their intimate sins to you. Is that true?" asked the Inquisitor.

Gremper took the pipe out of his mouth and coughed, wheezing. "Well, no. I mean, I hear all confessions. Who told you that? Was it Nezetta? Piera?"

"I desire to save all their souls. Tell me more about Nezetta's sins," asked the Inquisitor.

"Father, you know that I cannot divulge sacred confidences. Canon law provides that I would be sent into a monastery to do perpetual penance if I reveal what is told to me in the confessional."

"But you also know that Canon 21 of the Fourth Council of the Lateran provides that if a priest should happen to need wiser counsel, he may cautiously seek the same without any mention of a specific person," replied Institoris.

"But why would I need wiser counsel?"

"Because I will place a lit torch under your genitals if you do not cooperate."

Gremper went silent.

"Therefore," the Inquisitor continued, "you are hereby authorized to tell me details. If I happen to discover on my own accord whether vile acts were done by Nezetta, Piera or someone else, is of no consequence to you."

"I simply cannot do that," declared Gremper, preparing to walk away, despite the Inquisitor's seemingly credible threats.

"I happen to know what you did with Agnes and Caterina. In fact, I happen to know that both were with you together at the same time in bed, is that not so?"

"Where did you hear that lie?" asked the frightened Gremper. He knew he couldn't trust those two.

"I am sure their parents would be displeased," said Institoris. "Now, I am going to inventory several deadly and mortal sins for you. I want you to tell me whether they were committed in this Diocese, and when. There is no need to give names. Leave that to me. Let us begin." Institoris took out his book and opened it to a fresh page titled *Buchel*. "Adultery," he said.

The priest stammered. "Th-there is a woman here consorting with many men, not her husband."

"Go on," the Inquisitor made a note. "Continue, please."

"She is not only committing adultery, but she also performed love magic. It drew the man to her. She also fornicates with many others in a barn," he said. "She uses her mouth to pleasure them and they, her," he whispered.

"An incubus, no doubt," commented the Inquisitor.

"A what?"

"Scripture speaks of incubi and succubi, demons that lust after women, yet nowhere do we read that they fall into vices against nature. We do not speak only of sodomy, but of any other sin whereby the act is wrongfully performed outside the rightful channel. So if a woman uses her mouth on a man's member for oral pleasure, such is often a sign of an incubus or succubus."

"I see," said Gremper.

"Witches infect the minds of men with an inordinate love of strange women, and so inflame their hearts that by no shame of punishment, by no words or actions can they be forced to desist from such love. Similarly, witches can stir up such hatred between married couples that they are unable in any way to perform the procreative functions of marriage. Indeed, in the untimely silence of the night, they will cover great distances in search of mistresses and irregular lovers."

"Interesting," replied Gremper.

"If a tempted man has a beautiful and honest wife, why else would he wander from the marital bed other than to a waiting witch?" the Inquisitor asked.

"I suppose…" said Gremper.

"Lust," continued Institoris.

"Must we continue?" asked Gremper, becoming more and more uncomfortable with this process.

"Lust," the Inquisitor said again, not answering his question.

Gremper continued to detail three years of confessions he heard from those who lived in Buchel, trying not to offer too many names. But by the time he was done, the Inquisitor had enough information about virtually every soul in town to easily figure it out.

Gremper divulged all the many times that Margaret Segerin admitted that she was fornicating with Dorothy Bydermans. He divulged the time that Ludeck Tobel confessed to him that he had murdered Hilmar Hagen over a feud involving stolen cattle. Tobel never faced any punishment, even though the priest had requested that he turn himself in to the civil authorities. The Hagens had been told the death was accidental.

And he told Institoris that there were a few elderly women who were suspected of placing curses on the farmers' fields, as they had lain fallow for two seasons now. And he told them all about Alice, Horace, Diago and all the men in the barn.

"Good," said the Inquisitor, finally closing his book.

"Nezetta and Piera, they will be left out of this, yes?" asked Gremper.

"That depends," replied the Inquisitor.

"Depends on what?" he asked.

"Whether they tell the truth about what you did, when I spend my time with them in the dungeon," he said, grinning.

MORIGNY

After dark, when Sebastian had settled into his room at Mont-St-Michel Abbey, he lit a single candle, barred the inner door, and looked more closely at the book he had absconded with from the crypt.

In two different places the name Brother John of Morigny was inscribed. He looked at the map that Mudazzo had given him in Barcelona. It showed a tiny dot for the town of Morigny only two days ride from the shoreline near here.

Sebastian went to sleep that night, troubled by the prospect that this book had been circulating for an unknown time before it was relegated to the basement of the Abbey. He thanked the Abbot, and hailed a ferryman to take him back to shore during daylight when the tide was in. The seasons had shifted from Autumn to winter in the space of a fortnight.

He had previously stabled Epona in La Caserne. Once he was reunited with her, he felt reinvigorated. He could stash the large grimoire in one of her side saddlebags. Heinrich Institoris would commend him for stealing the tome from the crypt.

But when he passed through Morigny, if he blinked, he would have missed it. Other than a few small farms and an outpost for exchanging coins for milk and meat, there was only a dilapidated building that once constituted a Benedictine monastery. The building's roof had practically collapsed and there was no longer a cross at the apex, where one once stood. The walls had massive holes in them, and weeds grew both outside and inside it. It looked thoroughly abandoned.

He approached a farmer in a nearby field.

"Brother John?" replied the farmer. He spit on the ground. "Died back before my parents were born. Had no children. You need to ask Tomas. He might know if he left anything when he died." The farmer wiped his hands on his leather apron.

"Where is he?" asked Sebastian.

The farmer pointed at the collapsing monastery.

"In there?" Sebastian asked incredulously. The farmer nodded and went back to his work.

Sebastian walked over to the crumbling edifice. Inside, he found an ancient monk wearing a ratty brown Benedictine robe. All around were leaves that had blown in from the outside.

The monk was bald and painfully thin. He was seated at a table in the back of the dark room, holding a cracked mug, staring at a wall. His eyes were completely white, and his skin was practically translucent. He did not look like had left the collapsed building in ages.

"Hello?" Sebastian said, as he walked inside.

"Yes? Is someone there?" asked the blind monk, looking around frantically as though he might see someone.

"Yes, my name is Sebastian. How are you, Brother?"

"Are you here with my puzzles?" asked the monk, smiling exuberantly.

"Puzzles?" Sebastian, confused, looked around to see if the monk was talking to someone else.

"Did you bring me puzzles?" asked the monk again.

"Uh, I am sorry, I do not know what you mean," said Sebastian. "I am the only one here."

"Every month, Jacques comes by and brings me some food and wine, and my puzzles. Old wood pieces that I can play with, and stack and piece together. I cannot see anymore."

"I am sorry, Brother, I do not have any puzzles for you today."

"Piecing puzzles together is a joy. Do you not agree?"

"Yes, yes I do. I am looking for information about a monk that I believe once may have lived here. Brother John of Morigny?"

The blind monk's face deadened. "What do you need to know about him?" he asked grimly.

"I saw his name in a book at Mont-St-Michel Abbey. I came here to see if he might have left any other books—"

"Sit down, pour me wine, and I will tell you about John," said the blind monk. "My name is Tomas."

Sebastian peered at the wine in the carafe on the monk's table, leaning over and smelling it. It had turned entirely to vinegar. Instead, he reached in his flask and poured the monk a little wine that he had left over.

The monk sipped it, thanking him. Sebastian sat down.

"John had a friend, a doctor, named Jacobus de Terramo. I believe John grew up with Jacob before he became a doctor. He was the one who put him up to it, I believe."

"Put him up to what?" asked Sebastian.

"Since he was a child, John thirsted after enlightenment," the monk said. "But its pursuit filled him with fear and dread for his soul. You see, when he arrived here at this place," the monk gestured around at the rundown monastery, "he had visions. They filled the sky and shook the earth. He found them frightening and suspicious. He did not know if they were scenes of heaven or hell."

"Visions?" asked Sebastian.

"From those damned books!" exclaimed the feeble monk, slamming his bony hand on the table in front of him. "John learned a great deal from the spirits. He used his art to learn about these visions. He taught the two of us how to practice the arts as well. His younger sister used it to learn ten languages but she had the visions, too."

"I do not understand," said Sebastian.

"It was that doctor, you see! He gave him the books. I think the doctor had stolen them, myself. I think he got them from a Turk. But John learned everything in them. Eventually, he copied one of them called the *Ars Notaria* by hand. But when we tried using it, even more dreadful things came to pass. One by one, each of us suffered black visions. I went blind. Then the deaths started. John and Jacob fought viciously. John killed Jacob first. Then he turned on his sister. Killed her in her sleep. By then, John tried to put an end to it by burning his books. He threw the ashes down the well. But still, the spirits plagued us day and night. May more in this town died by murder, including John by his own hand."

The monk pointed up to a rafter which had the remnants of rope hanging from it. "Behold, the symbol of our destruction." The monk then pointed at the wall he had been staring blindly at. On it was scrawled in blood the same symbol that was next to John's name in the books.

"*Glasya Labolas*," the monk said. "He made us do it."

"Go on, please," asked Sebastian, nauseated by the sight.

"An apothecary got hold of a surviving copy we did not know John had made. Then he had the visions. He set fire to his own household. They burned up to ash. All of them died. Family, servants, even the horses trapped in the barns."

"So what happened to the book?"

"We believed the book was lost—burned up in the fires. But," he said, leaning forward and tapping the table with his long fingernail, "I heard a rumor that the last copy had survived."

"Do you know where it might be?" asked Sebastian.

"Northgate—Michael Northgate—spirited it to London. Good riddance, I say. Let them keep it on their filthy soil. Let the city burn for it."

"Another book that was mentioned to me was called the *Goetia*'?"

"*Goetia* is the Greek word for sorcery. That book is in Hibernia, at Clonmacnoise Abbey. So many men who have dabbled in such things, like Pietro de Abano. A remarkable physician who took an interest. Destroyed him too. His family as well. Jacobus and John were not the only ones...The Church came and took the other books away, thank God."

"What did the *Ars* look like?" asked Sebastian.

"It looked like something that was forged in hell where it came from," said the blind monk. "Now, please leave. I must go back to playing with my puzzles."

LONDON

After Morigny, Sebastian was confounded. The blind monk had told him the *Ars Notaria* might be located somewhere in London. But that was merely conjecture from an old man, and he only had a name—Michael Northgate—to start a search there.

But the city was far beyond the Channel and populated by tens of thousands of people. Finding a single lost book would not be easy, even assuming the information was credible. He had more authoritative information from the Cardinal in Paris that additional books were in Hibernia, but that was even more distant.

He developed a strategy. He would first explore London for the *Ars Notaria*. If he found nothing after a fortnight, he would travel to Hibernia directly. If he chose to forego the opportunity to seek the *Ars Notaria*, he might never make it back to London, and Institoris would be displeased that he did not follow up on a lead to collect a critical text. And if Sebastian allowed a book as notorious as the *Ars* to remain in permanent circulation, it could lead to tragic consequences. He had enough extra gold to afford the travel.

So, he rode Epona due north back to Cherbourg. He found a large-sized ferry that would accept Epona and paid the first mate three gulden to ensure safe and quick passage to Portsmouth. Due to good weather, they crossed the Channel within three days. He was making good time.

Once he arrived in Portsmouth, the first mate told him that London was a three days' journey. The weather was becoming colder here, and Sebastian realized that he had failed to take weather into account when formulating his plan. Here, most of the roads were dirt tracks which only remained visible and free from growth because of frequent use. Most carts and wagons had spiked wheels and blacksmiths set up forges near the roads and made a good trade shoeing horses and repairing wheels. Travel was hazardous in these winter months when rain or snow could obliterate the dirt tracks. Villages were few and far between and signposts a rarity. However, after two days of asking directions, Sebastian neared London. Like Paris, when he arrived at the city center, he needed to stable Epona and enter on foot.

The city was quite a sight. Streets were narrow and filthy. The upper floors of timber houses hung over the roads and were quite closely packed together. Everywhere he looked were fishmongers, goldsmiths, tailors, haberdashers, vintners and clothworkers. In the nicer parts of the city he saw two-story wattle and daub houses painted with white limewash.

He decided to invest a few gulden in a strong wool cloak sold by a clothmaker at an outdoor market outside Blackwell Hall. It was thick and provided excellent warmth for the price. Once he got his bearings and ate some roasted fish, he decided to enter a small bookshop in Charing Cross, a street in a circle that had a large cross erected in its center.

The shop was named Bryars & Bryars Books. It was tiny and quaint. He entered it and asked for the proprietor. The man introduced himself as the elder Bryar, whose great-grandfather had established it. Their sign said they specialized in selling bound, handwritten copies of manuscripts that were mostly monastic and alchemical. They displayed many beautifully calligraphies of Bibles in every size imaginable.

"Hello, my name is Sebastian. I heard in Paris that a book may be in this town. It is entitled the *Ars Notaria*."

"The *Ars Notoria*, you mean? The book of the notorious arts?"

"Oh, I suppose that is correct. I misunderstood its name."

"That book is now called *The New Arts*, or *Ars Nova*. At least once John copied it and added his own doctrines."

"Oh, so you are familiar with the book and John of Morigny?"

"I have never seen his book with my own eyes or touched it. Once it reached these shores, we received a dozen bids for it in this shop alone. Anyone who possessed it had perfect memory of all things, you see. A Lord offered us his weight in gold if we could acquire it for him. But we never did. And I was glad of it. The rumor was that a curse would lead to murder and deaths by fire anywhere it travelled. Last thing London needs are fires."

"Do you know where it is now? I heard a name, Michael Northgate?"

"Michael of Northgate. He was a parish priest once, but his interests veered into the…esoteric. He amassed obscene wealth for a priest and became a boundless benefactor of the Abbey at Canterbury. He moved there and hired four monks. They collected more valuable books about magic than the entire library at Oxford."

"What happened to him?"

"Library was looted. Far too precious a cache for a monastery to defend. They slaughtered him and the others and set fires. Terrible sight to behold."

"All the books were lost?" asked Sebastian, dejected.

"Sometimes Michael's books will come back on the market, but typically the less valuable ones about alchemy or the movements of the planets. We never came across the *Ars*. We have no idea if anyone owns it or if it was lost in the mists of time. Michael's was the only surviving book, so I can only assume it is gone. Good riddance, I say."

"May I ask where Canterbury is? I have come all this way. I would very much like to exhaust all possibilities and see where it all came to rest."

"Certainly. For a gold piece, I can sell you a map…here…" The man reached down and pulled out a cheap map of the area.

Sebastian offered him a few gulden, as the man had been more accommodating than anyone in weeks, and the map would be helpful.

He unscrolled it. Unfortunately, it appeared that Canterbury was a fair distance from London and would require at least a few additional days overland to get there. Nonetheless, Sebastian wanted to follow all leads to their end.

CANTERBURY

"Michael's room." Inside the monastery at Canterbury Cathedral, the page pointed into a room that had scorch marks on the walls and floors.

The structure was familiar to Sebastian, even though he had never visited the grand Cathedral before. It had been a Benedictine monastery for centuries, and it had many of the same features as Mont-St-Michel. Parts of it were still under construction as every King of England had desired to improve upon its perfection somehow.

But this part of the complex was where the Benedictine monks lived and worked, and so it was far less ornate and impressive than the main building.

"Burnt up," the page said, running his finger along the sooty windowsill. "Empty for as long as I can remember."

"Thank you," said Sebastian, offering the boy a silver coin for his troubles. "Is there anywhere else he would have stayed, perhaps a scriptorium or library?"

"There was a section under the main Cathedral where some of his books were once kept. But it's all empty now."

"May I see it?" asked Sebastian, fishing around in his pouch for a gold coin. He passed it to the page.

"No harm in it." The page tucked the coin snugly in his vest pocket and led Sebastian through the courtyard toward the Church itself. Surrounding them were the soaring arched windows of Canterbury Cathedral. There were a few flat gravestones throughout the yard, a few trees, and stone benches.

"In summer, this garden's full of roses. In winter, though, nothin' but thorns."

A strange bird with incredible plumage strutted past them. "Peacocks!" the page exclaimed. "We have 'em here. Mournful crying, if ever you hear it. We hear 'em echoing around the gardens. This one'll try to bite you if you got too close." He chuckled. "That was his spot," he pointed to a bench on the other side of the courtyard. "Michael's bench. That is where he'd read his books. All tangled up in roses now, no one wants to cut 'em. Can't tell you how many times I get pricked over there," he pointed to the morass of dried rose bushes that desperately needed pruning.

When they arrived at the door to the empty library chamber under the Cathedral, the page opened it and displayed the room to Sebastian. "See, nothin' here."

The page was right, there was absolutely nothing to be seen. Bare walls. Sebastian was disheartened. He had come all this way only to be brought to a dead end.

He thanked the page and walked back into the courtyard alone. He wandered over to the stone bench on which Michael of Northgate reportedly sat decades earlier. He could not even sit on it, as the thorny roses had totally taken it over. He inspected it more closely and saw a small inscribed stone slab underneath it on the ground.

He assumed that the slab must have been there a very long time, as thorns had grown over it completely and it remained untouched. He went over to a groundskeeper who was standing on the other side of the courtyard.

"Sir, may I trouble you for your rake?" he asked, flipping a silver coin at the man.

"Have at it, my friend." He smiled, enjoying the excuse for a break from his work.

Sebastian walked over and used the rake to spread aside some of the thorny branches that had grown between the bench and the slab. Once the rock was visible, he could make out the symbol inscribed on it, but he still did not know what it meant.

Once Sebastian cleared the ground a bit more, he realized that he could use the metal tines of the rake to tilt the slab up. He pried up the stone slab and underneath was an empty space, about nine inches in diameter. He flipped the remainder of the slab off and reached inside. It was a deep hole. He kneeled and plunged his hand down into it, not sure if a viper or spider might lie in wait.

His fingers brushed against something that felt like leather. He tugged on it and his fingers wrapped around it. It was a small book, not much thicker than a prayer missal.

He yanked it out of the hole. He badly scratched the back of his hand on thorns and started to bleed. He covered his bloody hand with the wool cloak. On the front of the book were the words "*Ars Notoria.*" He flipped it open. On the first page was the symbol of a peacock with a human head and the word "Andrealphus" and the familiar name "John of Morigny."

Michael had evidently secreted it in a place that no one was likely to dig; under pricking thorns and a cursed stone bench in a monastery courtyard. Sebastian had finally found what he came here for.

FINAN

It was nearly noon on a blustery day late in December, and a numbing blast of wet arctic air continued to blow steadily from the north. Shivering, Sebastian rode Epona westward through the farmland of County Galloway.

It had taken him several weeks to arrive in Lahinch on a ferryboat from Dover. He had spent four days looking for a ship that would transport both him and Epona, as he knew that finding a mare of this quality in Hibernia would have been near impossible.

The relatively small ship had tossed and turned in the icy waves, and even Sebastian was worried that it might capsize. When he had spent time on fishing boats in Bretagne, the captains had always returned before wintry waters would get that rough.

Eventually, when the battered ship arrived in Lahinch, it took him and the horse two days to recuperate from the trip. Now firmly on land again, he found that he had made a wrong turn and ended up traversing a wasteland that the map called "The Burren." He had wasted hours going in circles and now hurriedly tried to make up for the lost time. After passing through Lisdoonvarna, he was convinced that he was nearing the end of the Earth itself.

Sebastian hoped that he could soon thaw out his frostbitten fingers and toes in front of a blazing fire. The gloves and pelt that the Abbot had offered him at Mont-St-Michel were still of tremendous value to him here. He had not even taken them off since then, sleeping with them on. With teeth chattering, he rode up a rocky path through walled gardens, and finally arrived at the freshly built Leamaneagh Castle.

It belonged to Finan O'Brien, feudal lord of western County Clare. Being new, the castle lacked many of the defensive features that many older fortifications had. It had no moat or portcullis, but the eastern portion did have a five-story tower with a stone vault on the top floor with a few narrow vertical slits for archers, just in case of unlikely attack.

Sebastian relinquished Epona's leather reins to the two knights stationed in front of the entrance to the squat castle. An affable young groom took the horse's reins from the knights and handed Sebastian a flask containing an unidentifiable beverage. He took a gulp, and it burned his throat, but the warm feeling was a glorious delight after his frigid trek. The knights informed Sebastian that they had summoned Finan, who was eager to meet him, but that he was saying the Angelus prayers at noon upstairs in his private chapel with his wife and children.

While Sebastian had been lingering in Galloway for two days to get his footing, he had asked the traveling merchants that he had befriended who was the most fitting lord to find rest with in far western Hibernia. Everyone bestowed on him the same advice. They all said that Finan O'Brien was the benevolent—and extremely rotund—lord of the County, and that as a devout Catholic, he would likely welcome any pilgrim, especially one officially dispatched by the Church. They uniformly told Sebastian that once you were in the O'Briens' good graces, you were as safe and as well fed as you could ever possibly be in Hibernia. Unlike some upstart magnates in the south and east, they told him that Finan had inherited his lands from his ancestors, and their ancestors before them, but that he was nonetheless advanced in his thinking.

Sebastian passed through an entry archway, which led to a great reception hall. He removed his scroll of introduction from his satchel, and he presented it to Finan who had been expecting him.

The traveling merchants had not been joking. Finan was an extremely heavy man, obviously given to great love of food and drink. His round face was pink and jovial, but Sebastian could detect maturity, leadership, and profound confidence behind his eyes. He wore several layers of clothing made of wool, leather, and pelts, making him appear even larger.

Finan's devotion to all things religious was certainly not exaggerated either. His home was practically a chapel itself, adorned with countless relics, icons, statues, and frescos in every room.

The roaring fire Sebastian had prayed for did not disappoint. Once Finan saw that Sebastian's hands were sufficiently warmed as the fire hissed, he called over a servant who offered them a bewildering array of beverages—all of them very alcoholic. Sebastian accepted the hospitality by selecting hot cider, figuring it was the least potent. He was wrong. It burned his throat as he sipped. He peeled off his gloves.

"Me good boy, yer welcome to remain in me house as long as ye desire," said Finan in English affected by a heavy brogue. "I am tickled that ye decided to cool yer heels in this 'ere remote territory."

Sebastian was grateful that Finan was trying his best to communicate without relying on a local dialect of Gaelic that Sebastian would undoubtedly find impossible to comprehend.

He offered Sebastian a comfortable seat near the massive stone fireplace, which he accepted without a second thought. Finan reclined on an armchair, which was itself covered with at least half a dozen pelts and skins.

"Me father Turlogh O'Brien just built this 'ere castle, but sadly passed away last year. Now, as for me self, I am not the full heir of the O'Brien clan in County Clare. Me cousin Liam O'Brien, of Bunratty Castle held that title until he died."

Finan bowed his head, pressing his jowls together unattractively, crossed himself and then continued.

"Liam left his son Murrough to be the Earl of Thomond, ya see. He made me his protector to care for the boy until he grows up.

"Now, as for we O'Briens, we are the largest clan in Hibernia. Me entire family has been loved and respected for centuries, ya see, because we have the blood of the High King of Hibernia Brian Boru." Finan pointed to veins in his portly arms, and then to a large sword and shield painted with a colorful crest, hanging above the mantel.

Finan explained that there were various branches of the O'Brien clan. There were the O'Briens of Ara in north Tipperary, a territory they had acquired from the O'Donegans centuries earlier. There were those of Limerick, which gave their name to the barony of Pubbelebrien. Yet another branch was located around Aherlow by the Galtee Mountains, and another south of the Comeragh Mountains on the rich lands near Dungarvan. Finan and his heirs ruled the western regions of Clare.

It was clear to Sebastian that Finan's social status imposed a lifestyle of conspicuous consumption. The pelts, furs, gold, and tapestries in the reception hall alone would have taken generations to acquire. And they were valuable enough that a substantial number of well-financed knights would need to guard the castle against rogues and brigands all night and day.

"In this 'ere County alone, I have two 'undred and twenty-four tenants sharing ten thousand acres, each givin' me a hundred pounds in cash rents, ten pounds of pepper, eighteen fowls, and ale, me boy. Now, we O'Briens are loved for we give the local villages in this 'ere county respect, ya see, me boy."

Finan proudly explained how he depended on his tenants to bring laborers to his fields, gold to his coffers, and chickens, cheese, beef, and ale to his table. In exchange, Finan said everyone in Clare understood the O'Brien family would take care of their material needs. In exchange for their fealty, he provided his tenants with food and shelter.

Finan also described how he shared a centuries-old judicial function: his manor courts dealt with a range of civil and criminal cases that provided him with fines, fees, and confiscations. In addition to dues that he regularly collected from his dutiful tenants on the occasions of their marriages, deaths, and inheritances, he enjoyed the "ban," a monopoly on certain activities. For example, Finan derived rent from anyone grinding grain or baking bread in western Clare. In exchange, Finan said that bakers could earn a decent living, and prices were regulated so that poor villagers always knew what they would be paying for a loaf of bread in a month's time.

He was pleased if he could depend on the certainty of rents and dues from his tenants, the efficient operation of his demesne, and sound prices for wool, grain, and, naturally, ale.

Finan bragged that one of the most important functions the O'Brien family had regularly provided was strong military and police protection. Tenants were required to furnish the services of one knight for every two hundred and fifty acres they held. If a tenant could not provide knightly services, he was required to augment his cash rents to cover the purchase of comparable mercenaries, at no small cost.

However, Finan said that because of fierce loyalty to the O'Brien clan, many families had pledged at least one of their sons to military service per generation. Thankfully, because Clare had not experienced any major campaigns in hundreds of years, their service consisted chiefly of keeping drunkards off the highways and catching poultry thieves. Nonetheless, the O'Briens were reputed to have at their disposal over four hundred well-trained knights. Additionally, potentially thousands of cavaliers and infantrymen were ready to do battle at Finan's word should it become necessary.

After giving his proud and lengthy explanation of his family's background, Finan put his stout mug down heavily on a table nearby, splashing ale.

"So, what would our Most Holy Father in Rome have to do with us humble folk in a remote land, would you say now?" Finan leaned forward curiously.

"Well, I am conducting research . . . on behalf of the Inquisition," Sebastian replied.

"Aye, me friends in Galloway tell me yer huntin' witches," Finan whispered.

Sebastian was mortified. "That is not quite the case, sir. I am researching folklore. Local legends, pagan customs, that is all. I am also seeking certain books that may reside near here."

Sebastian hoped Finan would not have spoken at great length to anyone about his mission, but somehow that seemed like a dream to him now, given the apparent love of gossip.

Finan leaned back in his chair. "Her name is Brigantia," he announced. "She's yer witch, 'tis herself." Finan nodded. "Aye, I can point ya to the way there, so ya can go have a gander at 'er yerself if ya doubt me."

Sebastian was startled by his candor. "You actually *know* that she is a witch, sir?"

"Are ya jokin', now, me boy?" Finan's hearty laugh resonated throughout the room. "Me gran' used to buy charms and trinkets off her mother Dagda. Her father was named Dubhthach. He was a pagan king; some say he was Druid. May God give peace to all their souls." Finan bowed his head and crossed himself again.

After a pause, he continued. "Brigantia's good folk. But she still makes a livin', mostly off the simple. The bog is given over to such things. That's why the tinkers wander about un'armed, too. They are afraid of those who folla the old ways."

A servant came over and refilled Finan's mug for the third time. Sebastian politely declined a refill of the cider.

Finan thanked the servant and loudly slurped another mugful. "As for meself, the Blessed Virgin Mary and Saint Patrick care for us and the pious who reside in this 'ere manor. But we pay Brigantia and her kind no heed. None at all."

The look in Finan's eyes turned grave. He leaned forward slowly. "Son, do ya wish her harm, now? Because if ya do, I won't lead ye to 'er. Brigantia may be pagan, but she's still good as any. Now, I ain't superstitious t'all, but I won't be responsible for bringin' no harm to 'er kind. You understand me? I have heard what your Henry-man's been doin' to 'em! Cooking 'em up, I hear!"

It was obvious that Finan was not a man to be trifled with, so Sebsatian agreed wholeheartedly. He dismissed Finan's strange joke about Institoris as drunken folly, nothing more.

"Yes, the Pope has merely given me the charge of investigating their ways." Sebastian recalled Institoris's warning that he was merely to *inquire*, nothing more.

"Aye, well, I have heard that the Church is going after 'em, them that still folla the old ways. We're good Christians in this 'ere manor, but this land is old, older than Christ Jesus Himself, and there are many here who have not yet accepted Our Lord and Savior. But it is our lot to teach 'em, ya see, me lad, not harm 'em. That's what will lead 'em to the Lord."

Sebastian quickly responded.   "I mean her no harm at all, sir. I promise that I will speak to her kindly, you have my word. Thank you, my gracious lord. Your reputation as a generous nobleman has been proven yet again today."

Sebastian was dumbstruck by Finan's acceptance of a known witch in his lands. Apparently what he had heard was true—this region was chock-full of folk still practicing heathen ways, and those who lived here were more tolerant of them than anyone else in Christendom that Sebastian had yet to come across. He would make note of that in his research.

Finan motioned to the servant to bring over a large, rolled map. Finan unfurled it on a table and showed a small portion of it to Sebastian by the light of the hissing fire.

"Here, have a good look, me boy. The old bridge in Kilfenora is out, ya see, and Ennistimon to the southwest is too dangerous for a boy like yerself without soldiers. So, take yerself north to Ballyvaughan, along the Burren Way. We call it the Green Road. You'll pass through Ballynalackan and Doolin." Finan pointed to several dots on the map. "Yer Brigantia is northwest of the old town o' Liscannor."

Sebastian peered at the map in the flickering light. Brigantia appeared to live on the western coast, where stood the legendary Cliffs of Moher. The map beyond the coast showed nothingness, just the endless ocean to the west, until the end of the earth.

"You will find 'er up near the grand cliffs, in a bramble to the left of an old oak grove. Look for the old well and the weepin' willa tree." Finan directed him to an unmarked spot on the map. "Three streams meet here. Brigantia and her kind are mighty shrewd, so be prepared."

The drunken warning, given with a wink, was too ambiguous to be helpful, but Sebastian figured he would take his chances. He thanked Finan and retired to his room. He had been looking forward to encountering a real witch since his quest had begun many months ago in a warm church in sunny Rome.

BRIGANTIA

After waking before dawn in his plush private guest chamber at Finan O'Brien's castle, Sebastian held his rosary beads and knelt at his bedside. He recited a decade of the rosary, reflecting on the Mystery of the Annunciation, in which the Archangel Gabriel announced to the Virgin Mary that she was pregnant with Jesus. Sebastian mulled over something Finan had said—about Father Institoris cooking women—and dismissed it again as drunken foolery.

After finishing his morning prayers, he sat at a desk near the arched window and made detailed entries in his text about the O'Briens' tolerance of pagans. He noted that while they themselves were devout, they seemed to freely tolerate seemingly occult practices in their lands.

He then prepared for the winter day's journey ahead of him. Even the bedrooms here had fireplaces, and while the fire from last night had been reduced to burning embers, the room was still warm and cozy. He didn't want to leave.

But he packed his leather text into his crude satchel and wrapped himself in two thick red fox pelts. He returned to the outer door by means of the castle's dramatic spiral stairway. He fetched Epona from the groom, who had fastidiously brushed the mare's coat until it was shiny and smooth. When Sebastian mounted the horse, she seemed well-fed, rested, and eager to gallop.

He headed north on the main road, until he spotted a strange configuration of massive boulders on the horizon. He drew Epona to a halt and stared at the rock formation which was posed dramatically against a bright morning sky. Four mammoth stones stood upright, topped by one flat slab that must have weighed a hundred tons. The resulting shape reminded him of the mysterious Greek symbol pi.

This is not something of nature. This is the handiwork of someone who wanted to make a dramatic statement, he thought to himself.

He yanked his text out of his satchel and made a note of the stones' location and odd shape.

After leaving the outcropping behind him, he continued riding north, circling past the quaint town of Ballyvaughan. He then trekked down the western coast using the Green Road, which was nothing more than a muddy path that had been eroded and sunken by the traffic of people, beasts, and barrows. He noticed that many cottages had large portions of butter and milk placed on their outer windowsills.

Why are villagers wasting valuable food in the middle of an icy winter when stores are dwindling, he wondered.

He stopped and made note of this observation in his text as well.

On the way into Doolin, he passed several squads of men-at-arms, who studied him briefly and, perceiving him to be no threat to the peace, allowed him safe passage to the town center. He heard the familiar sounds of villagers at work and play while in town: the voices of the peddlers, the rattle and squeak of cartwheels and the clop of horseshoes, infants crying, and the squeal of swine being slaughtered.

After a solitary hour of traveling, he began to wonder if he had miscalculated the route Finan had given to him. He slowed Epona to a trot.

Did I pass the oak grove? But where were the three streams? Maybe I should turn back . . .

He was pondering his recourse when he made out the unmistakable sound of rushing water. He peered far ahead and caught sight of a wobbly bridge crossing over the junction of three flowing streams. Beyond the currents stood a huge oak grove. To the left of the oak forest was a dense, extensive gray thicket of rowan trees that seemed impenetrable.

He rode closer to the bridge. Pails were strewn around, surrounded by piles of dried flowers. The milk in the buckets either had been poured out or was still inside them, sour.

After nervously crossing the shaky bridge, he dismounted Epona, patted her thankfully on the shoulder, and tied her to a nearby oak. While still on the horse's back, he had not been able to observe the pathway that led through the dense thicket of rowan trees, but now at ground level he could see it.

The walkway was clear of branches as if something had prevented the morass from ever growing there. He ambled down the narrow walkway, now uncertain of the wisdom of this course of action. He spotted a clearing ahead of him, deep in the woods. A round stone well jutted up in the center of the clearing. Next to it stood a willow whose branches hung low to the ground. To the left of it was an apple orchard.

Beyond the trees was a tiny gray cottage.

Wispy trails of smoke wafted out of a thick chimney, but the scent was not that of ordinary wood or timber being incinerated. He recognized it as the earthy smell of turf burning in a hearth. He had learned that for heat, the poor often burned hard black logs of petrified moss that they carved out of the bogs. The peat logs gave off a heady smell when burned, one that stayed with you long after the fire had died out. The smell trapped in your garments forever, it seemed.

The cottage was in miserable condition. It was a timber frame with graying exterior walls of wattle and daub, which had become rotten after endless wet and dry seasons. A dark brown thatched straw roof was falling in, and it likely harbored a menagerie of mice, rodents, hornets, spiders, and birds. A variety of herbs and plants hung out in large bundles to dry, tied to rusty iron hooks on the exterior walls of the cottage. He identified rosemary, dill, basil, celandine, heather, chamomile, and red clover. Others he could not. A leather-handled sickle dangled from a rusty nail.

Brigantia? Sebastian thought to himself, walking toward the shack.

"Yes, Sebastian. It is I." A woman's voice came from somewhere, seemingly emanating out of the air. Frightened. he turned around quickly and saw a young woman standing a few feet behind him. There was no way that he missed her. And he had not said her name aloud, of that he was certain. The rowan thicket was far too dense for anyone to have passed through undetected, and she could not have come up on him from behind.

More shocking than her inexplicable entrance was that far from her being an old, hunched-over hag as Sebastian expected a witch to be, the woman was tall, young, and vibrant. Her hair was flaxen blonde with a hint of strawberry red, cascading to her waist. Her skin was smooth and pale, her eyes as green as the rolling hills he had crossed to get here. She wore a thin white gown that draped to her feet, her figure gracefully slender yet curvy. The neckline of her gown plunged deeply, and Sebastian could not help but notice the immodest outline of her full, firm breasts that it offered. Her cloak was woven from soft lambswool that had been dyed a deep hue of green. It was fastened at her neck with a gold brooch fashioned in the shape of two crescent moons, facing back-to-back. A thin gold tiara in the shape of a serpent devouring itself rested gently on the top of her head, its eye a lustrous emerald.

Sebastian had never been in the company of an actual witch before, much less a woman this stunning.

"Finan could not have forewarned you of my arrival," he stammered. "And how did you know my name?"

She laughed, her green eyes flickering in the sunlight. The sparkling gem in her tiara complemented her gaze perfectly.

"You are far younger than I expected," she said in a mellifluous voice. "Inquisitors are usually gray-haired old fools chasing their own tails. But you are a boy. We do not encounter many of your kind around here." She eyed Sebastian from head to toe, and then back again. "You came alone, too. Brave."

"Well, you are far younger than I expected, witch. I had anticipated that you would be an old hag."

Brigantia beamed at him with a dazzling smile. "Well, it is funny you say that. I am as old as the cliffs, but I do not appear a day over 20, do I?" She winked at him playfully.

"You are lying. Do not bewitch me."

Unfazed, she chuckled at him. "Come inside my home, Sebastian. I have been waiting for you for ages." She walked past him to the doorway and motioned for him to enter.

He hesitantly approached but spotted a five-pointed star made of branches that was posted above the lintel of the doorway. He stopped dead in his tracks.

"What is that?" he demanded. "A mark of the beast, no doubt. I will not pass under it."

"Sebastian, you have much to learn. It is a five-pointed star called a pentacle, a symbol of balance."

She walked under the lintel and pointed to the star-shaped figure that had been formed from rowan branches. "See, each of the five points represents an element. Earth, air, fire, water and spirit. With the fifth point facing up, the human spirit is elevated above all matter. This one is facing up to represent humanity's triumph over the base forces. When the point is down, well, that is the opposite," she said.

He was unconvinced and stood motionless.

She smiled. "It will not hurt you; I promise. Was not the Child Jesus announced by a star in the heavens?"

Sebastian nervously crossed himself, ducked under the lintel and scurried into the cottage.

She followed closely behind him and laughed to herself under her breath, "I love Christians. More superstitious than pagans!"

Despite its exterior appearance, the interior of the rundown cottage was impossibly huge and was in excellent condition. The walls consisted of solid oak beams and were carved with intricate details on all the moldings. Dozens of leather-bound books were crammed onto book-shelves. Their titles were inscribed in a strange language.

A massive stone hearth contained a roaring blaze within it. Lighted candles made of rolled beeswax were lodged in every niche and crevice of the home. The cottage glowed with the cozy orange warmth of fire.

A satiny black cat was curled up in front of the warm hearth. It raised its head and squinted. Its glowing green eyes opened to survey Sebastian. Sensing nothing threatening, it put its head down and went back to sleep. An iron pot swung on a hook over the fire, brewing some concoction that smelled of herbs. Despite its appearance from outside, the roof was intact and sound when viewed from within.

"Please, sit with me awhile." Brigantia removed her soft wool cloak, tucked her dress underneath herself and pulled up a chair in front of the flickering flames. "I know why you are here, Sebastian."

He sat down on a chair across from her, finding himself oddly comforted by his surroundings. She picked up the sleek cat off the floor and gingerly placed it in her lap. The cat began to purr but never opened its eyes. "This is Bastet, my familiar. Is she not beautiful?"

He stared at the cat but gave no response to her question. "I have many inquiries," he stated tersely.

"I will permit you to ask them, but you must allow me to explain the old ways to you in good time," she said, stroking the cat's black fur gently.

"How is it that this cottage appears different on the inside than the out? Is it a bewitchment? A glamour? A fascination, perhaps? Are demons manipulating my mind?" His questions were now coming rapidly.

"Sebastian, how do you see it?" she questioned him, smiling.

"With my eyes," Sebastian replied without thinking.

"No, we perceive with our minds. Our souls. Two people look at the same object or event and witness two different things, yet they both have eyes, do they not?" she asked.

"I suppose," he reasoned, "but that is because they are viewing it from different angles. They have differing powers of vision, perhaps."

"No, the soul is the explanation. Where one person perceives beauty, another sees atrocity. What we expect changes everything. Do you understand?"

"I have not a clue what you are talking about," he said.

She sighed.

"For instance, a man walking on a plank at a great height falls, because in his fears he visualizes he will fall. But if the same plank were positioned on the ground, he would not fall, for he would have no reason to fear falling. Sebastian, his expectations make his fall happen. Appearances are likewise changed by our expectations. One may perceive me as a hag because that is how they expect a witch to look. Others see worse. But you, you do not see things that way any longer, do you? You are changing. You are seeing things through different eyes, Sebastian. You are starting to see me as I am. If you had truly expected a hag, you would have seen one."

The cat jumped off her lap and found a comfortable spot near the hearth and curled up again.

"But, what of the appearance of this cottage? It is not large when seen from outside. In fact, the roof was falling in!" He pointed at the ceiling.

"The same logic applies to all things," she replied. "Your mind is opening to new possibilities. While your intellect expects evil and malice, your heart knows that our ways are not evil or malevolent. You are starting to see value in the old ways, whether you realize it or not."

"And what are *your* ways, Brigantia? Is this trickery your religion?"

"Trickery? The only trickery is convincing oneself to see only black and white, truth and heresy, when life consists of shades of gray and is far more complicated."

Sebastian paused for a moment and extracted his weighty leather-bound text from his satchel. "Please explain your heathen beliefs more fully, Brigantia. I will take notes if you permit me."

"Do as you will. In fact, that is the whole of the Law. Do you comprehend, Sebastian? But harm none."

"I missed that. Start over, please." Sebastian unearthed his quill, put his inkpot precariously on his knee, and began to scribble furiously.

"Do as you will. Harm none, lest you receive that harm thrice in return." Brigantia spoke deliberately. "That is our way. And *that* is the whole of the Law."

Sebastian finished writing her words down and looked up at her incredulously.

"I can see from the look on your face that you do not accept this belief? You are doubting the foundation of our ways."

"But what does it really mean?" he asked.

"Is it not plain? The world is made up of many different powers, but the most pertinent one is that of the threefold return. When you cause harm, you upset the natural balance, the natural order. As a result, the harms you have wrought will return to you threefold. Within those bounds though, you are free do whatever you will. In fact, that is what you *should* do."

"So, I can do anything I please?" he asked.

"Do whatever you will, Sebastian, but harm none in so doing. Therein is true freedom. If all humanity followed the old ways, there would be no murder, no theft, and everyone would be happy and free."

"But what about sin? When a man sins, he disobeys God's laws, does he not?"

"As long as you harm no one, you have done no wrong. If you have harmed others, then harm will come back to you threefold. Sin is not a concept we embrace."

She paused and looked at the fire. "But our ways are fading. Not in small part due to your Church's murderous Inquisition—would you enjoy a drink?" she interrupted herself, her tone changing from ponderous to gleeful. "I love to make tea with the sacred herbs I have grown in my own garden."

"That depends," Sebastian said, looking up from his book. "Will you poison me?" he asked, only half-jokingly.

"Well, that depends. Will you burn me at the stake if it tastes bitter?" She smirked.

"Brigantia," he said emphatically, closing his book. "I want to make it clear that I have not come here to harm anyone. My objective is to inquire, to research. My Church solicits information from you only."

"You are but a boy who has come to learn about my world, yet you have much to learn about your own, Sebastian. I hope that the Fates allow you to before it is too late." She stood up and walked over to the pot brewing an earthy liquid. "Let us put all this heavy talk aside and share my tea. We must walk to the Cliffs of Moher before twilight. It is becoming cold outside, but I have essential preparations I must make for Imbolc."

"I have heard the Cliffs of Moher are beautiful," he said. He surprised himself by looking forward to spending more time with her.

She walked over and put a ladle into the brew.

"Preparations for what?" he asked as she poured the tea into small earthen vessels that would function as mugs.

"All in good time, my dear Sebastian. All in good time. Now, drink."

Warily, he sipped the hot tea. After a while, he said, "You were right."

"Oh?" she replied. "About you being ridiculous, immature and knowing nothing about your own world?" She smiled wryly.

"No. About the tea. It is delicious." He smiled back.

DEAN

"Is witchcraft heresy?" asked Professor James Sprenger, the Dean of the University of Cologne, infamous for employing a harsh Socratic method while teaching advanced theology. "Brother Thomas, stand and edify us."

A young brash student with blonde hair and blue eyes stood up in the large classroom.

"Yes, it is, Professor. A witch is a heretic since she rejects one or more of the fundamental dogmas of the true faith."

"But if a witch denies the existence of God entirely, is she therefore not an apostate, rather than a heretic, Thomas?" The Dean was departing from the written materials he had assigned in advance of the class.

Thomas looked down at his notes, which contained nothing that would allow him to answer the question.

"Uh…I do not understand, Professor."

"Well, heresy differs from *apostasy*, does it not?" The pleasant, aged professor continued. "An apostate wholly abandons faith in God, yes?

"Yes," Thomas replied confidently.

"But the heretic always his retains faith in God, albeit erroneously denying particular doctrines of faith, yes?" asked the Professor.

A deafening silence fell over the lecture hall as the student stood mutely staring at his notes.

"So, tell us, Thomas, if a woman practices witchcraft, is she a heretic or an apostate?"

"Well, it stands to reason, Professor," he hypothesized, "that she is an apostate. As a witch, she rejects God, I must assume."

"But you just said she was a heretic. Which is it?" Dean Sprenger smiled at his student, who was now thoroughly bewildered.

"It depends on whether or not she believes in God?" he guessed.

"Are you asking me or telling me, Thomas?" The class snickered.

"I suppose I am telling you then, Professor."

"Well, let us argue the hypothetical some more, Thomas."

The student winced.

"Suppose a witch professes a sincere belief in God, but uses potions and herbs to cure the sick and merely engages in rituals to honor the beauty and balance of nature—then is she a heretic?"

"Yes, she is still a heretic."

"Why though, Brother? Why is a profound respect for God's creation and the use of potions and herbs necessarily a violation of some necessary doctrine of faith?"

"Uh . . . because the witch is employing the devil's tools," he said confidently.

"The devil's tools? Surely, a potion made of natural leaves that makes one feel relaxed is not a devil's implement, Brother Thomas. If it is, I am in deep trouble with the Lord for my tea." The class laughed.

Thomas scrambled for an answer. "The potion may rely on the powers of a demon, which makes it anathema or accursed."

"Oh, I see," mocked the professor. "So demons are now in the habit of making tea. Are they apothecaries too? Did they attend this university to learn how to fashion healing elixirs? If so, I may need to consult one; my back has been terribly aching."

The students laughed once more.

Thomas became exasperated and said, "But does it truly matter, Professor? Doesn't the Inquisition treat all witches the same way, by burning them alive?"

The classroom hummed with disbelief. Everyone in his class knew that a crude and flippant answer about the Inquisition was not what Dean Sprenger wanted to hear.

"'Does it truly matter?'" Sprenger repeated the student's question with sudden derision. "Well, let us consider that question, my doubting

Thomas. For centuries, canon law has strictly held that there can be no forgiveness for those who have willfully denied God. Apostasy belongs, therefore, to a terrible classification of sins for which the Church enforces execution, perpetual penance and excommunication without hope of pardon, leaving the forgiveness of the sin to *God* alone after death."

Thomas just stood and listened silently.

"Heresy, on the other hand, Thomas, entails a subtle matter of degree you apparently lack. For instance, adherence to an erroneous doctrine contradictory to a point of faith clearly defined by the Church is heresy pure and simple, heresy in the first degree, so to speak. We can all agree such a heretic is not very nice."

The students chuckled.

"But if the tenet being defied has not been expressly defined or is not clearly proposed as an article of faith in the ordinary, authorized teaching of the Church, a belief opposed to it is only a personal opinion approaching heresy, and having an odd personal opinion is not necessarily evil, thank goodness!" He chuckled at himself.

"Next, a doctrinal proposition, without directly contradicting dogma, may yet implicate logical consequences at variance with revealed truth. Such a proposition is not even heretical, it is a *propositio theologice erronea*, that is, purely erroneous as a matter of theology."

The students in the class scribbled notes.

"We can certainly forgive that. The Lord knows your examinations contained these errors, Brother, but I haven't burned you at the stake, yet."

Thomas' face turned red.

"Therefore, it stands to reason that if someone we are calling a witch was well-intentioned, with a clear personal conscience and did not deny that God nor worship Satan or consort with demons, but merely used natural herbs and potions without contradicting any fundamental Catholic principles of faith, we should not execute her, and in fact she could be permitted to live a full life. But if we automatically define all witches as apostates, as you recommended, there is not even a doubt that her automatic sentence would be the scaffold or stake, and eternal absolution prohibited, yes?"

"I don't know, Professor. I suppose so." Thomas sat down.

"To answer your absurd earlier question—yes, it all matters. It all matters! These are not idle conjectures gentlemen! Inquisitors must make mortal decisions based on these theories, and there cannot be any uncertainty in our minds that the offender is worthy of the dire sentence.

"So, study harder, Thomas. Someday, you alone may be pressed to judge whether someone should burn in hell for all eternity or be absolved to dwell with the angels in heaven." The professor made a gesture simulating a bird's wings. Students sitting near Thomas giggled at his misfortune.

In the rear of the large lecture chamber, a robed figure had silently slipped into the gallery and was listening to the professor's words very carefully. Sprenger began concluding his lecture.

"Important questions of heresy and apostasy should be on all our minds today, gentlemen. Foul winds have blown from the East. In my lifetime, I have witnessed Constantinople fall to infidels. As you are aware, the Knights Templar are still undefeated in many parts of the Christian world. The Holy Father has remitted me and many others on crusades to instruct the masses. However, it is important that you know and respect your adversary. If heresy were manifestly incorrect on its face, no one would believe in it! One must investigate blasphemy, grasp a heresy's inherent logic and its appeal before it can be vanquished. That is all for today, gentlemen."

Once most of the class had exited, Heinrich Institoris removed his long hood and walked up to the dais, where Professor Sprenger was gathering his notes and packing up a satchel heavy with books.

"Respect heresy? Learn from blasphemy? That is something a fool says, not an Inquisitor Extraordinary appointed to root out heretics."

"Oh, I did not see you there, Heinrich," said Sprenger.

"All witches must burn—you know that the Bible commands that, James. Suffer not a witch to live, it is written in the Book of *Exodus*. It is better called the heresy of witches than of wizards, since the name wizard is taken from the more powerful party," said Institoris.

"Well, you know what Euripides wrote. Talk sense to a fool and he'll call you foolish." The professor smiled, feigning innocence.

"And who is the fool in that story?" Heinrich retorted.

"That depends on who you ask," Professor Sprenger muttered. "Have you spoken to the young fisherman in Rome yet?"

"Yes, he began his research some time ago. I told him to submit a substantial draft by next year. I believe that will give us adequate time to edit it and have it printed for distribution throughout all of Christendom."

"Yes, well, you are the one who is going to edit it, Henry. I will doubtless be very busy next autumn, what with my teaching schedule here, plus now that I am dean, I have countless formal events to attend. This book was all your idea anyway. However, I am looking forward to reading what the boy discovers."

Institoris picked up a scholarly book from the desk, examining it mindlessly. "You need to discontinue this pointless academic career and embark on a real campaign. I naturally still make time for teaching, but the substance is in the *execution*." Institoris looked up and smiled coldly, dropping the book back on the desk with disdain.

"That was a very poor choice of words." Sprenger picked up the book, dusted it off and packed it in his satchel. "I heard that you had some snags with the tribunal in Innsbruck," he asked, relishing the question.

"Georg Golsen is a bastard, that is what happened. He released all of them! Every last damned one! He had the gall to announce that he had 'found the devil,' and that 'the devil was in the Inquisitor, not the witches.' After I departed Innsbruck, the Archduke hired Ulrich Molitor and Conrad Sturtzel to explain this whole witchcraft business to him. Georg made me a laughingstock. He will pay."

Sprenger suppressed a laugh. "I recall how he used to preach to Father Ferdinando in class. I think the Pope finally made him a bishop just to drive the rest of us mad."

The elder professor interrupted himself, wanting to change the subject again to calm Institoris down. "Who is your friend I see lingering by your office every day? Tall fellow, middle-aged. Wears the garments of a barrister, I believe?"

"He is Arnold Kolich; he is a mere notary. Pay no heed to him." Heinrich suddenly looked oddly uncomfortable for the first time.

"A notary? Why on earth do you need a notary, Henry?"

"He freely offered his services and . . . I accepted. That is all there is to it." Institoris looked at Sprenger with a cold, empty stare.

"Interesting. Well, if I ever need a document formally sworn, I suppose I now know who to ask—"

Institoris interrupted him. "I will have to tell you more about what I cooked up in Brixen...but I am late to a more important meeting with some business associates in the main faculty room. I will stop by your offices later today."

"I wish I could say it was good seeing you again, Henry, but lying is a venial sin." Sprenger smiled.

Institoris just walked away.

MOON

Sebastian lay flat on his back in a bed on the second floor of cozy Leamanaugh Castle, staring at the coffered ceiling. Even though it was very late, his body and his intentions were not cooperating with each other.

His mind was relentlessly picturing the beautiful Brigantia, walking with him along the cliffs. Each time he saw her face in his mind's eye and remembered some new detail of their conversation from earlier in the evening, he would smile sheepishly and nervous energy would coarse through his body, making sleep impossible. Her beautiful smile was infectious even when it was just recalled.

He vigorously turned onto his right side, growing frustrated and angry at himself. This position wasn't working, either.

He stood up and walked over to the tall window, overlooking the front of Finan's estate. He stared out at the full moon which draped everything with pale light as it rose higher into the sky. The stony garden outside of Finan's castle took on an eerie white glow as if the rocks themselves were drawn down from the moon.

He tried to remember Institoris's specific instructions and pictured what the Inquisitor would say if he knew his secret thoughts.

Stop it, Sebastian. You are acting like a fool. You must stop this madness and focus on the task at hand. This woman is a witch, a heretic cast into the outer darkness, in bed with devils. These strange feelings you are having are the product of phantasms, spells, and evil magic. Your only weapon is your intellect. Protect your soul with it.

But if that were true, why did he feel this way? He did not believe for an instant that Brigantia was capable of malice. He had looked deeply into her eyes, and he did not detect a single ounce of evil. But she was a witch; she had told him as much. How could this be?

He walked over to the edge of the cushioned bed and sat on it. It sank deeply under his weight. If he did not get enough sleep now, he would not be able to find the strength to ride all the way back to Hag's Head and see Brigantia by noon. Even though he now knew the way, it would still take an hour or more. He lay back down on his side.

Sleep only came begrudgingly. But in his dreams, her eyes were even more entrancing.

The next morning, mists hung over the copse of oak trees outside. Sebastian had eagerly departed from Finan's castle at dawn, approaching today's meeting with Brigantia with enthusiastic curiosity. Gone was the dread and fear of the unknown he had wrestled with only yesterday.

When he arrived, he noticed the dried herbs that had hung on rusty hooks were gone. Brigantia was kneeling in a grassy patch near the stone well, bundling stalks of herbs into a straw bushel basket. She was wearing a different dress today, but one that was just as flattering.

"Hello, my Sebastian." she said and smiled. She stopped tying the stalks together and stood up. She was not wearing her cloak or her tiara today.

"Good morning, Brigantia," he said, beaming.

"You are early. How was your night?" she asked sweetly.

"Troublesome. I could not sleep," he said, surprising himself with his own candid answer.

"I have a treatment for poor sleep. It is called valerian root. If I make a tea for you from a sachet, you will sleep soundly the whole night through. Would you like me to prepare you some?" she offered.

He considered it for only a moment and then rejected her offer. "Thank you, but no. I must conduct my research with a clear mind."

She looked disappointed and frowned.

He cleared his throat to seem more serious. "Shall we discuss more of these preparations you appear to be making?"

"Yes, come and see." She motioned for him to walk over. She pointed to a variety of dried leaves and flowers of different colors laying on the ground in bundles. "These are the herbs of Imbolc. I cut them yesterday with the sacred boline, a scythe dedicated to cutting roots and herbs that honors the life they have provided to us. We will burn them tonight and scatter them to the four quarters."

"Imbolc?" he asked, looking at the herbs in the basket. "You said that yesterday. What does it mean?"

"A sacred day in our calendar in which we honor the first stirrings of life." She pointed to a patch of soil where a few small green crocus blades were valiantly pushing up through the soil.

"Flowers and plants that will begin to appear when it warms? What is special about that?" he asked.

"There is so much more to it than that, my Sebastian."

He noticed that he liked the way she said his name as "her Sebastian." It stirred something deep inside him.

"How so?" he asked.

"Like the quickening of a child that occurs in the belly of a mother, plants have already begun their life long before their blades are seen above the ground. We honor and respect the powers of life unseen by the eye."

"But why are plants and bushes sacred? Is not God the author and source of all life?"

"All life is sacred. How can you claim to honor and worship God but murder his creatures without thought?" she asked.

"The Bible gives us dominion over all inferior creatures," he said definitively. "God made them to serve us. Trees, plants, animals…they are not as sacred as man, who is made in His image," he retorted, remembering his Catechism.

"Yet, man cannot exist without them. So, who needs whom?" she asked.

He pondered her comment for a moment and then abruptly sat down on a nearby log, opened his satchel and removed his text, quill and inkwell, balancing them on the log. She smiled and returned to bundling herbs, kneeling on the ground.

"I am surprised that you are so learned," he said, preparing to write. "Where did you acquire your learning and powers of persuasion?"

"You are surprised that I can read and write because I am a woman."

"I mean…well, yes,. Also, because you are very poor."

"Your own powers of persuasion leave something to be desired, Sebastian." She laughed at him.

"Oh, I did not mean that. I mean, I was just . . . I am sorry." He bowed his head, embarrassed, regretting his thoughtless choice of words.

"It is fine; I know that it is uncommon for a poor woman in the countryside to be educated. That is yet another thing about our worlds which differ. But to answer your question, my mother and father taught me to read and write, and my coven provided me with many books."

"And yet you studied philosophy and rhetoric, as well?"

"I study things as they are, Sebastian. Subjects are just different facets of the same diamond."

He began to scribble. "Imbolc," he spelled the word out slowly. "Where does that word come from?"

She tucked her dress under her and sat on the log next to him. "Oimealg, our word for lactating ewes. It is the midpoint of the dark half of the year when the bellies of pregnant herd animals will swell to give birth in spring."

"Dark half of the year," he said, skeptical. "Dark as in evil."

"No, you see the year is divided into light and dark halves. The darkest point is Yule, on December 21."

"Yule? Oh, you mean Christmas," he said, "on December 25, on which we celebrate Jesus Christ's birth."

"Yule before Jesus," she reminded him. "It was your Church who stole and renamed *our* day. Jesus was not even born in December. Surely, you knew that!"

"Of course, I did," he said. He wrote it down anyway.

"The brightest point is July 21, the midsummer feast day of Lughnadasa."

"I see," he said, scribbling again. He looked up. "So, when will you hold this ritual circle?"

"We begin at midday. I would invite you to watch, but I do not know how my coven will react to your attendance. It would teach you much to see the old ways being practiced, though."

"I am not sure. It is one thing for me to learn by inquiring, it is quite another for me to witness the rites themselves," he said. "I understand your hesitation, as well as the concerns of your coven. However, it is only through mutual understanding that we can come to accept each other."

She stood up, brushing herself off. "I will leave the decision to them. For now, we need to eat. Do you like fish?"

"You ask a sailor if he likes fish?" He laughed.

"Well, you ask your own share of foolish questions!" she said, pushing him lightly on the chest. Losing his balance, he fell backwards off the log, landing on his back in a pile of leaves. Ink spilled out of the inkwell onto the ground, and his book landed next to him.

"Oh! I am so sorry!" she said, trying to pull him back up while giggling. He laughed even harder as he could not get his footing and fell back down into the soft leaves, his book underneath him.

He had never felt like this before. Brigantia's knowledge was intoxicating, and he felt like time did not exist when he was with her. In fact, he constantly found himself losing all track of time and worrying about whether there was going to be enough daylight for him to get back to Finan's castle.

Yet, in that moment, he did not care if he had to spend the night sleeping under the moon. To be able to spend more time with Brigantia would be worth suffering through the frigid wintry night.

PRINTERS

The tall Inquisitor strode into the room and sat at the head of a long mahogany table in an ornately carved chair usually reserved for the Archbishop of Cologne. Once he placed his breviary down on the table, he cleared his throat. The room instantly fell silent.

"Good morning, gentlemen. Thank you all for traveling so far and wide to be with us in Cologne today. I trust that you all had a prosperous New Year. Seventeen years ago, a great man died in Mainz. Many of you knew him."

A dozen men had convened around the table in high-backed wooden chairs, each seat and chairback appointed in rich red velvet. Without enough seats at the table, another dozen men stood. The room was humming with anticipation as they muttered to one another, debating the purpose of this meeting with the Inquisitor.

None of these men wore clerical vestments. Instead, they wore the colorful garb of opulent merchants from distant lands. Some of the men wore impressive garments of fine linen, silk and other luxurious fabrics that boasted of exotic origin in the Far East. The room reeked of expensive tobacco and rich liquor.

The faculty at the University of Cologne usually used this impressive main meeting room as a conclave for making important decisions about the future of their school. Enormous Flemish tapestries, oil paintings and detailed maps covered the room's stone walls. The long rectangular room overlooked a magnificent, cloistered courtyard on one side, and the center public square of Mainz on the other. An enormous marble fireplace housed a roaring fire. High ranking ecclesiastical officials also made important political decisions there. Dean James Sprenger had reserved it for today, but not for his own use.

Today, Heinrich Institoris, the Grand Inquisitor, had requested use of the large room for an undisclosed business meeting with two dozen visitors. Dean Sprenger knew nothing about the substance of this meeting. He had endorsed the request because Heinrich usually handled business transactions without him.

"Others here did not have that privilege," Institoris continued. "I knew him in my youth. His name was Johan Gutenberg, and we all owe him a great debt." Heinrich nodded toward a frail, elderly German men hunched over the table to his immediate right.

The hunched, elderly man cleared his throat loudly and spoke in a hoarse, strained voice, looking at Heinrich first, then around at the other men. "Gutenberg was a good man, but his investments turned out to be more profitable for his successors and partners than they were for himself. His former partner bankrupted him with a despicable lawsuit."

The man pointed his finger into the air accusingly. "He spent his savings on wine and foolishness because no one was loyal to him!"

He then looked at Heinrich lovingly. "But, thanks to you, Father, he was well taken care of in his later years by the Church. You served him well, Heinrich." The man nodded his head toward the Inquisitor who grinned, pleased with the offering of respect.

"Thank you, gracious Herr Fridenperger. It was my pleasure to convince the Archbishop of Mainz to grant Gutenberg a pension, plus food and lodging in his old age."

The Inquisitor stood, picking up his breviary. He walked behind Fridenberger and gripped the back of the man's tall chair. "Allow me to tell you all a story."

Heinrich walked over to stare out the window down at the peddlers hawking their wares in the square. "In Schlestatt as a youth, I trained in the fine art of calligraphy. I spent years as a diligent scribe, learning how to transfer the sacred characters of the Bible from one text to another." He opened his breviary, demonstrating his handiwork.

"It was tedious, but necessary to hand the Word of God down. But while I was toiling away, the world witnessed the invention of something profound in Mainz—movable type.

"I came to realize that by this simple yet brilliant invention, at that instant, Gutenberg created the opportunity for us to reach all Christians, infidels and pagans. No longer would books take years to copy by hand. No longer did manuscripts need to be lavish and expensive, read only by clergy and those wealthy enough to possess a personal library. We are all indebted to him, but you are each here because Johannes Gutenberg made you wealthy."

He stood behind the chair of a fat, bald man decked out in elaborate red and blue silk Florentine garments. He reached over and examined one of the red silk tassels that swung daintily from the obese man's cloak, examining it, then dropping it in disgust.

"You owe your personal successes to this great man."

A young German man with long brown wavy hair spoke up from the far end of the room.

"Yes, yes. We all know this, but what was the point of dragging us all the way here? To celebrate a Requiem Mass for the dead?" The young man laughed sarcastically. "We will buy Gutenberg an indulgence. Better yet, I will print him twenty!" The meeting room echoed with a mix of wry laughter and fearful whispers.

Heinrich grew characteristically stern, tensely gripping his breviary. "Herr Stahel, your disrespect toward me and your ignorance about Gutenberg's achievement is telling and immature. Perhaps Herr Preinlein will benefit from this endeavor in Brno instead." The room grew silent once again.

A middle-aged Venetian man stood up and interrupted the exchange, his gestures flailing to calm the two men's nerves. "Please, please! Let us not act as wolves; we are all educated men of God here!"

He turned and looked at Institoris, his expressive eyes pleading for calm. "Inquisitor, please pardon my lack of graces, but with all respect, what is the endeavor you speak of? I—we—are all curious to hear about it." Others nodded in agreement, happy to defuse the tension and eager to get to the point of their long travels.

Heinrich paused and walked back over to the Archbishop's chair, sitting down again. "I present to you a book to rival the Holy Bible."

One of the men laughed and said, "Inquisitor, as a learned man, you must know that the Bible has been the bestselling book anyone has ever printed. We have never had much success with anything else. Last year, at my press, we tried printing ten new titles, including that crazy book *Poliphio Struggles for Love in a Dream*. He sounded like he was always making love to buildings. It was terrible." The room erupted into laughter.

The bald man wearing the tasseled cloak spoke up, the fat of his cheeks causing him to slur his words. "About ten years ago, we experimented with a book by Signore Aligheri, called a Divine Comedy, but despite its title, it wasn't funny." There was more laughter. "All churches want to buy is the Bible and nothing else. I want to print more prayer books, more breviaries, and sell more indulgences—"

"Allow me to introduce this well-dressed gentleman to those in the room who do not know him," Heinrich interrupted him. "This well-fed man is Herr Numeister. He was Gutenberg's own student. After Gutenberg's death, Numeister settled in Foligno and has been making an abundant living ever since. I hear your villa is stupendous. Paid for entirely by indulgences, is it not?"

Numeister grimaced in disgust, but Heinrich continued. "According to Numeister, nine Venetian ducats and the Lord will forgive you for robbing a church. Eight gulden gets you away with murder. According to his one-page indulgences, you can be free of sins not yet committed!"

Neumeister was becoming angered by Heinrich's searing criticism of his business practices. He leaned over, slapping his chubby hands flat on the table, and addressed Heinrich directly. "I simply meant that we are all struggling businessmen, as was Gutenberg, God rest his soul. Printing is a difficult business these days. Costs before profit include presses, typecases and fittings, rent, handmoulds, metals, ink, paper, vellum and wages." He leaned back and counted on all ten of his stubby fingers as he rattled off the list.

"A printed paper Bible sells for twenty gulden, a vellum copy for fifty, but it takes a long time to print one! Indulgences can be printed by the thousands in the same amount of time, and they cover these costs and generate profits."

He leaned over to address Heinrich's gaze directly again. "If you were a businessman and not a lazy priest, you'd—"

"Please, please. Heinrich, tell us about this book. Do you have it here with you? I would like to see it." the hunched-over Fridenberger interrupted in a hoarse voice.

Heinrich had expected this understandable question, and having it come from Fridenberger made it even harder to deflect.

He looked at the old man and answered softly. "No, Herr Fridenberger, it is not written yet. It is being researched as we speak. But the ideas expressed in it are tremendous, I personally assure you."

"You have dragged us to Cologne to present us with *ideas* that you think will outsell the Bible?" A sharply dressed young man emerged from the shadows, his speech dripping with sarcasm. "I see that this long trip was a sound investment of my time. Ciao." He began to walk toward the door to leave.

"Aldo Manuzio, do not forget that the world is now very competitive! I know you are friends with the nephews of Prince Pico of Mirandola, but you are not here today because of your relationships with princes. I invited you because you were ingenious enough to spot the need for Greek typeface in the market, and I admire originality. Your twenty-year monopoly on the printing of Greek books in Venice will be profitable for our venture. So listen instead of speaking."

"Well, then, what is this brilliant idea that will outsell the Bible?" Manuzio scoffed, turning back and crossing his arms.

Institoris looked around the room and responded with a rehearsed speech.

"Gentlemen, there is a growing need to fight an old heresy in Christendom. Witches have gained great power, and they are spreading to every town, village, and hamlet, in every country. This book will be the fundamental tome used in combating the powers of the Devil. It will be named *The Malleus Maleficarum*."

"*The Witches' Hammer*?" asked Fridenberger, translating from Latin in his head.

"Yes," responded Heinrich. "*The Witches' Hammer* will reach Satan's followers everywhere and will combat the growing tide of witches in our midst. The book will even be purchased by all secular authorities, for it will teach them how to properly try witches in court, a required text for all Christian judges and magistrates. From a business perspective alone, it is going to make you all even more wealthy."

"Tell us more," requested Manuzio, who had suddenly softened his posture.

Disgusted by his evident greed, the Inquisitor glanced at him and continued. "The purpose of my book is to educate the masses about the terrible dangers of witches and to provide civil judges with a guide for detecting this heresy in the accused. The book will contain detailed information about what I have learned from the witch trials I have already conducted. As we speak, a brilliant researcher of mine is collecting all the scandalous practices of the witches and pagans, which will be described in the book. I guarantee you that graphic stories will be included, so that even your dullest readers will remain interested to the end."

"Wait, are we to understand this book will contain specific information about the unholy practices of pagans and witches?" asked the bald Numeister, eager to find fault with Heinrich's proposition. "How is that not heresy itself to print? It might be heresy to print a book that even professes a belief in witches! We must respect the papal authority, of course."

"Do not forget that I was authorized by the Pope himself to act as an Inquisitor in combating witchcraft, Numeister. You know that I would never print anything that did not contain the personal imprimatur of Pope Innocent himself. Dean James Sprenger is my co-author. The distinguished faculty of this university will approve the book's contents. I will be responsible for acquiring all pertinent ecclesiastical and scholarly approbation, which you will place prominently in the front when you print it. These approbations will give you comfort but they will also accord the book great weight and credibility throughout Christendom. Your role is that you will produce copies of this book in large quantities and sell it to everyone in the world who can read any language."

"As you said yourself, printing has become competitive," said Manucci. "There are over fifty presses in Italy alone, over two dozen in Germany. I now see printed books coming out of Holland, Spain, even Belgium. Let us assume the book is successful in sales. How would we each make a profit if we all sell this same book?" he asked, still skeptical of Heinrich Institoris's proposition.

"Under my authority, you will each print and exclusively sell *The Witches' Hammer* in the region where you have established your own printing presses. If you do not have a press established yet, we will set a region aside for you. Herr Rodt, you are setting up a new press in Pescia, correct?"

A German man sitting near Heinrich leaned forward and responded, "Yes, Father. We are building it now."

"Excellent. You will print and sell all copies there. Herr Fridenberger, I am delighted that you will print and sell in Verona. Herr Han, as an elder printer for many years, you will of course have the lion's share in Rome."

"A thousand thanks," an old man responded quietly from the far end of the table.

"Konrad Sweynheim?" asked Heinrich, looking around the crowded room to find him.

"Yes, Inquisitor. I am here, along with Arnold Pannartz, my new business partner." A short German man stepped forward, standing squarely beside Sweynheim.

"Your old monastic scriptorium in Subiaco outside of Rome is well situated to supply the Church in Rome with all the copies it desires to purchase. You two will work with Han to accommodate all of Rome's needs. I suggest dividing the city into ecclesiastic and secular markets.

In this manner, you will each be able to supply all necessary demand in Rome."

"We will do that, Inquisitor," responded Han in a raspy voice.

"Agreed," responded Sweynheim, Pannartz nodding his eager concurrence.

Institoris continued.

"Venice will be handled by von Speyer, of course. Genoa by Scopo, Siena by Dalen. And while they are not here today, Gering, Friberger and Crantz will publish in Paris. Their presses have been running for years. Herr Winterberg, is your press running in Alakraw in Moravia yet?"

Yet another man stepped forward and responded. "Yes, Father. Last year we began. Thank you for this great opportunity." Heinrich nodded at him, acknowledging his thanks.

"I intend to reach out to William Caxton, the Englishman who had the good sense to study here in Germany, and yet returned to London to set up shop there. He wastes time in his old age printing nonsense like *The Canterbury Tales* and *Le Morte d'Arthur*, but I am sure he will have the good sense to supply Westminster Abbey and all surrounding areas of London with this important book. I especially want this book to reach Hibernia. I will speak to the rest of you privately about any remaining regions."

From their satisfied looks, the roomful of men seemed pleased with their respective wheedles.

"If you encounter competition from unauthorized sources, you will refer them to me, and I assure you they will face the unbridled ire of the Inquisition."

Heinrich surveyed the room and concluded the meeting.

"My motives are not yours, gentlemen. But now, we all share the same goal. This book must reach every soul in the world. And when we succeed, we will all reap the fruits of our labors."

CLIFFS

Two people from very different worlds silently tread on the same meandering path that led to the Cliffs of Moher. What had been the faint scent of salt water became pungent and strong. The rocky cliffs were usually shrouded by mist and buffeted by arctic gales, but the sight they offered was always breathtaking. The frigid wind off the sea was bitter and biting.

Brigantia was the first to break the silence as she and Sebastian walked down a well-worn path along the edge.

"They call this point Hag's Head," she said, wrapping herself tightly in a pelt. "They often call us witches hags. It pains me."

"It is a beautiful cliff," he responded. "It is very remote though. Does it not feel cold and lonely at times?"

"At times," she whispered, now barely masking the profound sadness in her voice. "My coven only sets rituals twice a year. That is the only time I see them."

The rocky cliffs presented a dramatic panorama. Over six hundred feet below them, the foamy sea was in great turmoil. Enormous white waves crashed upon the stony shore. Green moss clung in various places to the black shale and sandstone strata. Hawks, gulls, guillemots, shags and ravens nested in thousands of crevices along the face of the rocks, trying to find shelter from the misty rain that seemed to endlessly fall here.

They reached a spot where they could view the entire coastline and stopped.

"This is a place of power, Sebastian."

"Yes, I do feel the presence of God here. All of nature is God's creation, and it reflects His perfection," he responded.

"We believe that it represents three of the four elements. Earth, air and water are all in great abundance here. My coven will present the other two elements of fire and spirit tomorrow to balance and honor them all. I must prepare the instruments for the circle tonight, though."

"Fire? A magical circle? A coven?" Sebastian remained deeply concerned with her mentions of such things.

"A coven is a group, Sebastian. Like your Church. We will light candles and face each of the four cardinal directions and reflect on what each represents. We only honor the balance and power of nature. We will meet within a great stone circle that has stood here for thousands of years to remind us of our ancestors, as well."

"But I thought a magic circle was used to conjure demons?" he asked, remembering his previous research.

"That is something we would never use. That is sorcery. That is from *your* world, not mine."

"Witches do not conjure demons through sorcery?" he asked, perplexed.

"No, a true witch does not call upon spirits. They rarely interfere in the affairs of humans unless the Fates require it. Despite what your Church teaches, spirits are not even 'good' or 'evil' any more than humans are entirely all one or the other. Some spirits have a pleasant inclination, some are mischievous, and others are just cruel—like men."

"I was taught that demons and angels were involved in our daily lives," he said.

"Spirits usually treat humans the way we might treat a fish in the lake. We might ignore it entirely or not notice it because it lives its life entirely in water and we breathe the air. The fish, like an angel or demon, is a being existing in a different element. But a true witch honors balance and respects the role we each must play. Conjuring spirits to suit our own ends upsets the balance and is selfish and destructive."

Sebastian looked confused.

"It is *sorcery* you speak of," Brigantia explained. "Sorcerers attempt to manipulate demons and the powers of nature to their own selfish ends."

"I see, so a sorcerer is different than a witch?"

"Indeed. For one, sorcerers are men, and witches are women. But more importantly, sorcerers have no respect for anything except their own desires. Witches respect the balance of the universe and seek to do no harm. Your Church Fathers see us unfairly. They consider us their enemies."

He would make a note of this interesting distinction in his research and discuss it at length with the Inquisitors when he returned.

She started walking again, along the precipitous edge of the cliff. Icy wind whipped against them harder than before. She pressed up against him to stay warm.

"Where are you from, Sebastian? Originally." she asked softly as they walked, changing the topic.

He slowly treaded alongside her. "There are five fishing villages that lie on the northwest coast, also on cliffs at the edge of the sea. I was born in one of those villages, called La Spezia, near Riomaggiore, but ... I did not grow up there. I spent most of my life in Bretagne as an orphan. The Church raised me until I went to Rome to study."

"And what of your father and mother?" she asked.

Sebastian had dreaded the day that this topic would arise. He lowered his head and spoke more quietly.

"I do not remember my father. He was an important man in Tuscany, I believe. I remember my mother, but she abandoned me when I was six years old. She sent me to Bretagne, and I never heard from her or saw her again."

"There must have been a reason, Sebastian. No mother would leave her child without a very good reason."

Tears welled up in his eyes. He suddenly looked extremely uncomfortable.

"I am sorry," she said. She turned toward him, stopped and put her head on his shoulder.

"Please do not be," he said. "I just have never understood why my parents left me. How could my mother send me off to Bretagne and have forgotten about me? What could ever explain why she did that to me?"

Sebastian shocked himself. He had never uttered these painful words to anyone before, especially not to a woman—much less a witch—but Brigantia had a profound effect upon him that he could not explain or control.

She looked up at him and saw the enormous pain in his eyes. Nothing she could say at this point would alleviate that suffering, and she knew it.

"My parents raised me here," she whispered. "When they were very old, they went there." She pointed through the misty haze at the fuzzy outline of several islands on the distant horizon.

"Where?" he asked. "I did not see any islands on the map beyond this shore."

"Those are the Aran Islands," she said. "The oldest and safest places for us to go to hide from your world." She shivered. "It's getting cold and dark now."

He reached over, wrapped his arm tightly around her shoulder and pulled her closer to him. He felt her body shivering underneath her green wool cloak and pelt.

Their eyes locked, only inches apart. He desperately wanted to kiss her fully on the lips at that single moment. Nothing else existed around him, only her. Everything else just faded away.

But Brigantia broke the silence and turned away from his hypnotic gaze. "We should get you back to Epona so you can return to Finan's castle before dark. I must do my preparations at the grand circle."

Sebastian was heartbroken, but he hid his disappointment by looking away at a raven that had landed nearby.

"Yes, I should be heading back to Finan's estate, I suppose. I might just encamp near here."

He suddenly turned back to face her. "Wait . . . how did you know my horse's name?" he asked.

She displayed her dazzling smile. "Will I see you again tomorrow? I would very much like that."

"You probably already know whether you will see me or not," he joked.

"Well, then, I will see you before noon." She smirked at him.

They walked back on the same path together, holding each other closer than before.

CATS

"You would not believe the atrocities in this district as of late." The fat judge belched, his bloated belly painfully pressed against the edge of a long banquet table. He yanked barely cooked meat off a bone while reclining at the table covered with hearty plates of food and steins of beer.

"I believe the Devil himself has taken over Strasburg," the obese jurist mumbled as he swilled a mouthful of frothy beer. "These people make my skin crawl!" His voice echoed as he spoke into a mug while still drinking, suds dribbling over his jowls, then down the front of his voluminous judicial robes.

"We have always had our fair share of thefts and bickering among the townsfolk here, Father," said a wiry magistrate in a hushed tone to Heinrich Institoris. The Inquisitor sat across from the judge while the thin magistrate sat on a short, narrow bench along with two other scrawny magistrates, one on either side of him. Perched so closely together on the narrow bench, the three of them resembled the proverbial monkeys who neither heard, saw or spoke evil, and their demeanor did not resist that image.

"When too much beer has been drunk, many fools pick a fight that leads them to end up in the stocks or pillory. But lately the crimes have become more violent and distressing," piped up another magistrate, speaking directly to Heinrich.

"You may trust that I have witnessed many atrocities in my day done in Satan's name, Your Excellencies," said Heinrich. "But are you able to give me a specific example of a noteworthy offense committed in your region that would lead you to suppose diabolical influences?" the Inquisitor asked, looking directly at the judge.

"Certainly!" the fat judge bellowed, while spooning huge piles of thick brown gravy onto his plate of rare mutton. "In fact, there is a workman imprisoned in the deepest dungeons of our tower who beat three women of this town. They lie in their own beds unable to rise or to move because of that bastard."

"Two of our servants found him and brought him to the bailiff," said the wiry magistrate.

With both of his plump elbows resting squarely on the table, the judge leaned forward, shaking a lamb shank emphatically, unchewed food still dangling from his open mouth. "I have sent this beast to the lowest level of the dungeon where we keep the offenders awaiting execution."

Disgusted by this lack of table manners, Heinrich grimaced, then turned and looked at the magistrates. "They each accuse the workman of these same heinous acts?"

"That they do," said the thinnest one.

"Did he explain his motive? Why would a workman do such a thing unprovoked?" Heinrich asked them quizzically.

"That is my very point, Father! The Devil is behind this!" The judge pounded his fist on the far end of the table, rattling the silver serving plates and steins. "This workman has been held for three days now and has done nothing except demand to know why he is being held! He has been complaining to the prison guards that he does not know what crime he committed! But I have refused to hear him! After seeing the women's wounds for myself, I would only see him from a distance and refused to entertain the pleas of this inhuman beast—"

Heinrich interrupted. "I can surely understand your desire to mete out God's good justice, Your Excellency, but we may be able to deduce some information from his pleas, perhaps some nugget of keen interest."

"If you are asking me to entertain his plea, Father, I refuse to honor it!" the judge said angrily.

"But he is no rogue or brigand; he is a workman whose Christian life is previously without blemish," pleaded one of the magistrates.

"I know that!" the judge snapped, throwing a bone he had been sucking on, which rattled down onto his plate. "But I will not hear a criminal who dares to proclaim his innocence to me!" He threw up his grimy hands in an expression of frustration.

Silence held the room captive. The magistrates kept their heads down, their faces pale.

Heinrich carefully wiped his mouth with a linen cloth, licked his lips, and then spoke slowly and confidently. "I fully appreciate that this heinous criminal is entirely within your jurisdiction to punish as you see fit under the law, Chancellor. However, I believe that your earlier allegations that the devil is present in Strasburg countenances that we allow the man to present himself for a hearing. From his testimony, the Inquisition may gather pertinent facts about whether this may be the work of the Devil. I must insist that we determine if there is evidence of diabolical mischief." Heinrich paused, then added, "You see, that is why the Pope sent me here."

The judge squinted and looked at Heinrich for a while, then surveyed his magistrates, who continued to avoid eye contact. He then nodded slowly. "Yes…I see your point. Then prepare the hearing room for tomorrow," he said, licking his chops.

The next morning, an enormous bailiff and several armed guards dragged a husky, bearded man into a small courtroom in the Strasburg Chancery. His chains rattled loudly. From the deep cracks in his lips, it was clear that the prisoner was severely dehydrated. His brown hair was matted and unkempt, his workman's clothes torn. He looked exhausted as he lay on the floor in a heap, wheezing.

Heinrich stood in the dark corner in the rear of the room, his arms tightly folded. The three magistrates stood in front of the decrepit prisoner, incessantly conferring among themselves. The portly judge walked in and propped himself up behind a large bench in the front of the room, his eyes averted from the prisoner.

"What have I done, your Excellencies? Please, for the love of God and His Saints, have mercy and tell me of my crime! I beg of you!" the man cried out repeatedly, weeping.

Still, the judge looked away and did not utter a word. From his flushed complexion, he appeared to be growing angrier with the prisoner's ongoing petitions.

The prisoner then turned and looked at the three magistrates, who seemed to be the only men in the room capable of listening to him. He threw himself at their feet, his shackles and chains clanging against the cold stone floor. "Please, my lords, I beg of you, why am I here?"

The judge finally stood up and bellowed at him, "You most wicked of men! How can you still not acknowledge your crime? You are fully aware of your guilt. Over a fortnight ago at sunrise, you beat three respected matrons of this town so that they still lie in their beds! How dare you proclaim your innocence!"

The prisoner stared at the ground, apparently lost in thought.

He finally looked up at the judge and said, "Never in all my life have I struck or beaten a woman, and I can prove that at that time, on that day, I was busy chopping wood! Ask your bailiff and servants! When they came for me, I was still chopping wood!"

The judge exclaimed in a fury at the magistrates, "See how he tries to conceal his crime! These women are bewailing their blows, they exhibit the marks and bruises, and publicly testify that he struck them."

The prisoner stared at the ground in silence. Finally, he raised his head, and declared, "On that day and that hour, I do recall striking some creatures, but they were not women."

The judge scoffed in indignation, but all three magistrates gasped and came forward, looking astonished at his comment. "Tell us, what sort of creatures did you strike?" the thinnest magistrate entreated.

He looked at the magistrates and explained in an animated fashion, "Your Excellencies! At dawn I stood at the rock near which I typically chop the wood to burn in my house. A large black cat appeared and began to attack me. I was driving it off with the axe handle I was holding, when another, even larger black cat came and attacked me even more fiercely."

The magistrates looked on in amazement at his testimony. "Tell us more," he insisted.

He continued breathlessly, "and when I again tried to drive them away with the axe I was holding, behold, all three of them jumped up and together attacked me, jumping up at my face. They were all biting and scratching at my legs as well." He pointed to his legs which were bloody and scratched.

The magistrates looked at each other in amazement.

"I must say that I was in great fright and was more panic-stricken than I have ever been!"

"So, what did you do?" asked one of the magistrates, eager to hear more of the explanation.

"I did what any of Your Excellencies would have done! I crossed myself, in the name of the Father, and of the Son, and of the Holy Ghost!" The prisoner demonstrated how he made the sign of the cross on himself, his exaggerated arm movements limited by the heavy chains and shackles attached at his wrists.

"Then, I fell upon these cats which were swarming all over the wood and again leaping at my face and throat. With great difficulty, I drove them away by beating one on the head, another on the legs, and the third on its back." The workman used dramatic physical gestures to show how he swung the axe handle at them.

"I must say, that is quite a story," said Heinrich Institoris, slowly marching forward out of the shadows toward the prisoner, who had apparently not detected his presence until now. The prisoner recoiled fearfully at the Inquisitor's approach. The priest's arms remained tightly crossed, the prisoner not sure what to make of him.

Heinrich walked past the prisoner and up to the judge's bench. He motioned for the magistrates to join him at the sidebar.

"Tell me, what do you know of the three matrons?" Heinrich whispered to the judge.

"They are quite well respected," the judge said, looking confused.

"Why do you ask?" asked one of the magistrates, whispering to Heinrich.

"Well, Your Excellency, it would appear clear from this man's story that you were correct. The devil *has* taken hold in Strasburg. These three matrons are witches, who were actually present at the workman's scene, converted by some glamour into the shapes of those beasts who attacked him."

The judge and magistrates looked stupefied. "Tell us more," the thinnest one begged in horror.

"You see, they were urged to do so at the instance of the Devil. Having been turned into beasts by some devilish glamour, they had to attack the workman. No doubt, this transformation was accomplished by some mutual pact between these women and the Devil himself."

The judge and magistrates were visibly shaken. They crossed themselves. The prisoner looked on, trying to determine his fate, but he could not hear their conversation.

"You see," Heinrich continued explaining, "the wounds they suffered on their bodies were the same wounds the workman inflicted upon the feral beasts that attacked him. Once they returned to their homes, and their appearance returned, their human forms exhibit the same injuries."

"What do you propose we do, Father?" the thinnest magistrate asked, sounding mortally frightened.

"Since these women are clearly engaged in the dark work of Lucifer, we must release this poor man and allow him to return to his work unharmed. However, he must be ordered to speak of this matter to no one."

"And what of the three witches? What shall we do about them, Father?" the thinnest magistrate pleaded.

"You may leave the three witches to me," said a smiling Heinrich, pleased with his newfound trophies.

IMBOLC

When Sebastian awakened on the morning of the last day of January in Finan's warm castle, he was startled to count a dozen melted candles surrounding his bed. They had all burned out. For an instant, he worried that someone was casting a hex on him while he slept.

He dressed in his usual robes but added two light gray fox pelts given to him by Morgan, Finan's wife. He went down to meet Finan and Morgan for a hearty breakfast of blood pudding, sausages and other unidentifiable "delicacies," and intended to inquire about the odd assortment of candles.

While he was enjoying himself, Sebastian greatly missed the food of the warm Mediterranean. He had grown up eating mostly seafood in Bretagne, and while studying in Rome, he remained partial to all manner of fish and crustaceans mingled with fresh olive oil and vegetables. He regretted that he had not eaten a light meal in months. It seemed that even at breakfast, the knights and guards happily drank ale and ate heavy meats with Finan.

But he was glad to be meeting with Brigantia again today and looked forward to studying the rituals of Imbolc that she had begun telling him about. Sebastian found himself thinking of nothing but her. He thought that he may have dreamed of her, as well, but the memories of his dreams were fading.

As he came down the circular stairs, he found Finan standing at the hearth with his wife, daughter and several of his sons, who all looked like younger versions of Finan.

"Aye, we are lookin' for tha' club," Finan turned and said to Sebastian.

"The club?" Sebastian had no idea what Finan was talking about.

"Aye, tha' club!" Finan replied with a chuckle. "Me wife dressed up a sheaf o' oats last night. We even put candles by yer' bed, did ye not notice?"

"Yes, I did, and was meaning to ask you about their significance," Sebastian replied.

"If tha' shape of a club is found in the fire's ashes this mornin', we will have a good year. We call it Laa'l Breeshey," said Finan.

"Is that a Christian practice?" Sebastian asked.

For the first time, Finan looked intimidating.

"Now, that is none of yer business, boy. I allowed you to stay in me home during all yer travels. But don't be writin' about what we do in this manor in that…that book of yers'. You'll be good to remember where ye are."

Sebastian was instantly reminded that he was a guest in the home of a powerful man. If Finan suspected for a moment that Sebastian's research for the Inquisition was a threat to himself or his family, Sebastian would be spending a long time in the dank dungeons underneath their feet, if he was lucky.

"Of course not," Sebastian quickly and emphatically responded. "I am just curious, my Lord."

"Aye, not all our ways are church ways," Finan responded. "But that don't make 'em wrong. Spend some time with Brigantia, Sebastian. In fact, tomorrow is *her* day."

Sebastian was not sure what he meant, but heartily agreed with Finan.

Suddenly, there was a soft knock on the inner door. Finan's daughter Philomena walked over to it, seemingly knowing who was there already, and pronouncing loudly, "Failte leat a Bhrid."

None other than Brigantia entered the room, glowing with her usual incandescence. She looked more beautiful than Sebastian even recalled.

"Beannacht De ar daoine an tighe seo," she said smiled.

"God bless the people of this house, as well, thank ye, me dear," said

Finan, apparently understanding her. "Will you join us for breaking fast, my dear love?"

Brigantia smiled back. "No, thank you, my Lord. I am here to collect my possessions," she said, gesturing toward Sebastian.

"Aye, 'tis so!" Finan laughed heartily.

Sebastian felt like a discomfited schoolboy, as the whole room laughed at his expense.

"Yes, well, I suppose it is better to belong to her than any other," he said, trying to sound charming.

"Ooh!" said Philomena. "I see we have lovers in our midst!"

"Oh, dear, do not do that—you are embarrassing them!" said Finan's wife Morgan.

For once, Brigantia and Sebastian blushed simultaneously, as they hurriedly walked out the door toward the waiting horses.

"Not even a hello before interrogating me again. We may need to teach you some courtly manners," she joked.

He always felt both comforted by her presence but embarrassed at himself.

"Oh, I was just teasing you. I was wishing Lord Finan's family the traditional blessings. You see, tomorrow is Imbolc."

"Yes," he said. "I have been meaning to ask you about it. Is it the feast day of a Saint?"

"You could say that," responded Brigantia with her usual brilliant smile.

Sebastian assisted her with mounting her horse, even though the grooms standing nearby were jealously waiting for the opportunity to do so first.

When Sebastian tried to mount Epona, one of the grooms said to him, "Be careful with that one. Sh'll steal yer heart right well."

"Are you talking about Epona or Brigantia?" he joked.

"Aye," the groom laughed. "Be wary of both!"

Sebastian and Brigantia rode in silence for a long while. Even though it was still late January, they could smell and taste spring coming in the air. Almost as if reading his mind, Brigantia said, "new life is stirring in the womb. The trees will bud soon enough."

They spent the day riding back to the Cliffs, and just talking about the weather, food, and the verdant countryside.

The next day was Sunday and Sebastian regretted that he could not attend Mass. He had planned to set up a camp to sleep overnight near the Cliffs to be nearer to Brigantia during Imbolc, but the bitter cold made that impossible. Instead, he rode until he found an old stone structure that was abandoned and outfitted it for his brief overnight stay.

The tightly built stone room was perfect for a short-term camp, as he could build a small fire near the corbelled doorway to cook some fish, and which kept the inside remarkably warm. The tanned grey fox pelts Finan had loaned him also let him sleep comfortably. Even without a front door, it stayed warm inside the building.

He was awakened in the early morning by the most mellifluous sound he had ever heard. He looked outside and saw Brigantia sitting on a boulder, singing. The song was a language he did not recognize but it was intoxicating.

Brigantia stopped singing and spoke to him. "Good morning, my Sebastian."

"I did not expect you this early. I am groggy from my winter nap." He smiled, trying to compose himself while waking up.

"I did not sleep; I was making the preparations," she said.

"Imbolc—is that how you pronounce it?" he asked.

"Yes, you are learning our language well." She smiled. "My coven will arrive at noon, so be prepared."

"Remind me, how many are in a coven?" he asked, pulling out his journal, and rubbing his bleary eyes.

"Twelve plus myself."

"Jesus' apostles," he commented.

"The number is the perfect circle."

"Twelve, perfect circle, twelve apostles" he scribbled, then set the journal aside.

"But come, it is too early for such weighty things. Awaken and come to my cottage and I will give you more tea and pleasant food."

At noon, the first woman arrived on foot. She was at least sixty years old and had a hunched back, weathered skin and flowing gray hair. Sebastian thought she looked like the image of a hag.

Brigantia introduced them.

"Sebastian, this is Aife. She is the oldest member of our coven. Aife, this is Sebastian. He is here doing research for the Church…for the Inquisition."

When Aife heard the word, she started to shout and began to flee. "Murderer!" she shrieked.

"No!" shouted Brigantia after her.

"He will burn us, they do!" screeched the terrified woman, clutching her chest.

"No, he is a kind soul," said Brigantia, trying to assuage the woman's fears. "Finan sent him to us."

Aife started to calm down. Six more women walked up from behind Aife, hearing the din.

"You invited the Inquisition here?" a woman named Saiorse demanded to know. "Finan has been good to us and allowed us to live in peace. But you know that the Inquisition from Rome will not heed him. Why did you invite him here and put us in danger?"

"I do not believe we are in danger. Sebastian, this is Coamhe, Saoirse, Ciara, Niamh, Roisin and Cara," said Brigantia. "They have traveled great distances. Roisin has recently given birth to a beautiful daughter named Orla."

He introduced himself. "My name is Sebastian Alberti. I am here under the auspices of Finan O'Brien, who I know you respect and trust. He directed me to meet Brigantia, who has instructed me in some of your ways. I want to ensure you that I am here only to research.

"My objective is only to *enquire*," he said, echoing Institoris's words to him in Rome at the Pantheon. "This is only a preliminary investigation. I am nothing more than a field researcher. I brought no arms or weapons and no soldiers or knights. My mission is peaceful, and I am only here to learn. I mean you no harm, and you have my word that I will not seek to do you any violence."

Another woman who had joined the group stepped forward. "I am Clodagh, and this is my sister Aisling. Our ways have been hidden for hundreds of years, since long before my great-grandparents were born. They instructed us to keep our rites away from the Church. Only two things could come from the Church: death or destruction."

"How did the Church destroy your ways?" Sebastian asked.

"They learned of our holy days, our rituals and practices and stole them. We do not lightly forget," said Aisling. Three other women had now joined the group, so all thirteen were now present before him.

"I cannot speak to what my forefathers did, but you have my word that I am merely seeking enlightenment," he replied.

Brigantia stepped forward, turned and spoke to them, "Sebastian is my guest. Today is my day. I bid him welcome."

The women skeptically looked at each other. Roisin finally said to Brigantia, "Indeed it is. Sebastian is welcome." She nodded her head at Brigantia.

Brigantia relaxed. "He has also agreed to carry our heavy sacks to the circle." As she pointed to a large volume of parcels tied up nearby, she smiled at Sebastian.

"Yes, yes I did," he said, putting his book down and dragging one of the heavy bundles up the hill. Overlooking the Cliffs was a great stone circle consisting of twelve pillars. In the center was a flat rock that resembled a table or altar. Sebastian placed the sacks down on the ground, and the women began to unpack them and remove their contents. One woman created a small fire.

Niamh pulled out a small copper crown that held four candles. "This is the Crown of Lights," she said to Sebastian. "Brigantia will wear it."

Clodagh walked up to them and placed a bundle of straw about a foot long, with a straw crosspiece for arms on the altar. It was dressed like a doll. "This is called a Brideog," she said to him. Another woman placed a long branch with a pinecone on the tip. Nearby the altar was placed a broomstick and a small iron cauldron filled with twigs of evergreen, holly, ivy, and other herbs and plants.

Brigantia told Sebastian to step back, which he did. She then stepped up to the stone altar. Roisin went over to the smoldering embers of the fire and lit a branch. She then blew on it and lit the four candles and placed the crown on Brigantia's head.

Roisin said, "in the midst of the deep darkness, I set these candles aflame. In the time of cold, I bring warmth. In the depth of winter, I carry the spring. May the sole flames of these candles set the whole earth ablaze."

Each woman stood at one of the twelve pillars, with Brigantia in the center. The four women at the four cardinal points raised their hands to the sky. Sebastian scribbled feverishly.

Cara raised her hands and said, "Guardians of the Watchtowers of the East, Powers of the Air, blustery winds and gentle breezes of the spring, I invoke you."

Clodagh, who was standing directly across from Cara, raised her hands and proclaimed, "Guardians of the Watchtowers of the South, Powers of Fire, crackling fire of the hearth, growing sunlight, I invoke you."

Niamh raised her hands and shouted, "Guardians of the Watchtowers of the West, Powers of Water, crystal ice and melting snow, I invoke you."

Aisling stepped forward and loudly proclaimed, "Guardians of the Watchtowers of the North, Powers of Earth, fallow fields and first buds of flowers, I invoke you."

Sebastian tried to keep up with his furious notetaking, but it was all happening so fast now.

Roisin stepped forward into the center near Brigantia and spoke, "Lord of death and resurrection and the giver of life; Lord within us whose name is the Mystery of Mysteries, encourage our hearts, let thy holy light crystallize itself in our blood, fulfilling us with resurrection, for there is no part of us that is not of God. Descend, we pray thee upon thy servant and priestess Brigantia. Blessed be."

All twelve women spoke simultaneously, "Brigantia is come,

Brigantia is welcome!" This they repeated three times. Roisin went over and tied back Brigantia's flowing hair. She looked more beautiful than Sebastian could have imagined. He had to stop writing and stare at her for a moment.

Roisin draped a green wool shawl over her bare shoulders and proclaimed, "Behold the three formed goddesses; she whoever was Maid, Mother and Crone. Yet is she ever one. For without spring there can be no summer; without summer, no winter, without winter, no new spring!"

When she had finished, Roisin took up the broomstick and made her way slowly around the circle clockwise, ritually sweeping the ground clear of all the old branches and rotting pinecones that were strewn about, having amassed there over the winter. Two women walked behind her in stately procession. Roisin then replaced the broom beside the altar, and the three women resumed their places around the circle.

Brigantia turned and kneeled before the cauldron. She picked up each of the evergreen twigs and set fire to them from the candle. She then blew the smoking twig out and put it in the cauldron. As she did this, she declared, "Thus we banish winter, thus we welcome spring, say farewell to that which is dead and greet each living thing. We banish winter, thus we welcome spring!"

The women sang the exquisite song that Brigantia had sung earlier when Sebastian was awakened by her.

He finished scribbling in his journal, looked up again and took stock of what he had just seen. It was a simple ritual that seemed to harbor no malice whatsoever. In fact, it seemed like a beautiful way to regard the end of the frigid winter and welcome a warm spring; a sentiment that he shared exactly.

When all twelve women walked out of the stone circle and back toward Brigantia's cottage, he approached Brigantia.

"That was a beautiful ceremony," he said.

"Thank you. I trust you will describe it fairly?" she asked.

"I promise. I frankly expected something quite different."

"I do hope that I did not disappoint." She smiled at him.

When they arrived back at Brigantia's cottage, the women came out with trays of cakes. Sebastian ate one, and then another. They were delicious beyond belief.

Roisin walked over, holding a baby. "Sebastian, this is my daughter Orla. She is twelve weeks old. My eldest daughter has been watching over her."

"What dazzling child," he said.

"Would you like to hold Orla?" she asked.

"Uh, I have never held a baby," he said.

"Here, she doesn't bite—yet," Roisin joked.

Sebastian held the baby delicately, as he was terrified to drop or hurt her.

"You would be a better real father than a priest father," joked Cara.

Brigantia blushed, seeing Sebastian's face, as he cooed at the baby.

CRIB

"You tied your son to a crib?" asked the senior magistrate in Speyer, looking up at the woman skeptically as he took down copious notes.

Belinda sat in an uncomfortably tall chair in the precinct of the magistrate's chamber. She looked worn, beaten down by years of quarrels with Emmeline, her neighbor next door.

The arguments between them had started simply enough. Emmeline's two sons had been showing up at Belinda's doorstep all hours of the day and night, stirring up trouble. Sure, they were only boys, but Belinda could not seem to control their behavior when they were always coming around her home uninvited.

The mischievous boys were constantly banging on her chamber door, looking for food, while their mother was home drinking wine and entertaining guests. Their mother was not married. She had the boys with several men, and apparently had no intention of marrying any of them.

Belinda believed in the sanctity of marriage. She had listened to the priests preaching every Sunday about how important it was for a woman to marry, especially if she had children. She listened to those sermons intently and married a good man.

But her husband Bernard had been gone for months, traveling as far as Alsace to serve their lord on martial campaigns. And during his time away, Belinda had given birth to Alexander. The boy had been colicky. He was waking up five to six times a night. Belinda was barely sleeping and was starting to have difficulty sleeping even when she knew that she should be.

After Belinda frequently brought up the boys' misbehavior with their mother Emmeline, the arguments finally boiled over. The women upbraided each other in a manner unfitting Christian women. Emmeline had cursed at her.

"That baby cries all day and night! I cannot sleep, I cannot eat, damn him!" shouted Emmeline over the baby's cries. Belinda crossed herself. They were devout woman, after all, and blasphemy and cursing babies was never appropriate.

"Go ahead and see what happens with your God damned son, he will grow up to be just like his worthless father, always risking his life and limb for money," Emmeline screamed at Belinda. "Just like his father, he'll love his women and wine while he is away from home." Belinda slammed the door in Emmeline's face. Emmeline had crossed the line.

That night, when Belinda went to place her little one, who was still nursing, in the crib, she reviewed in her mind all the terrible things the women had said and done toward each other that day. Belinda felt guilty about their quarrels, but also grew apprehensive of the danger to her son. Emmeline and her sons simply could not be trusted.

She put a little exorcized salt in Alex's mouth, placed some blessed plants under him and sprinkled him with holy water. She made the sign of the cross on the child's head and tied him carefully to the crib with ropes. This way, if that damned sorceress Emmeline were to try something, the child would be safe and secure.

She replied to the magistrate, "Yes, and I will tell you why…around midnight, it was my habit to confirm that my son was sleeping. However, I heard him cry out. So, I went in to caress him. I moved the crib to reach him. He was gone!"

"Where did he go?" asked the magistrate, looking up from taking notes again.

"I thought I had lost him. I was trembling and in great distress. I got up and lit a candle and found my little one crying in the corner under the bed but without harm."

"And where was Emmeline?"

"She had moved the child. There is no other way he could have escaped the crib. The ropes were tied tight, I am sure of that. She is a witch, you see."

"Did you see her untie your son?"

"I did indeed," she said.

The magistrate looked up at her skeptically. "You needed to light a candle to find your boy. And you found him safely. How could you have seen this…'witch'?" he asked sarcastically, looking back down at his notes.

"You just tell the good priest traveling from Rome that I will accuse that woman with all my might," said an indignant Belinda, holding Alexander closer to her chest as he began crying again. "Shhh, do not cry, son. You will be safe from Emmeline now, I promise," she sobbed as she whispered to the baby in her arms.

DUTY

Once again Sebastian found that he could not sleep. He had returned to Finan's castle after the Imbolc ritual ended. His lavish private bedroom, warm fireplace and soft linens offered no comfort. He started to dream that he had kissed Brigantia at the Cliffs. He wished he had kissed her but at the same time he knew it was wrong to think as such—or was it? Groaning, in the middle of the night, Sebastian woke up and rolled out of his cozy bed and found his way down the spiral staircase, wandering the castle without any purpose.

"I reckon ye could not sleep?" a voice said out of the darkness. A man was sitting on a large chair in a dark corner of the room. The fire in the hearth had not died out yet, but it was down to smoldering embers. Finan sat with a large goblet of dark brown liquid in his hand. He laughed, swirling the content of his ware, then taking a small sip.

"You have no crime before ye, nothin' to frighten ye," Finan said, chuckling.

"Oh, but I feel that I do," Sebastian mumbled under his breath as he made his way towards the cold hearth where a second armchair sat.

"Come, join me, I have a flask full but no one to share it with. What burdens ye? I would have thought me beds were warm and soft enough." Finan grabbed a second goblet, sloppily pouring some of the sweet-smelling wine into it and handing it to Sebastian.

"Thank you," said Sebastian, barely sipping it. "The Church teaches that the ways of Brigantia are the way of the Devil. Heretics are to be burnt and sentenced to torture. But I documented her acts and I watched her ceremony and they are nothing short of the very same way I pray each morning. Purer, in fact."

"You saw her rituals then?" Finan asked. "I cannot believe she permitted ye to witness it."

"And it was nothing like I expected," Sebastian said, twirling his ware as he stared at the small flames dancing around the charred wood in the hearth.

"Aye, we will never reckon the Old Ways. Brigantia may practice 'er own, but they be pure and true, harmin' no one. There are those who aim to cause nothin' but harm," Finan said, looking into the fire like one in a trance. Sebastian studied his host silently. He rarely had the time to privately talk with the man.

"I have been brought up to distrust those like her," Sebastian stated sullenly. Finan chuckled lightly as he watched the young man glare at his wine like it was to blame for all his struggles.

"Ye came under me roof to study the Old Ways for our Church. And ye have a duty. Does it not say in the Holy Book to do what ye must do well? Ye must find yer own path. Ye have been led to believe and now you understand more of the Old Ways. The ways of us men are but fleetin'. Complete yer task first and then return to her if ye so wish. But don't forsake duty and cleave unto the woman," Finan emphatically said.

Sebastian continued to stare at the brown liquid in his own goblet, pondering what he had just heard. His research would indeed be accomplished within the year, and there was nothing stopping him from returning to Rome to submit his text. But he had never felt something so strong with someone before and he wanted to stay with her and forsake all duty.

"When I was young, I traveled far. But while I wanted to keep wanderin' forever, I knew that I had a duty back here. Me family needed me, aye, this manor needed me. I came back for duty." Finan stretched. "I must retire, but do not forget. Ye have duties. We all do. But let not yer heart be troubled," Finan said as he stood up slowly, heading for his bedroom. "Ye will find yer own path, please God."

"Thank you. Farewell, Finan. I leave for Clonmacnoise before you awaken on the morrow. I must then begin my trip back to Rome. I have spent far more time than I should here," Sebastian declared, having made up his mind. "But your beds are indeed warm and inviting."

Finan nodded at him and smiled. "I pray ye find all you set out to, my friend. It was an honor having ye under my roof." He knew Sebastian would someday return to these shores.

REGRETS

B efore daybreak, Sebastian headed out to Finan's stables and packed up his belongings on Epona himself, as the grooms were still asleep. Soon, he found himself atop Epona, galloping towards Brigantia's cottage. The weather was cold and drier this morning, but he did not even notice the icy wind beating against his face this time.

The conversation he had with Finan late last night was fresh on his mind. He knew he had to complete his duties, no matter how tough or painful it may be. When he finally arrived at his destination, he found Brigantia by her garden. He was once more struck by her beauty and grace. He started regretting his decision instantly upon seeing her.

"You should not creep upon a defenseless woman in such a way," Brigantia called out, not even bothering to turn toward him. Sebastian laughed.

"You are anything but defenseless," Sebastian replied, a small smile on his face. Brigantia patted the dark soil tenderly then stood. She was clad in a pale pink dress. Her fair hair was braided down her back with flowers entwined into the rather intricate-looking braid. Sebastian wished he could run his hands through her silky hair, but he knew he shouldn't. It would only make leaving harder. He cleared his throat uncomfortably, causing Brigantia to look up at him. A small frown appeared on her face.

"What is it, my Sebastian?" she asked as she walked closer to him. Her frown deepened when Sebastian took a step back from her. "Do you want to discuss more about our lives, and perhaps take another walk with me?"

"I am departing today, Brigantia," he blurted. Her head tilted to the side as she looked at him. "I have tarried here longer than I should, and I believe I have documented all I needed," he finished, looking down at his feet like a sheepish boy.

"Must you truly leave?" she replied as she took a small step towards him.

The smell of the nearby woods and herbs around her filled his lungs and he once again wished there was another way.

"I know you must, and I understand, but I did not expect that it would be so soon," she said. "I thought we had more time," she mumbled, lifting a hand to touch his stubbly cheek but then deciding against it, dropping it to her side instead.

"I cannot stay any longer. It is like your duty to your coven," he said. "You offer rituals at a specific time and season. You respond when you are summoned, and you follow the law."

"Can you not send your research so the book arrives safely in Rome without you?" she asked, already knowing what his response would be. Sebastian reached out and held her hands. He sucked in a breath at the smoothness and smallness of the hands in his palm.

"I wish there was another way, but I took an oath. I have been entrusted with dangerous documents and it is of utmost importance that I return to Rome to ensure the safe passage of my text, lest it falls into the wrong hands," he said as he brushed a little hair away from her face. She sighed.

"When do you leave?" she whispered, not willing to hear his response, for she knew Epona stood a little way off, already saddled with his belongings.

"I came to say goodbye. I leave today," he said as he squeezed her palm gently.

"I have some herbs for you," she said as she pulled him toward the cottage. Sebastian opened his mouth to object, but she continued, "Including the tea you loved so much the first time you visited me." She smiled broadly at him.

Brigantia began bustling around as she quickly packaged the herbs.

Some were dried and others crushed while some were seedlings. She wrapped them in small woven light green cloth and proceeded to stack them atop each other. Sebastian watched Bastet as she wove in and around Brigantia's legs, purring as she went. Brigantia hummed lightly as she worked, a tune that seemed familiar.

"Is that the song of Imbolc?" he questioned as he looked at her. She picked up her small stack of herbs and walked over to him.

"I am surprised that you remember," she said as she stood beside him. Bastet immediately curled up at her feet, shutting her green eyes.

"One does not easily forget a song like that," Sebastian responded, eyeing the parcel in her hands. "What are those? I thought it was just the tea you intended for me?" he asked and Brigantia smiled at him.

"This first one is to repel evil creatures as you sleep," she said as she placed the herb packaged in green woven cloth. It had an intricate design atop it.

'What marking is that?' Sebastian asked, running his finger over the design.

"I knew you would ask. It is the old language of witches. As old as the Aramaic of Christians. Not many remember this language, but it has existed long before Jesus came. It has actually existed before Aramaic was used." She caressed the design softly as she spoke.

Sebastian watched, in awe of her intelligence; how well-spoken she was. Once again, conflict arose in his head as he questioned all he had been taught and told.

"Do not fret, my Sebastian. Remember, where there is good there is bound to be evil. Did Finan not tell you the very same thing last night? There are sorcerers who have forsaken the ways of old and veered into the dark arts," she said.

"How do you know what Finan and I spoke of?" Sebastian asked, once again puzzled by her knowledge of things he was sure he never mentioned. Brigantia smiled brightly at him.

"The walls have ears, my Sebastian. Nothing said or done will remain hidden forever," she responded as she picked up the second and third parcels. "These are the teas I had made for you the first time we met. It will help you sleep and keep you well rested and strengthened." She finished, placing the parcels atop the first. Sebastian noted that this time the herbs were wrapped in a pale weave and another intricate design lay atop. He nodded at her and she picked the last parcel.

"This is poison to whoever wishes you harm. They are crushed clove seeds; I have tied them in small bags. Hang them in your room and whoever enters with intentions to harm you would instead cause harm to himself."

Sebastian immediately began shaking his head at the last parcel of woven moss green that seemed almost black in color. "I cannot accept this," he mumbled. How would he even explain the other parcels? At least they could easily pass for tea and repellents, but this was pure enchantment, and he could not take it back with him.

"It would bring no severe harm, just minor inflictions enough for the person to faint and for you to escape. You need not explain to anyone the occurrence," she persuaded as she proceeded to tie up the parcels with a string of her fair hair wrapped around in a ribbon.

They stepped out of the cottage and toward Epona, Sebastian clutched the parcels in his right hand, fighting the urge to hold onto Brigantia's hand.

"Will I see you again?" Sebastian asked as they stopped by his horse.

'If we are meant to be together, my Sebastian, then I trust that the Fates will bring us back to each other," she replied.

"Goodbye, Brigantia," Sebastian said as he looked at her, committing her face to his permanent memory. Unwilling to let her go. Brigantia saw the conflict in his eyes and smiled up at him. Leaning forward on her toes, she pressed a chaste kiss to his jaw.

"Until we meet again," she whispered in his ear, giving it a little kiss.

Sebastian mounted his horse as Brigantia untied Epona from the tree. She handed him the rope as she smiled at him. She made a clicking sound at the back of her throat and slapped Epona lightly. The horse immediately thrusted into a gallop. Sebastian turned to bid Brigantia farewell but just like the first time that she appeared suddenly. This time, she was gone.

RAVENSBURG

Rodrick used a rusty iron rake to comb through Agnes the Bathkeeper's clumpy ashes, looking for any leftover jewelry that hadn't fully melted. He had already found remnants of a silver ring in Anna of Mindleheim's' pile, but he had to fish it out by hand, and her heart hadn't fully disintegrated from the fire. Even skulls usually burned up by now, but the hearts didn't always go, because they were big, tough muscles. He hated having to touch the hearts.

Back when he was working in Ravensburg, they had many more jobs for him compared to here in Constance. But Institoris had kept him occupied.

"We had a savage hailstorm from this one," he remarked to his friend Lodwich, who was in charge of setting up the pyres. "Remember it? Stones as big as pebbles." He continue to comb through the ashes.

"Oh yeah," Lodwich replied. "The one two years ago?"

"For a mile! Crushed my garden, Jarl's crops and even his vineyards. So bad that they still haven't come back yet!" said Rodrick, rubbing his dusty whiskers.

"The hail was because of Agnes?" asked Lodwich, his face streaked with sweat.

"Some notary claimed that, I forget who. He started it all. Then the farmers started in. They put Agnes in the old prison, and Anna in the new one. Separated 'em."

"Smart dealings," said Lodwich, putting down a burnt rope and replacing it with a fresh one. "They can't get their stories all straight then!"

"One didn't even know the other was arrested," said Rodrick. "They kept 'em apart."

"So, how'd they figure it?" asked Lodwich with genuine interest.

"Agnes went first. They hung 'er up by the shoulders, Gehler did it," said Rodrick.

"Ooh, Gehler. He's a tough one. Crazy, they say," said Lodwich, brushing off his shoe with his gloved hand.

"Look, I found it!" said Rodrick.

"What you find then?" asked Lodwich, stopping his work to peer over Rodrick's shoulder.

"Another silver ring. This is less melted. I might keep this one," he said as he held it up to inspect it.

"You not keepin' the other?" asked Lodwich.

"No, Institoris wants a trinket from each girl," he said. "Keeps them like little trophies." He shuddered. He put the ring in his coat pocket. "I will just sell this one."

"Agnes didn't say a word, though," he continued. "Weird thing is that when she finally did speak up, they say she screamed like a man. I heard she even got violent on Gehler."

"She give it up?" asked Lodwich.

"Institoris took the chains off her arms. Her arms were all broke anyway. She confessed," said Rodrick.

"Without a single witness against her?"

"Not a one," said Rodrick.

"What she admit?" asked Lodwich.

"She said for eighteen years she slept with a devil."

"I didn't know she was married, ha ha!" laughed Lodwich, grinning and displaying yellow teeth.

Rodrick laughed too. "She weren't! She said she had a demon or something livin' in 'er beds. Anyway, they asked her about the hail-storm. She admitted she did it."

"How she do it then?"

"Well, she said she was in her house. Devil told to her go out to Kuppel."

"The field?" asked Ludwich.

"Yeah, the plains. Devil told her bring some water. He said he was goin' to make it rain or something. She said she saw the old bastard standin' under a tree. The one across from the big tower."

"Go on," said Lodwich, stopping his work again to look at Rodrick and listening intently.

"She said he told her to dig a hole and pour the water into it."

"Then what?" he asked.

Rodrick stuck out his little finger and swirled it around in the air. "She said she stirred the mud with her little finger, and it all disappeared. Devil took it up into the air, I suppose."

"Right," said Lodwich. "How'd old Anna get caught?" he asked, going back to his work setting up the kindling.

Rodrick said, "she said she saw Anna nearby, under a tree."

"That's it?"

"So, then old Gehler went with Institoris to the new prison. They asked Anna all about it. Hung her an inch off the ground with chains while they did. Anyway, she said nothing. But when they took her back down, before they strung her arms up again, she confessed."

"To causin' the same hailstorm?" asked Lodwich.

"Yeah, heh. And she said she was sleepin' with a demon for twenty years!"

"Same demon?" asked Lodwich, laughing.

"Yeah, same one," laughed Rodrick. "He gets around, that one. Busy fuckbeggar. And she also admitted to makin' lightning."

"From the sky?"

"No, from my ass. Of course from the sky, yeah, she said she could do that as easy as hail."

"Well, they both gone now," said Lodwich.

"Yes, they are," responded Rodrick emphatically, taking his hat off and placing it over his heart. "I will keep the melted ring, and let Heinrich keep the good one."

"Better for business," said Lodwich. "Have to keep the man happy."

"Yes, sir," said Rodrick, putting his cap back on. "Better for business," he repeated, and continuing to comb through Agnes' ashes.

CLONMACNOISE

Since leaving Finan's estate, Sebastian had thought of nothing else but Brigantia.

Every time he looked at his detailed notes, he could only think of all the topics Brigantia had discussed with him. No one had ever made him think about the world the way she did. He seriously considered turning around and riding back to her. But he had to complete his mission; Finan was right.

It was warm for the last day of April as Sebastian finally approached Clonmacnoise Abbey's grounds in County Offaly. He had spent weeks traveling through County Roscommon, meeting with local people, as well as travelers and priests. After Ballinasloe, he stopped in Athlone, in the center of the country. Villagers there directed him to Clonmacnoise. He tied Epona to a rock wall three pastures away and walked the remainder of the way.

Clonmacnoise rose on a breezy mount overlooking substantial verdant pastures. Its majestic stone towers and stately spires were visible from miles away, and it had stirred generations of monks to glorify Christ, as well as to study literature and art within its walled enclosures.

As he approached the Abbey, he could see a few large gray Celtic crosses revolting against the sky. Buried on the Abbey's grounds were the remains of great warriors and pious priests alike. The crosses marked the site of graves and were haphazardly positioned anywhere that an influential lord or noble could manage to attain the sacred real estate.

Sebastian had read that Clonmacnoise was established a thousand years ago by Saint Ciaran at the point where the major east-west land route through the bogs of central Hibernia crossed the River Shannon. Within this rectangular-shaped complex stood a grand cathedral which had served as the main church of central Hibernia for centuries. Several smaller churches and chapels had been added by assorted kings and lords over the years.

What had inspired Sebastian the most, though, wasn't the Abbey's reputation for notable architecture. It was the fact that during the dark times when the barbaric hordes overran the countryside, the wise monks of the Abbey took care to guard their most sacred assets within its main, impregnable, windowless tower—their treasure trove of books.

The monks recognized that the throngs would ignorantly destroy the priceless tomes, and in doing so, rob Christendom of the classical knowledge of the saints and doctors of the Church. Sebastian now appreciated that many brave monks had lost their lives to safeguard these humble handwritten books as though they were fashioned of gold and jewels, and he was proud and appreciative that they had grasped the priceless value of recorded scholarship and knowledge.

Always the diligent student of monastic architecture, he knew that the thick, rocky outer walls he was nearing marked the exterior perimeter of the cloistered courtyard within. But from what he could see in the dusky twilight, the entire complex was unkempt and overgrown. It was utterly crumbling and covered with wayward vines and strangling fauna that seemed to sprout right out of the large rocks themselves. Entire sections of buildings were missing or strewn yards away. In the churchyard, headstones had been toppled or were sharply missing portions, as if irately battered with swords or clubs and not just eroded at a snail's pace through the passage of time.

Sebastian concluded that, sadly, Clonmacnoise was no longer the epitome of monastic accomplishment. It would now take an inventive imagination to envision what this mighty complex might have once looked like in its prime. Standing at the boundary of the blighted buildings, Sebastian pondered for how long these sacred grounds had lain abandoned by the Church. Perhaps a better question, he realized, was *why* was it lying in trampled ruins?

The central cathedral was missing most of its roof and an entire exterior wall, making its interior almost wholly visible from outside. Sebastian dearly hoped that inside its crumbling edifice there would be some remnant of the high altar, nave and transept that once made a soaring tribute to God.

Suddenly snapped out of his thoughts by fear of dangerous reality, Sebastian thought he noticed the occasional flicker of what might be the flames of torchlight emanating from somewhere deep within the remaining stone structure. Instinctively, he knew he had to observe the central cathedral and furtively venture to a higher, safer vantage point to effectively do so.

There was a nearby tower that might furnish excellent height and a safe distance to survey the landscape. Its interior was now accessible through a gaping space in its base. More importantly, several thin vertical windows facing in all directions had been carved through this smaller tower's circular walls. Hopefully, he thought at least one of these narrow slits, once probably used for firing arrows against the barbaric hordes, might prove a good vantage point into the cemetery and church structures below.

Without hesitation, he traversed the defiled graveyard, and briskly entered through the large hole in the tower's base. He instantly discovered that its interior was exceptionally cold. Even if getting warmer by the day, it was still damp on the last day of April, and he had come to expect that seasons meant little as a fact of life here. But this was different. The empty sensation pervaded his being and cut to the bone.

He stared blankly into the yawning gloom above to get his bearings. As his eyes grew accustomed to the darkness, he looked up and managed to detect that access to any of the small windows was only attainable by climbing up numerous flights of shaky, brittle wooden steps. Sebastian had no idea if the tower's steps would be capable of withstanding the slightest touch, much less supporting his full weight. But because there simply was no other way up, he painstakingly began his slow ascent.

When he reached the fourth level of the citadel, Sebastian rested and peered out of one of the windows facing west. The sun had set, and it was only the full moon that furnished the primary source of light now. He wearily reached the fifth and highest level of the spire, relieved that the uneven timber steps had not given way.

There was a tiny room at the apex of the tower. In it were strewn about papers and leaves that had blown in from the windows. On a broken shelf, he spotted a small book entitled *Goetia*, and perused it in the dim candlelight. Paralleling the *Clavicula* from Mont-St-Michel, it utilized bizarre words, but finally he found an entry that succinctly articulated what at least some of these words meant. According to the anonymous author of *Goetia*, it was a list of the infernal leaders of hell. The authors purported to enumerate the hierarchy of hell itself, which included Astaroth. That name had also appeared in the *Clavicula*. He flipped to an entry relating to Astaroth:

> Astaroth is a great and a strong duke, comming foorth in the shape of a fowle angell, sitting upon an infernall dragon, and carrieng on his right hand a viper: he answereth trulie to matters present, past, and to come, and of all secrets. He talketh willinglie of the creator of spirits, and of their fall, and how they sinned and fell: he saith he fell not of his owne accord. He maketh a man woonderfull learned in the liberall sciences, he ruleth fourtie legions. Let everie exorcist take heed, that he admit him not too neere him, bicause of his stinking breath. And therefore, let the conjuror hold neere to his face a magicall ring, and that shall defend him.

In the distance outside, Sebastian suddenly made out the sound of a mournful groan that sounded like a person in great pain. Now alarmed, he hurriedly ascended to the next flight of rickety steps, shuddering from the frigid cold, and praying slightly more urgently.

He peered out of the easterly window slit. From this high vantage point, he could decipher the silhouette of the entire Abbey. In particular, he directed his observation to the central cathedral.

He could make out the shape of the main altar but not because of the dim moonlight. Rather, the rectangular stone table was ringed with ignited torches, held aloft by twelve robed figures, standing in a semi-circle. Their robes and hoods were long and covered them almost entirely, but they were clearly the robes of monks. Their torches formed a bright circumference of flickering orange light which surrounded the stone altar. On the flat table itself was a collection of implements, some of which glinted in the flickering torchlight. A brass bell, a large silver chalice, some form of clay figurine, and four or five scrolls were placed in various locations on the flat surface.

A curious and elaborate set of shapes and characters were etched onto the stone floor below the altar. The odd markings seemed to almost glow as they reflected in the moonlight. One of the symbols looked like the one he had seen in the mines.

All the figures walked over and stood within the center of the large circle. One was holding a large wooden staff and seemed to be whispering to the others, but Sebastian could not hear anything. Inside the triangle to the east of the circle was a large metal brazier that burned noxious incense. Sebastian could smell its fetid odor of sulfur and noxious gases as the fumes occasionally wafted in his direction. The smell was awful and nauseating; it almost made him gag.

Another robed figure took out two strange swords and laid them on the ground, crisscrossed. A thirteenth figure with a staff entered from the southwest, moved closest to the eastern edge of the circle and then spoke very loudly, in clear and distinct Latin. His voice sounded like that of an older man, and projected great confidence and strength.

"I invoke and conjure thee now, Lord Astaroth. Fortified with the power of the supreme majesty, I strong command thee by Baralamemsis, Baldachiensis, Paumachie, Apoloresedes, and the Most Potent Princes Genio, Liachide, Ministers of the Tartaraean seat, Chief Princes of the Seat of Apologia in the Ninth Region.

"I exorcise thee by Adonai, El, Elohim, Elohe, Zebaoath, Elion, Escherche, Jah, Tetragrammaton, Sadai, do though forthwith appear and show thyself until me, here before this circle, in a fair and human shape, without any deformity or horror. I command thee, O Spirit Astaroth by Him who spake and it was done."

Once he completed his bizarre speech, there was a long pause, but nothing happened. He then raised his voice a second time and shouted a variety of words Sebastian had never heard before, "Anexhexeton, Schemes, Amathia, Hagios, Jetros, Athenoros, Agla and Saray!"

Still nothing happened. There was another pause, during which everything was silent. Sebastian had no idea what they were expecting to take place.

The third time, the figure raised his voice even louder and added several other names to his odd list of words, "Prerai, Inessensatoal, Putumaton and Itemon!" His voice boomed throughout the stony ruins of the building. Sebastian tried to commit the strange words that the celebrant had uttered to memory so that he could write them down in his journal, but he was not sure he could.

Sebastian's eyes were drawn to the small brazier within the triangle. He could have sworn that a form momentarily appeared within the incense smoke rising out of the censer. It was not visible or solid, but something with substance seemed to flicker.

Sebastian assumed he was imagining this, but it seemed that the robed figures saw it too. The celebrant seemed unfazed by whatever was occurring. He lowered his voice, and said toward the censer, "Welcome, most notable Lord Astaroth. I called thee and have bound you to remain affably and visible before this circle, within this triangle of art, so long as I need thee and depart not without my license, until thou hast truly and faithfully fulfilled all that I desire."

Sebastian swore that he heard a gravelly sound. After a minute, the strange noise faded away. The celebrant seemed pleased with whatever he thought he had heard, and said, "Lord Astaroth, because that has diligently answered my demands, I do hereby license thee to depart without injury to man or beast. Depart and be willing to come whenever duly exorcised and conjured by the sacred rites of sorcery. The sacrifice of innocent blood that you demanded will now be offered." Each robed figure slowly left the circle and began to ascend the steps to approach the high altar, torches in hand.

As the orange glow began illuminating the sanctuary behind the high altar, Sebastian spotted something which paralyzed him with dread. He saw two massive wooden beams behind it, fastened together with rope to form a large wooden crucifix. The corpus on the cross appeared to be dripping with fluid which was pooling and congealing on the smooth floor.

Sebastian became alarmed when he realized that the body on the cross was quivering. It was not a statue, as he has expected. The form appeared to be that of a woman. She was tied by ropes to the two wooden beams and appeared to be struggling to remain conscious in spite of blood loss.

His first instinct was to rush down the steps, scramble into the abandoned church and try to rescue the young woman, at any cost to himself. However, as he began to stand up, he paused and thought for a second. Impetuousness may serve no good, as the robed men would undeniably overpower him and just add him as another human sacrifice. Deeply disturbed, he decided that at this moment he could do nothing more than wait and crouched back down to observe more closely. Perhaps there would be an opportune moment when he could save her. Plus, he was continually hoping he could be able identify one of these people if they removed their hood.

Sebastian began to make out a slow, masculine chant emanating from the robed group. Unlike the Gregorian Chants in Latin that he had frequently heard in the monastery, this one was guttural and not in Latin. From what he could make out, there was a hymn or recital by the tall, robed figure, and occasionally an antiphon recited by the remaining figures, vocalized in response.

He could hear and comprehend nothing specific of what was being chanted. He had never heard such strange words uttered and could not even detect what language they were using. The wind died down slightly, and he could make out voices more clearly now.

Four of the participants departed the circle and surrounded and faced the cross from each of the cardinal directions, with the remaining watching from a distance. Their positions reminded him of the ceremony at Imbolc.

The first figure facing the cross from the east spoke first and said in a loud voice: "From the watchtower of the East, I am sent by Lucifer to pierce this woman's right hand." He then took up an iron nail from the ground that had been placed there and used a mallet to nail it into the right hand of the young woman. Sebastian heard a horrible yelp. The girl was not dead. Sebastian averted his eyes from the horrible spectacle.

A hooded figure facing the cross from the north announced: "From the watchtower of the North, I am sent by Lord Belial, to hobble her feet so that she may forth no more to spread her disease." He then stepped back and handed the mallet to the next figure. The girl was now breathing quickly but was wheezing loudly.

Sebastian again considered rushing down to save her but was reminded that they would just kill him on sight.

The next figure moved toward the girl and said, "From the watchtower of the West, I am sent by Leviathan, to pierce her left hand." The girl had stopped yelping and seemed to be losing consciousness again.

The final one of the four men approached from the south and could be heard to say, "From the watchtower of the South, I am sent by Satan to ravage her mind." The girl was dead. The main celebrant took a large torch and set fire to a bundle of straws and kindling that had been placed at the foot of the cross. It instantly ignited.

Sebastian turned away. He desperately tried to remain as quiet as possible, as he had no idea how the sound might travel from this height. He gagged and vomited as he smelled burning hair.

The cold chill in the tower suddenly became a freezing wind he had never experienced before, even in a blizzard. He started to feel that he wasn't alone in this tower. He felt the sensation of eyes watching him from the dark.

Sebastian ran for his own life, down the steps three at a time, clutching the *Goetia*. Several flights down, he tripped on something warm and soft and lost his balance. A rat squeaked loudly, as Sebastian had crushed its backside underfoot. Sebastian landed on his lower back with a harsh thump.

Sharp pain shot through his body. He pulled himself up and continued the frenzied descent, ignoring the pain. Just as he did so, he saw another small, tattered book half-open on the dirty floor. It had an inverted cross and the words *The Sworn Book of Pope Honorious III* written in scarlet on the black leather cover. He grabbed it as he ran. It looked like one of the robed figures had dropped it, even though he had not seen anyone in the tower. He had to clutch one book under each arm as he ran.

When he arrived at the tower's base, he realized how dark it was outside now. Several dark storm clouds had just begun to form in the sky, blocking the moon's light entirely. He shot a quick glance back in the direction of the ruined cathedral. He knew the girl had already expired. He could see flickering firelight from her pyre glowing against the walls of the nave in the distance. He also knew he had to get back to Epona, who was tied to a rock wall several hundred yards away, to the south, to escape alive. He figured if any of these murderers had found Epona, he would never get away. He hoped he would be able to retrace his steps in the dark, back across the three fields.

As he went, he heard rustling sounds coming from the direction of the main church. Instinctively, he began to run at full speed away from them. When he reached the outer wall, he had to feel his way to one of the gaping holes to allow him to escape the perimeter of the Abbey. The rustling behind him grew louder.

Sebastian kept stumbling over the hem of his own robe and nearly dropped the book he was holding. Once he had crossed a single field and reached the first stone wall, he turned and looked back, out of breath.

He could vaguely make out two of the robed figures moving about against the night sky. They were near the outer wall of the Abbey, only a few dozen yards away across the field. He hurdled the low stone wall and continued running. He was convinced that they had discovered that he had been watching them. Why else would they be running in the field?

When he reached his horse, he hastily untied her from the stone wall, throwing the two books into the saddlebags. He kicked Epona into a full gallop toward the south. He was profusely sweating from the run, but the cold chill he had felt in the tower still hadn't left him.

CASHEL

Sebastian felt like his heart was beating out of his chest and his lungs burned. His mind was filled with images of the girl's bloodied body and the glassy look in her dead eyes as she hung on the cross. He wished he could cut off his ears and wash them clean of the sounds he still seemed to hear. Epona neighed as if feeling her owner's discomfort, jolting Sebastian from his thoughts.

"Faster, girl," he shouted to Epona, leaning forward to rub her flank soothingly—or maybe it was more to sooth his own frayed nerves.

As he rode, Sebastian wondered what description he could offer for what he had just seen. He knew exactly what he saw and there was no denying the fact that the robed monks had been practicing sorcery and committing murder. He had to bring them to the Church's good justice.

He would get to Cashel and report all he had seen to the Catholic and civil authorities of the region. There was sure to be dire consequences to those men for this blasphemous act and he would be sure to see it to the end. He feared they would call him mad and accuse him of heresy, but he hoped the Archbishop of Tipperary would understand and help.

Epona neighed again and Sebastian knew he had to find a place to rest. There was only so much his horse could take. Finding a rundown inn, he sought shelter for the night sleeping under piles of straw in their stable for fear that he was still being followed.

He hid Epona after ensuring that she was given as much hay and water as she needed and as many carrots, apples, and sugar as he could give her. Sleep was hard to find as Sebastian violently tossed and turned under the hay. He said a prayer for the dead woman's soul as sleep finally found him. In his dreams, he was the one hung on the cross while face-less claws dug into his skin.

When he awoke before dawn, he anxiously wanted to reach the stronghold of authority where he could convey information regarding the murder. He also longed for a sanctuary to soothe his aching soul and give him a tranquil place to collect his thoughts and record all that he had witnessed.

He quickly fed Epona some more apples and sugar. He was de-termined to reach Cashel even before the sun fully kissed the sky. He found a stream close to the stable where he washed himself. The slightest sounds had him looking around as if expecting a cloaked man to jump out of the bushes and grab him.

He traveled southwest for two hours before arriving at the Rock of Cashel, the ideal destination to fulfill his needs. Rounding a bend in the road in Tipperary, Sebastian's heart finally lifted when saw the great fourth century fortification of Cashel, standing tall and proud on the plains. He was heartened since the largest building on the massive Rock was the 13th Century Cathedral of St. Patrick, which would give him everything he needed, including the presence of powerful regional authorities.

Once he reached the outer wall, Sebastian dismounted the mare, who was clearly exhausted. He handed Epona's reins and his scroll of introduction to the guards, who assured him that he was to be immi-nently greeted by the Abbot.

Sebastian knew that the Abbot was not the ultimate authority over the grand Cathedral on the Rock of Cashel; that was a high ecclesiastical office held by the Archbishop of Tipperary. However, the Archbishop was not accessible to a young seminarian, regardless of introductory papers from an Inquisitor Extraordinary in hand. In contrast, the Abbot seemed to be an earnest, kind man who immediately appeared to pres-ent a sympathetic ear. He appeared to be delighted to encounter anyone from Rome.

"Sebastian, welcome to the Rock of Cashel. You good Inquisitors are always welcomed here," the Abbot proclaimed. They entered the complex through Cormac's chapel, under a large doorway decorated with chevrons and the heads of dragons and humans.

"Thank you, most gracious Father, but I must have a serious word with you first. It is a matter of the utmost urgency," said Sebastian, who had anticipated this moment and had practiced it in his head a hundred times during his journey. Nonetheless, it came out garbled anyway.

"There was a murder, a naked woman, nailed to a cross, a satanic rite. They burned her at the stake. It was horrible, a travesty of the Mass, she is dead. I believe they were conjuring a demon."

They stopped walking. "Are you feverish after your journey, my son?" inquired the Abbot, looking concerned.

"No, Abbot. I have journeyed from Clonmacnoise, which is deserted, and I have much to report about dark rites I witnessed there."

The moment the word "Clonmacnoise" crossed Sebastian's lips, the Abbot's complexion grew pallid, and his posture became more erect. "Sebastian, these are matters we cannot help you with here. The goings-on there are best left to Rome. However, I can get you a damp cloth for your head and we can freshen your garments before the matin morning prayers."

"Thank you, Abbot. You are kind. But I believe the Archbishop must be notified of this murder at once."

There was a long pause and Sebastian could hear a pin drop.

"As I said, these are purely matters for Rome," the Abbot painstakingly repeated. "Now, you will rest. We will get you settled. Vespers tonight are in the newly constructed Vicars Choral Hall. It is the only structure of its kind in Hibernia, you know."

"Yes, but the dark rites were conducted by fiends that I believe are Churchmen—"

"Sebastian, we have arranged a quiet room for you," he interrupted. "You will have access to the Cathedral and to the Church library which is wondrous for this part of the world. Not quite Rome, but astounding, nevertheless. Many grand classics are stored there."

The Abbot then whispered as quietly as he possibly could, "Do not breathe a word of what you witnessed to anyone until you are back in

Rome. The Archbishop will agree with me. I will not repeat myself," he warned, in a somber tone.

Sebastian was bewildered. Why would this stronghold be cowered by a few rogue murderers, he thought to himself. He decided to alter his approach.

"Thank you, most kind Abbot. I am obliged to you for your hospitality and kindness. I deeply apologize for my rantings and ravings. I am conducting intense research for my professors and I suppose my arduous work and hard travel has gotten to me. I plan on remaining at the Rock for a few days to rest my weary mind and soul, and benefit from the beautiful cathedral and library to which you alluded. May I do so with your gracious indulgence?"

Abruptly, the Abbot's jolly demeanor returned with a vengeance. "Certainly! We have *superb* cheese here. Have you ever heard of Cashel blue?" he said in a tenor that sounded more like that of an aspiring waiter than an Abbot.

"No, is it good?" asked Sebastian monotonously, fully aware of what Cashel blue cheese was.

"Is it good? It is stupendous! It is one of the preeminent cheeses in all God's creation. You will adore it. It has large blue flecks, made by the action of mold, but don't you mind that, it is delectable! It is one of the few blue cheeses made from cow's milk. We age it in caves far beneath the Rock. Roquefort doesn't even measure up to it in taste or consistency! It works wonders on the body when consumed alongside our legendary bread."

Sebastian found the Abbot's exhilaration for cheese bizarre in contrast to his abject refusal to hear details of a murder. Nonetheless, Sebastian realized that whatever benefit he could derive from his brief stay at the Rock of Cashel, it was not going to be from eating moldy cheese.

"Thank you, Father. I look forward to it." Sebastian replied, promptly, with thoughtful and considered prudence.

"Our good brothers will show you to your room and then to the Choral Hall for Vespers. God bless you, Sebastian."

With that, the Abbot joyfully departed, more skipping than walking.

Sebastian retired to his room, trying to figure out what to do next. He could never dispatch a scroll to Rome faster than he could travel there himself. No, his best solution was to gather the final material for his research and head to Rome immediately thereafter, as the Abbot had suggested. He had no confidence that the Archbishop would be of any greater use.

Once he knew that he was alone, he closed his door and looked at the books he had literally stumbled upon at Clonmacnoise. The *Goetia* was written in German and Latin but contained strange words in a language that he did not recognize. The rituals in the book seemed to reference up to 72 names of God and confessions, litanies, masses of the Holy Ghost and angels, the Office of the Dead, the Gospel of John and various prayers with gruesome sacrifices of animals and even humans.

It also contained detailed spellings of the strange words that he had heard the celebrant bellowing. According to the book, it was written by a man named Cencio Savelli who had become Pope and died over two hundred years earlier. In the book, he discussed the value of occult knowledge in the Church, and how by summoning or raising demonic entities, one could learn to control them. On the cover of the book was another symbol that looked like the others Sebastian had encountered before.

The *Goetia* contained invocations of demonic entities for every day of the week. It detailed how a priest needed to fast for a certain amount of time and sacrifice animals and humans in order to help with the binding of evil spirits. It also mentioned the same demon named Astaroth that he had come across in the other grimoires.

After evening prayers, Sebastian excused himself from dinner and crept into the underground Church complex, searching until he found the subterranean Church library. It was difficult to ascertain just how large an inventory of manuscripts it held because it was dark, but it appeared very well-stocked. There was no one minding the books at all, a testament to the disinterest the current fraternal inhabitants of the Rock had with dusty classics.

Sebastian grabbed a hefty iron candelabra and began to roam the stacks, which extended for many yards in a labyrinthine maze. He was seeking the tomes that Institoris told him were in residence here, but he could not tell how these manuscripts were organized, if at all.

"Someone should instruct them to classify books by topic," Sebastian muttered to himself. "And maybe even read them, God forbid."

After meandering for over an hour through endless stacks, he stumbled on one of the books he was seeking deep in a stack beneath at least a dozen other manuscripts that had nothing to do with it.

The large tome had the words "*Clavicula Solomonis*" on the cover penned in red calligraphy that was far more ornate than other books of this type. The book was bound in dark leather that was practically black in color from age and rot. In contrast, *The Grand Grimoire* was red with black calligraphy.

Oddly, this book's covers were sealed by a large, rusty lock. The keyhole was peculiarly shaped. Sebastian lamented that unfortunately the chain and lock would have to be broken. After his experiences at Mont-St-Michel, he knew that there was simply no way that he was going to lug this huge, esoteric manuscript back to the Abbot and inquire if anyone had a three- or four-hundred-year-old key to open it.

He pried the book open slowly. In due course, the centuries of rust gave way, and the lock broke and fell to the floor with a dull clang that reverberated throughout the stacks of books. There was no one around to notice the echoing sound.

As he opened the book, the spine creaked with age. He leafed through the yellowed pages, which seemed more like they were made of papyrus than paper. Thin copper plates were placed inside the center of the book, upon which were inscribed a variety of symbols, mostly circles surrounded by Hebrew letters. Some were pentagrams and hexagrams. Some of the seals had cloaked hands pointing to Hebrew words within them, and others contained what appeared to be astrological signs. While Sebastian had studied some ancient Hebrew, most of these words were unpronounceable and alien.

Like *The Grand Grimoire* and the book written by Pope Honorius, this book also purported to be a book written by King Solomon and claimed to contain the keys to conjuring and controlling demons and spirits. It was the ultimate guide to sorcery.

There was a large seal inscribed. He recalled the seal was also etched into the ground at Clonmacnoise in an upside-down pentagram, and he saw the same back in the mines in Paris. He remembered Brigantia explaining how a five-pointed star with the fifth point facing up represented the victory of spirit over the base elements. He assumed that the inverted pentagram must mean the opposite. He took out his scrawled notes from the Abbey and juxtaposed them with these entries in the old tomes.

Was it possible that the men at the abandoned Abbey were using these rites to try to conjure an infernal demon? It seemed incomprehensible, but here was startling evidence that the hooded figures had at least attempted to do so, if not succeeded.

It appeared that the dark robed figures at Clonmacnoise were using the information in these books to try and strike pacts with a king of the infernal spirits. The books seemed to suggest that the crucifixion ritual was an offering to Astaroth, the patron demon of the falsely accused. This must be what was happening in Paris, as well.

Sebastian closed the books, shut his eyes, and breathed deeply. It was now time to head to Rome to deliver these malefic books and report his findings to the Inquisitors. He put the other two books in his satchel and left the library as quickly as he could, weighed down by them both physically and spiritually.

No one saw him. He returned to his room to record and mull over his findings and these books in greater detail. When Sebastian arrived back at his room, it was after midnight, and there was a massive block of smelly Cashel blue cheese on a plate resting on a wooden table next to his bed. A dull rounded knife was sticking out of the cheese, and nearby were several pieces of sliced soda bread. Waiting for him on his bed was a note, undoubtedly from the jolly Abbot, that exclaimed "Enjoy our cheese!"

SCRYING

Brigantia sat in her cottage, gazing into a black polished mirror of obsidian stone that belonged to her great-grandparents, and their great-grandparents before that. She was told that it was forged in a volcano, back when such things were. Bastet was curled up at her feet.

As I scry, I can see in my Sebastian a growing power that I have never seen before. His insights into the Old Ways are growing, but he is still fearful. His beliefs waver back and forth, like dry reeds blown by the wind in autumn. He longer finds solace in mere repetition of prayers. I sense a longing for meaning that he can no longer find in buildings made by men.

She sipped her tea. Ever since Sebastian and her coven had left her after Imbolc, her loneliness was magnified.

Alas, there is a gorge growing in my heart. I know he must continue his fated journey and return to Rome, but I so desperately desire to capture and keep him here forever. I have never felt these feelings for a mortal man. He looks at me as if I am the only drink that can quench his thirst. I ache for his slightest touch. When he brushed my shoulder, the world fell away as if nothing else ever existed besides us. I cannot sleep without seeing his face and feeling his hands caressing my body.

I so desire to cast a spell of love over him. I mixed a powerful philter of vervain, wormwood and dittany of Crete. I even strengthened it with fennel, grains of paradise, motherwort, and lovage, but I could not bring myself to taint his tea and manipulate his will. If he is to love me, it will be without magic. I know that love spells are black magic the same as are those spells that commit murder, for it would rob him of his freedom. No, if he returns, he was always mine. If he does not, he never was mine to begin with. I know that I must accept my role in this age. It is not my will that I seek to do, but that of the Fates.

She then spoke aloud. "Hail to the Guardians of the East, South, West and North. I thank you for your protection and bless you forever. So mote it be."

There was a heavy knock on her door. She opened it to see Finan standing there. He had ridden alone all the way to her cottage from Leamanaugh Castle.

"Good morning, me dear," he said, kissing her on both cheeks.

"My Lord Finan," she said. "Please come in." She straightened her dress.

"No, 'tis alright. Thank ye. I just wanted to come by and tell ye that you are welcome at me home anytime, dear. I know that ye are out here all by yerself, and that may be the way yer mother and father liked it, but ye don't have to be that way."

"My Lord Finan, that is a generous and noble offer. But I must stay here, near the Cliffs. My coven needs me to guard these books, the dolmen and the stone circles," she said, pointing to the books on her shelves.

"Aye, but yer coven is only here a few times a year if I remember correctly. Ye can join them at the appointed times, but there is no reason ye need to be all exposed out here, to the cold, the rain, the snowy winter and God knows what else. Come pitch a cottage right next to me castle. I know Philomena adores ye, and Morgan would love yer company. I can appoint a hundred knights to guard yer precious books."

"I would love to, Lord Finan, but I cannot. Thank you for coming here, though. May I offer you some tea?"

"No, thank ye," he said. "But I also wanted to tell ye that I was the one who sent Sebastian away. I reminded him of his duties, to Rome and whatnot. It isn't that I wanted him to leave, Lord knows, I would have loved nothin' more than for him to stay in my lands. But we each have our duties."

"I know, Lord Finan. But I will see him again, I am sure of that."

"Aye, I reckon you are right, as always, dear. Well, do not forget about my offer. Ye can always come closer to Leamanaugh."

"Thank you, Lord Finan," she said, as she closed the door.

The loneliness hurt now more than ever.

EMPEROR

"Institoris must be punished!" Helena Scheuberin squealed, as she and her husband sat in their parlor in the burgher's lavish mansion in Innsbruck.

"We cannot afford another row with the Archduke," he declared confidently. "When Speiss died in your bed, it maligned our good name. I have not been able to sell a decent bundle of silk in ages. I imported hundreds of tapestries from Burgundy. And they sit rotting in a barn all winter! I cannot keep the moths out of them! No one wants to do business with us, after the Archduke informed everyone that you killed his Knight. Business was just started to resume, I had hoped."

"I do not care. Do you know the laughingstock we have become?" she asked, putting down her tea.

"Georg put a quick end to it for us, thankfully. But we can't just go around demanding priest's heads on platters. It is bad for business," he said.

"All you ever care about is your profit. How does it feel that your wife was called a witch and a harlot and humiliated in front of the whole city? A better man would have killed that bastard on the spot," said Helena.

"We cannot lower ourselves to his level," he insisted.

"Maybe you cannot, but I can. I do not care if you sold another gulden worth of those damned curtains again."

"I will ask Georg to write a letter complaining about him to the Archduke. Is that acceptable?" he offered.

"Make sure the Archduke knows that Institoris slandered him. And tell the Emperor how he slandered him—and his father, too! And I want the Pope himself to know of that man's depravity. Did you forget that he asked about my virginity in public?" she asked. "Did you forget what he accused me of doing with those two drunkards? I still cannot believe what he did."

"Of course, I did not forget, but the Pope? The Emperor? Do we truly want our names associated with this man in Rome as well as Vienna?"

"The Pope must discover that this Inquisitor is evil. His work must not continue."

"Yes, dear. I will ask Georg to write to all of them," he said sheepishly, still worried about his inventory.

"People confess nonsense when tortured," said Archduke Sigismund, biting into a pear while seated on a terrace outside his small castle. Spring had come early, and the weather permitted the importation of lovely fruit from far away. "I have seen it. A man with his testicles in a vise confesses to drowning his own daughters. Meaningless contrition. If you want to hear truth, offer a man a warm bed, a woman, beer and a hot meal. He will sing like a robin."

The Archduke had established a permanent residence here in Innsbruck since the early years of the century, making it more important politically, as it had served as the capital of the Tyrol region since 1429. The Emperor occasionally visited as well.

"You are absolutely correct, Your Excellency," said Ulrich Molitor, the legal scholar the Archduke had hired to address doubts that he had about Heinrich Institoris's teachings.

"The Witches' sabbats and rituals are illusions," the Archduke continued. "Heinrich has gone mad."

"Well, the Pope gave him the Bull, and ever since, he has been traveling through Tyrol, causing grief. Just last week, you received a letter from Georg," said Ulrich.

"Golser?" asked the Archduke.

"He wrote you a passionate letter describing how Heinrich came through here and conducted a frivolous trial against Helena Scheuberin."

"The woman who killed Speiss in bed?" asked the Archduke.

"Well, they never proved that." Ulrich smiled.

"I despise that woman. Do you know what she did?"

"I've heard the rumors," said Ulrich.

"Speiss was a great knight for me," said the Archduke. "As you know, I was in a dispute with Cardinal Nicholas of Cusa about the valleys. Speiss helped me by poisoning him before I needed to surrender. Speiss was loyal to the core," he said, patting his heart.

"He was a great knight," acknowledged Ulrich.

"Then, Speiss was afflicted with a strange illness," continued the Archduke. "It wasn't the plague. He developed sores and a rash, and eventually brain fever. I sent the best doctors from Genoa and Venezia to look at the cause of his maladies. After examining and questioning, they concluded that Helena had cast a spell on him. They told him to stop seeing her. He refused and he was then found dead in her marital bed. Her husband was not pleased."

"I would think not," chuckled Ulrich.

"Then," the Duke continued, one of my maids, Ingfried, told my wife a story of how Scheuberin cursed her too. Gave her the pox with rye or something..."

Ulrich changed the subject.

"I don't think Helena is really the point, Your Excellency. She may or may not be a witch. But she was not the only target of Institoris. He has apparently traveled throughout Tyrol and Innsbruck. They say he has taken two hundred souls in a fortnight."

"Two hundred, you say?"

"That is just what he admits to. The truth may be many, many more. Your Excellency, if I may bring in a man named Sturtzel. He is assisting me in this work."

"You may." He nodded. A distinguished-looking man walked in the room.

"Your Excellency, I am Conrad Sturtzel," he said, bowing.

"Explain this whole 'witchcraft' business to me," asked the Archduke, leaning back in his ornate chair. "I want to learn more about this subject. I have heard many rumors."

Ulrich began. "Your Excellency, as in all things, we start with Scripture. In Exodus, which Institoris cites frequently, it declares 'Thou shalt not suffer a witch to live.' He believes that this command gives him complete authority to root out all witches and destroy them, body and soul."

"Yes, I understand," said the Archduke. "So where is the ambiguity?"

"Our Scriptures are written in Latin. We received them from Jerome, who translated them from Hebrew and Aramaic," said Ulrich.

Sturtzel continued where Ulrich left off, leaning forward. "I consulted with the great Rabbi Yehuda, and he explained that the original Hebrew word for witch was misunderstood by Jerome. The word *mekhashepha* means root-cutter or poisoner. So, Exodus commands 'do not allow *poisoners* to live.' That is very different from a witch."

"Certainly, there is other authority. What about the teachings of the Church Fathers?" asked the Archduke.

Ulrich picked up again. "Their doctrines are all muddled. There is confusion about whether witches are truly raising tempests and storms. Some believe that it is all illusion from the Devil, and witches are merely fooled. Others believe it is *all* nonsense. I tend to agree with the latter."

"Indeed," said the Archduke. "I have oft wondered. Perhaps so-called witches are victims themselves, not heretics, or perhaps there are no witches at all. Maybe the real Devil is in the Inquisitor," he joked.

"Well, we do not know, Your Excellency," said Ulrich in a serious tone. "But one thing is certain—Institoris has killed many women and deemed them all witches after interrogation that amounts to nothing more than torture."

"Tell me more about that," asked the Archduke, leaning forward in his chair. "I have heard terrible things as of late." He picked up another pear off the table next to him.

"I have retrieved the written records of his so-called trials," said

Sturtzel. "I am a lawyer, and I can say that the questions that he poses are totally unrelated to the charges he brings and are scurrilous accusations."

"Describe for me an example," asked the Archduke, spitting out a seed.

"Certainly, Your Excellency." Sturtzel flipped open a small book. "In Ravensburg, he accused a young maiden of consorting with a horse. When she abjectly denied the bestiality, he used a hot poker to invade her eye sockets, blinding her. After this torture, she admitted the crime, and then he slowly roasted her to death."

The Archduke put down the fruit and made a face of disgust.

"No man of repute would consider such a 'trial' provable of anything," continued Sturzel. "For the fear of punishments incites men to say what is contrary to the nature of the facts."

"That was my point earlier!" exclaimed the Archduke. "These are not 'trials,' they are travesties. Why on earth is he doing such things?"

Sturtzel and Ulrich looked at one another. "We do not know, Your Excellency, but there are whispers that his bloodlust has no end. He is quite creative in that regard, actually. The methods of his torture and execution are not typical. He has been known to…cook them. Not just hang them or burn them at the stake once they are dead."

"Lord Jesus, I must consult with the Emperor," said the Archduke, who was no longer hungry. "Thank you, you are dismissed." The two men bowed and left his residence.

"He insulted my father?" asked the enraged Holy Roman Emperor Maximilian in Innsbruck, who was visiting Archduke Sigismund. The Emperor was reportedly considering moving here permanently, and if he did so, Innsbruck would likely become an even greater center of European politics and culture. A regular postal service between Innsbruck and Mechelen was already being established, making communications substantially easier.

"Yes, and I received this letter from Golser," said the Archduke, waving it. "He told me that Institoris has not only set fire to women and children but took delight in torturing them for no apparent reason. He would say that he was culling witches from our midst."

The two nobles sat on an outdoor terrace in Innsbruck, overlooking the nearby alps, which were covered in snow at their peaks.

"I received a similar letter from Golser. Witches, hah! That's what they all say when they want to kill who they don't like. Witches," said the Emperor sarcastically.

"I was told that the Bible says nothing about killing witches," said Sigismund.

"Is that so?" said the Archduke. "Well, I don't much abide by any of this nonsense. I just need the nobles to keep mining in Tyrol. I had to rent out my Swabian lands on the Rhine to pay debts. I also had a good idea. I issued a decree that instituted a new silver coin called the *gudengroschen*. Since I own the mines, I can just produce more coins."

"That is why we call you *der Munzreiche*," laughed the Emperor.

"'Rich in coins?' Who calls me that?"

The Emperor smiled. "Never mind. If you still need assistance in paying off your debts, take wares off the Venetian merchants from Bolzano. They have beautiful tapestries. Easily resold."

"Hmm, interesting..." said the Archduke, contemplating the implications of outright theft. "Imprison them and take their goods?"

"Certainly," said the Emperor. "They will bring them right to your doorstep."

"So, what are we to do with this Heinrich?" asked the Archduke.

"I will speak to the Pope," said the Emperor. "No one in Tyrol may insult me or my father."

Sigismund nodded in agreement.

RETURNING

"Palm trees," said a sea captain at the Ballygeary docks, pointing at the coastline. Sebastian had traveled overland with Epona from Cashel to Rosslare, a sea town on the southern shore. The spring had been early, and ferries started regularly transporting goods and occasional travelers from here up to Dublin, across to Holyhead, Pembroke or down across the Channel to Cherbourg for an additional fee. Rosslare was on the southeast coast and had a slightly milder climate more akin to Paris than Dublin, hence palm trees occasionally took root.

"Your horse stays. No room for her on a ferry," the captain declared.

Sebastian had ridden Epona the breadth and length of Hibernia but realized that his time with her was coming to an end.

"This is a Spanish mare," Sebastian said to the captain. "If you take her, I expect not only accommodation to Cherbourg, but substantial payment in kind."

"Aw, you'll be lucky to be rid of her. Not easy to use mares in these parts," the captain lied, eyeing the horse's muscular body. "Plus, I will let you use my captain's quarters."

As Sebastian patted her neck, he knew that even if he found a way to ship Epona to Cherbourg, he would have to sell her once he arrived back in Rome. The horse had become like a friend, even a family member, to Sebastian. He had bonded with the horse in a way that he did not expect, and he wanted to continue having that bond for as long as possible.

The ferry ride to Cherbourg took a week, which was relatively quick for this time of year. It was unseasonably warm, so there were no icebergs or floes to slow them down. However, the waves were choppy. He spent some time in the forecastle, so he could view the seas.

After Sebastian arrived in Cherbourg, he found transportation overland with a caravan led by a chieftain loyal to the Inquisition. The chieftain went out of his way to ensure that Sebastian had a comfortable wagon cart full of soft linens to sit on, so Sebastian could spend a significant amount of time sitting back and comfortably reading the source materials he had collected and prepared for Institoris's and Sprenger's careful review. Bumpy, muddy roads made it impossible for him to write, however. After a while, he fell asleep.

As he awoke suddenly, he smelled the pungent scent of cloves. A man was laying on top of him. Sebastian's books had fallen to the side of the wagon. It appeared that the man had tried to steal the books, inhaled the cloves and fainted. Sebastian realized that the unconscious man was the chieftain loyal to Institoris, who had been leading his caravan. The sachet filled with cloves that Brigantia had given to him were in his satchel, and somehow had fallen out.

Sebastian snatched his belongings and books and heaved himself off the back of the wagon onto the hard ground. He darted into the forest, lugging his heavy satchel, and hid behind a large oak tree until the rest of the caravan had long since passed. He was now alone in the forest with his books, belongings and satchel, but with no horse and no way to get back to Rome.

MONKEYS

"Monkeys?"

"Dogs, and goats, too, I do not jest," said Leofwin to Gilbert in a serious tone, wiping the foam from his beer off his mustache.

The two chief magistrates in Ravensburg were seated at a heavily scarred wooden table in a tavern. They had finished judging all their trials for the week, and their regular practice was to retire on Friday nights to snicker at the week's most memorable experiences over many, many beers.

"He told you that?" asked Gilbert, putting down his stein and gesturing to the servant girl for another refill.

"I swear it. Institoris told me flat out," Leofwine continued, "he was in his bedroom. He was sleeping and he woke up in the middle of the night, to pray."

"Praying in the middle of the night." Gilbert laughed and gulped his beer.

"Always praying, that one," laughed Leofwin. "Anyway, he says he hears noises right up from outside his window. He found that curious, he said, because his room was so high up that someone could have only reached his window with a very long ladder."

"Right," nodded Gilbert.

"He then says that he hears shouts and insults lobbed at him," said Leofwin, gulping his beer again.

"From right outside his window?" asked Gilbert incredulously.

"That is what he said. Then he swears he saw…monkeys."

"Monkeys can't fly," said Gilbert, in a serious tone, then belched. "They can only climb."

"Well, I know monkeys cannot fly," guffawed Leofwin drunkenly. "Not just monkeys, though. He said he saw female dogs, bitches he called them, and she-goats. All flying around outside his window." He put his stein down on the table emphatically.

"Were the monkeys female too?"

"Probably," laughed Leofwin.

"She-goats can't fly either. They can climb high, though," joked Gilbert.

Leofwin laughed heartily "Then Institoris says these monkeys were sticking pins in their linen headdresses, as if their intention was to insert their pins into his own head by using magic." He pointed to his temple.

"The monkeys were wearing hats?"

"I suppose so," replied Leofwin, looking down into his beer, still laughing. "Well, that's what he told me," insisted the magistrate. "He must have had quite a headache, on account of the flying female monkeys sticking those damned pins in his head."

"That one's plain mad," said Gilbert.

Leofwin nodded, staring down forlornly into his now empty beer stein.

PERESTRELLA

Sebastian trudged his way north to the closest port on the shore-line, which was Rouen. He approached several captains about a seabound trip to Rome. He walked down the pier when he saw a ship that seemed to bear a familiar name on its hull: the *Perestrella*. The captain was standing on deck. He immediately recognized the captain's similarity to his closest friend Amancio, who he missed terribly since he left Rome. The captain shared the same smiling countenance as his friend.

"Valentino?" Sebastian asked.

"Yes? Do I know you?" asked the captain.

"No," Sebastian replied. "But I studied with your brother Amancio in Rome."

"Ah! You are far from Rome. What is your name?"

"Sebastian Alberti. I have been traveling for a long year, and must return. But my caravan's chieftain tried to rob me. If I travel to Rome overland, it will take me ages."

"Well, come aboard! I am not going as far south as Rome, but after we round through Gibraltar, we will sail up to Riomaggiore. Is that close enough?"

"Yes, thank you!" said Sebastian. "May I pay you for your troubles?" Sebastian took out a handful of gold coins and offered them to Valentino.

"Not at all," said the captain. "If you must tolerate Amancio, that is payment enough!"

They laughed, and Sebastian boarded the ship. It was a large, sturdy galleon, three times the size of the other boats that he had traveled on. It had three decks with gunports and four masts.

Valentino gave him a tour. He explained that new methods of advanced navigation allowed the sailors to find their way quickly and safely. Cross-staves and astrolabes could be used to measure the altitude of the sun or stars. Consequently, the *Perestrella* could travel twice as fast and three times as efficiently as her competitors. The ship also had awesome firepower, as it carried both a long-deck bronze cannon as well as short-range guns in iron, so piracy was no real risk.

Sebastian was offered the finest wine, cheese, bread and meats to eat, and was offered the captain's own quarters, which had a sturdy desk. The space would give him ample time to review and finish his manuscript. After a hearty dinner in the galley, he retired to the captain's quarters. He read over all the text he had written in his journal in Hibernia, as well as on the trip to Cherbourg.

> As you charged me in Rome, I have investigated, researched, and uncovered the truth about witchcraft and sorcery. Many fine people, including Lord Finan O'Brien in County Clare, greatly assisted in my tasks and showed me great generosity. The Abbots of Mont-St-Michel and Cashel showed me great hospitality. They should all be commended.

> I have included a list of each of the cities, towns, villages, and hamlets that I visited, along with the names and locations of each of the helpful who assisted me along the way, such as Cecile of Limousin and the witches that assisted the beautiful pagan witch Brigantia: Aife, Caomhe, Saiorse, Ciara, Niamh, Roisin, Cara, Clodah, Aisling, Eeabha, Orla and Shana.

> In the event you good fathers desire to gather more information from the personages named above, they

visit the witch Brigantia at the stone circle near the Poulnabrone Dolmen in Finan's lands in County Clare twice per year including on the first day of February, when they welcome the spring season.

Point I: Witchcraft is Not Evil and Not a Threat.

Good Fathers, what is commonly called "witchcraft" is *not* heresy nor apostasy and is not a threat to the Church.

So-called witches believe in God and profess faith in Him. They view nature as a manifestation of divinity, not as a fallen creation. They recognize the female divine principle, as well as the male, in God. God is both genders and yet neither alone, as He contains all things within Him. This belief does not conflict with the Nicene Creed that we profess as Catholics.

They may call God by different names and use languages and images unfamiliar to us, but they do not reject the fundamental tenets of our faith. They dutifully honor the four seasons, the earth, the stars, and all of God's creatures in a manner that is wholly beautiful and perfect.

They respect the dignity of humanity and the expression of divinity in all things. They perceive sanctuaries in shrines such as natural springs, rivers, lakes, and woodland. They worship in the forests without using temples. Wellsprings of water are sacred to them and are associated with physical as well as spiritual healing.

These women are often midwives, and in in that role, they assist one other, often without expectation of financial reward. They assist one another with childbirth, with healing animals and rendering sage advice and wisdom.

They call theirs the Old Ways, and in matter of fact and truth, these are indeed much older than many of our own.

Further, it was remarkable to me that their calendar followed that of our own, and my first inclination was to assume that they had indeed modeled their calendar on the calendar established by Pope Gregory. Yet I was astonished to learn the opposite is true: our own Gregorian calendar was indeed derived from *theirs*.

For example, I learned that their most important festival of the year was on the first day of November, otherwise known as Samhain. During such time, they honored their dead at a gathering place. Indeed, our very own calendar honors all saints on this day, now known to us as All Saints' Day. Similarly, their annual festivals include Yule on the twenty-first day of December, which corresponds closely to our celebration of Christmas.

I must add that those who loyally follow the Old Ways are driven by a good and pure desire to use herbs, potions, and elixirs to heal rather than harm. Their methods differ slightly from the apothecaries we are accustomed to, but their goals (and many of their ingredients) are in common with our own. Again, our own Church would do well to learn from and study their practices.

In the land of western County Clare, I met the witch named Brigantia and her coven. This coven consists of thirteen women whose names and locations I have provided above.

This coven met on the first day of February on a feast day they call Imbolc. On that day, they surrounded a stone circle. At that site, these women showed great respect for nature and for God in a beautiful ritual. These women welcomed the season of Spring. No harm was done, and none was witnessed. In fact, the Old Ways teach that "harm none" is the whole of the law.

Point II. Sorcery is the True Evil Arising from Within the Church.

I must report with all urgency and despair that there *is* indeed a dark threat to the Church afoot, but it is *not* these witches whom the Church seeks out to destroy utterly. Rather, there are wayward monks, priests and rogues who are studying how to make pacts with demons and devils. They operate within the sanctuaries of our own churches and are committing *sorcery*.

These men are abusing the Lord's Holy Name and performing black magic; rituals that are perversions of the Mass to accomplish dreadful things.

First, at the Red Mountain near Paris, I personally witnessed evidence of a human sacrifice. The symbol on the stone altar corresponded directly with the later evidence of demonic activity discussed herein.

Second, at the formerly sacred site of Clonmacnoise Abbey, on the dark night of Walpurgisnacht on the first day of May, I was distressed to witness an atrocity committed by those who follow the Devil himself. Hooded men butchered an innocent girl, perverting the Holy Mass into something I call a "Black Mass." During this horrific rite, a murder was committed. These men apparently believed that they were conjuring a dreadful spirit named Astaroth by killing an innocent woman as some form of dark sacrifice. The sigil on the altar corresponded with that at the Red Mountain.

Finally, I have located and secured several books that corroborate my conclusions.

The first book is called *The Grand Grimoire*. It was in the crypt at Mont-St-Michel. I also secured the *Ars Notoria*, which had been copied by John of Morigny, although it was found buried at Canterbury. I also secured *The Grimoire of Pope Honorius III*, which was found at Clonmacnoise Abbey near *The Goetia*.

These are all blasphemous grimoires and other documents that prove my observations and had traveled as far afield as these places.

Each of the books was dedicated to propitiating a demon. Glasya Labolas caused murders and fires, as did Andrealphus. And Astaroth desires the sacrifice of innocent women's blood.

Their sigils are seals that bear their names which can be read clockwise.

These original texts are included herewith for your own review and they must be kept secure deep in the Vatican library's archives or destroyed.

In these tomes, it states plainly that the authors are sorcerers within our own Church who are conjuring demons. They are doing so for personal gain, including wealth, power and influence. But their practices only lead to death and destruction.

By my account, the witches who are being slaughtered are innocent *victims* and are intended to be sacrificial offerings by this dreaded group inside the Church to satisfy their demons' bloodlust.

There must be no delay! The Inquisition must immediately inquire further into these matters. You must release all the accused witches, and immediately investigate the dark sorcerers in our midst who are performing the Black Mass.

Yours in God's Truth,
Sebastian Alberti
1486 Anno Domini

Sebastian proudly closed his manuscript. Here in just a few pages was the culmination of all his experiences and research over the last year, which would hopefully be to their great satisfaction. He had unwittingly uncovered a massive, shadowy conspiracy within his own Church—one that had been carried on for centuries. Sebastian was particularly hopeful that his work would be reviewed by the Pope himself and deemed worthy of great public praise.

He closed his eyes and dreamed of the prestigious ecclesiastical post that he would receive. Perhaps he could become the pastor of St.

John Lateran, or maybe he could even become a Cardinal at a young age and wear the red cassock. Amancio would need to kiss his ring. He smiled at the thought. But just as he dozed off, his mind wandered back to Brigantia.

STREGA

The smell of rotten fish and salty sea met Sebastian with each inhale once the Perestrella arrived in Riomaggiore. It was late spring now, and warm.

He thanked Valentino and walked into town. La Spezia was one of the four fishing villages on the northwest coast near the larger fishing town. He could barely remember his time spent in the small hamlet as a youth, but he was determined to know what became of his mother.

Surprisingly, Sebastian could still remember the sandy road leading to the poorest parts of the village. Children ran past him screaming in glee, chasing large woven kites. They were poorly dressed in just pieces of dirty cloth, but they seemed to have joy and innocence in their eyes. Sebastian wondered if he had been like that. He noticed the stares his presence seemed to attract and decided to look for an inn. The sun was high in the sky and noonday was upon him. La Spezia was a very small town; he was sure news had already spread of his arrival. Eyes followed him as he found himself treading vaguely familiar paths.

He spotted a familiar house. It was even tinier than he remembered. He was thrust back to the past and he could smell the smoke that came from his mother's attempts at lighting a fire; the moss soaked in fish oil that she burnt to keep them warm through the night; the cloves, chamomile, and jasmine she planted to keep the gigantic mosquitos away from them as she sang him old songs to help him sleep.

Sebastian had initially considered that briefly stopping in the Cinque Terre region as a respite on his way back to Rome after a frigid winter in Hibernia would be refreshing. When he had arrived, though, he discovered that he was drawn to investigate as much about his own childhood as he could, despite the emotional pain it engendered. After arriving in town, he had asked several townspeople about any surviving family of his, and they all pointed him toward Diana, a midwife who lived in the small villa by the sea where he lived until he was six. He did not remember Diana, but he was assured that she would possess information about his family.

Sebastian did not realize his feet had been carrying him to the door until he stood right in front of it. He raised his fist to knock but dropped it almost immediately. He shouldn't be there. He didn't even know if this Diana still resided here. But he was here.

He politely knocked on the door, and a woman opened it and greeted him. He did not recognize her.

"Yes, may I help you?" she asked, eyeing him up and down.

"My name is Sebastian Alberti. I grew up in this home, or at least I think I did…"

"Sebastian," the squat, matronly woman said. "I have been waiting for you for years." She hugged him. "Please come inside and sit down," she said excitedly.

Sebastian entered the tiny villa. The rear was carved into a steep cliff perched over the crystal-clear waters of the Mediterranean. A fresh ocean breeze wafted through the airy house, which had wide, open windows permitting sunlight to stream in. The woman sat down at a tiny table where she had been cutting vegetables and putting the pieces into a ceramic bowl.

"I am Diana, Sebastian. Do you remember this place?" she asked him.

"I do now that I am inside. My mother sat at that very table, I recall that," he said, his nostalgia growing.

"And do you remember your mother's face?" Diana asked him.

"Only glimpses," Sebastian replied, as he walked over to the eastern window and stared out at the small fishing boats bobbing on the waves of the foamy sea. "I remember this view."

"I raised her," she said with a smile. "Come. Eat an artichoke. I soak them in garlic and herbs for flavor."

He took an artichoke from her, listening while pulling the soft leaves and sucking them dry. After many months of wintry travel, the fresh Mediterranean delicacy was invigorating.

"I was her midwife; you see, but I was also her great-aunt. Your mother was born in Volterra, inland. Her parents were strict. They wanted her to become a Benedictine nun. When she was nine, she defied them and refused. Her stepfather beat her. My niece sent me a message, asking me to take your mother in. I was more than pleased to raise her. I never had any children, and I considered her my daughter."

"Where did you live then?"

"Lake Nemi," she said.

"South of Rome?"

"Yes, I always loved living near water. Nemi was small, but it was so placid, I could look into it and see my reflection like a perfect mirror. I raised your mother there. We came here much later when we were forced to leave. The Church was not pleased with our . . . practices. I did not see eye to eye with the Church, or your grandparents, Sebastiano. You see, I did not raise your mother as they demanded."

He finished eating the dense artichoke heart and put the shell and leaves down.

Diana continued. "She was a *strega*, like me."

"A witch?!" Sebastian could not believe what he was hearing. He felt lightheaded. He had to sit down. He had barely made it to a chair when his knees gave out under him.

Diana smiled. "Stregheria is older than Christianity, Sebastian, and I despise the word 'witch'. It is a false word that your Churchmen created. We practice the Old Ways. Your grandparents never knew, though."

"A . . . witch? I am the son of a witch," he stammered, nauseous.

"Be proud of your family line, Sebastiano. In Stregheria, blood is directly inherited from the mother. Your fate is in your blood."

He felt even more nauseous. "But . . . how could my mother have been a witch?" he shrieked. "It is impossible! I was baptized, that I know for a fact. You are lying. . ."

"We do not reject God. In the Old Ways, we just see the world differently. We believe God is in each of us, and we honor nature and the seasons—"

"I have just spent the better part of a year coming to understand precisely. But I never could have believed that my own mother . . ." Sebastian's face was ashen.

"Your mother was a wonderful woman. She performed healing and was able to provide blessings to the villagers, and they loved her in return."

"Then why did she abandon me?" he asked, his voice cracking.

"Your mother never abandoned you. We heard rumors that the Inquisition was returning and diseased corpses in Riomaggiore were tossed in the back of wagons, hauled off to be burned. She was no stranger to the Inquisition or the Black Death. None of us were. But all these stories petrified us. Riomaggiore is walking distance from here, and she knew it was only a matter of time before it all reached us."

"The Black Death passed through here?" he asked.

"Yes, not only once. It took the lives of our family. They have no graves to visit. Their resting place is a spot in a field where ashes and bones were discarded along with hundreds of others."

He paused to think before saying, "I remember as a child, on the last day of October, my mother and I would make a pilgrimage to a meadow and throw flowers on the ground. She would often cry, but I had no idea why."

"Samhain. She was casting offerings where your grandparent's scorched bones lay." Diana became mournfully silent.

"I had no idea," he said.

"That is All Saints when the Church honors the dead. It is the same, Sebastiano. The Church renamed it."

She got up and walked over to the hearth, putting the vegetables into a pot of boiling water. "I taught your mother how the Black Death could be warded off. She knew these ways well since she had made a living off them. But this time, amulets and talismans were not going to work. No, the only way to cheat the Black Death was to run."

Initially, he had been reluctant to open the wounds of the past. But now, he wanted to know everything. A puzzle was falling into place as perfect pieces he had never seen or heard were handed to him.

After silently thinking a while, Sebastian asked, "What of my father?"

"In town, your mother met an older man, a lawyer. She told me that she had been struck by the thunderbolt of love upon seeing him as he stood at the edge of her town painting on a canvas. His name was Leone Battista Alberti."

"Was my father a lawyer or a painter?"

"Your father was a lawyer *and* a painter. He was also a poet, a philosopher, a musician and architect. He was older, so he charmed your mother. He told her that he amused himself by taming wild horses and climbing mountains. Despite her wisdom, she believed everything he said. She trusted all your father's promises, too. She expected that he would marry her and take her to Rome. She was just a poor girl, but she believed she could make Leone a dutiful wife."

"She did not?" he asked.

"Leone had lost much of his hearing, and she believed she could attend to his every need. She wanted to accompany him to all the Roman functions—or whatever events rich and important people were invited to there. But I think that he was always worried that people would ask about her background, so he never married her or even took her there.

"After you were born, your father let it slip to someone powerful and important that your mother was a strega. When you were four, she was accused of heresy for being a strega. The Inquisition was stirring up hatred all the way from Rome."

Sebastian could not believe his ears.

"The Inquisition came to town and stood us all in the square. They said that anyone caught practicing witchcraft would be set on fire. Now, I was a wise woman even then, so I was careful about what I said and did in public, but your mother was young and proud. She spoke back.

They shattered her knees as a warning to the rest of us. Then, they put hot irons through her feet so she could never walk again."

Sebastian swallowed hard as he envisioned his mother being tortured by the Inquisition.

"Of course, her suffering only made our beliefs stronger, but your mother was punished terribly at the hands of the Inquisition. She never walked again, but her faith made her only more powerful. Her teachings are legendary among us. We call it 'The Gospel of Aradia.' Is that not beautiful?"

Sebastian was silent for a long time. The enormity of the story sank in slowly. He reached deep into his memories. "I remember my mother not being able to walk, but I never knew why. She told me that she hurt herself."

"After she sent you to safety in Bretagne, your mother was heartbroken. The Inquisition visited this entire region, and it claimed many lives, including hers. When she died, her only prayer was that God would watch over you and keep you safe from harm."

"Were my parents unhappy that I was born?" Sebastian couldn't believe that such a monumental, life-changing question could be so simply put.

"Oh, Sebastian, they were both so happy when she gave birth to you! But she was left to raise you alone while your father traveled the world. Your father himself had been born in Genoa as the bastard son of a family of merchants. We expected him to be a better father. Your mother hoped that he would visit you more than twice a year, but he always said that his writing, music and travelling made that impossible. After she was crippled by the Inquisition, she never heard from him again."

"What happened to him?" he asked.

"I received word that he died about ten years ago."

He sat, absorbing a lifetime's worth of information.

"Sebastiano, your mother knew that even your father, with all his brilliance, could not stop the Black Death or the Inquisition. No, Aradia knew that the only way was for you to be sent away."

Diana put her hand under Sebastian's chin and looked him in the eye.

"Your mother was a great woman. You should be proud to be her son."

Sebastian weighed her every word, a lifetime of tears welling up in his eyes.

Diana stood up and went to a drawer where she pulled out a small scroll, wrapped in linen.

"Before he died, your father left you something," she said.

"What is it?" he asked, sniffling.

"You tell me," she said.

He broke open the wax seal, which was dry with age. He unfurled it. On it was written simply:

To my son. When you discover that all the forces of heaven are within each of us, then truly you will be living among the gods. Someday, you will understand who you truly are. Be proud of it, my son.

Sebastian stared at the words. "I think I understand now, Diana. I must return to Rome and complete what I began."

He hugged her so tightly, he worried that he was hurting her.

HAMMER

When Sebastian arrived in Rome, it was late summer again. When he had first returned, he had planned to deliver the heavy bundle of written materials, including the large tomes he had secreted, directly to Institoris. He dreaded seeing him again. Sebastian breathed a sigh of relief when he learned that the Inquisitor was traveling to Cologne and would not be back for a few weeks.

Instead, he learned that Dean Sprenger was visiting Rome. Sebastian approached the Dean when he was sitting and reading in a small room in the Vatican library, holding a book very close to his nose.

"Professor Sprenger?"

"Ah, yes?" said the man, looking up.

"I am Sebastian Alberti," he said.

"The very man I have been waiting for," he said, closing the book. "I trust your travels were safe and exciting, if not intellectually rewarding?"

"They were all of that, sir. I have brought you all the materials that I swore to collect and convey to the Inquisition." Sebastian plopped down a massive bundle of books and materials onto the table.

"My, that is quite a lot of reading. Did you carry those all the way here?"

"I did, sir, and you will find that the first book on top of this pile is my journal. I dutifully recorded all my observations along with quotations and summaries of selected materials. I trust this will be of value to you."

"Tremendous value, my son, thank you," he said flipping through the journal.

"As for the remaining books, they are extremely hazardous, and should be kept strictly secret," warned Sebastian.

"Yes, I believe so," said the Professor. "There are some things better left unknown by the vulgar mob, yes?"

"I agree. There are matters discussed in my journal that are of great urgency. I look forward to the final work that you and Father Institoris will accomplish with my research." Sebastian paused. "I do have one question, Father."

"Yes, my son?" The Dean listened intently.

"My mother...I had long believed she had abandoned me as a boy. But on my way back to Rome, I briefly tarried in the town where I was born. I was told that she was tortured and executed long ago....by the Inquisition."

"Oh my Lord," said the Dean. "That is terrible. Do you know any more information about her?"

"Just that her name was Aradia Alberti."

"I do not remember her," said the Dean. "I only joined the Inquisition two years ago, I am afraid. But I assure you that I have learned that many dark and terrible things happened before my time. Despite what we are taught, the Church is a human institution, Sebastian. And men are fallible. I am truly sorry if those horrendous things happened to her," he said in a gentle voice.

"Thank you, Father," said Sebastian.

He had done his sacred duty. The infernal materials were now safe in the Inquisition's custody. He hoped that the contents of his manuscript would spur an immediate investigation into the poor woman's horrific death at Clonmacnoise and the grim conspiracy he had uncovered. The Dean's words were calming and soothing. He understood that the Dean could not speak for the Inquisition's acts a decade earlier. He did not want to see Institoris again, at least until he was ready to. On the other hand, he was eager to discuss the promised promotion with him. He had thought long and hard about what specific role he could play in the Church, especially given his new perspective.

Sebastian decided that he would spend time away from the Vatican for a bit, to clear his mind. The last year spent traveling on the Inquisition's behalf had over the winter aged him physically and spiritually, and he needed to spend time recuperating. Over the rest of the summer, he would wander the gardens, go fishing and read. Once Institoris returned, he would be ready to discuss it with him.

He still had twelve gulden that were hidden away in the bottom of his satchel from his travels. He planned on returning them to the Inquisition but spending a couple for his modest upkeep in Rome for several more months wouldn't be a problem, he figured. Since it was summertime, there were few classes in session, so he would have to wait at least a month to get settled in again at the seminary to resume classes a year behind. He also decided to spend the summer living in a small room in the nearby Trastevere neighborhood.

After wandering on the cobblestoned streets of the city for a bit, he sat on a stone bench in the lush gardens of the Vatican, enjoying the sunshine. It felt odd to be lifted of the burden of the books, figuratively and literally. He had developed back pain from carrying them around.

The smell of hyacinths, violets, saffron, cassia, and thyme wafted through the air. Sebastian's mind turned back to Brigantia. He wondered what she was doing at that very moment.

Every day in good weather, he returned to this same spot in this garden again. He had made it his daily routine. He spent a lot of time thinking about his mother, and La Spezia. It had loomed so much larger in his memories as a boy. When he finally saw his childhood home, it was so much smaller than he had remembered. Some phantoms are like that, he figured. We build them up to be so much larger than real life. When we finally confront them, they are so much smaller than you recalled.

Amancio had been excited to see him upon his return. He told him all about the funny events that had happened while Sebastian was traveling, like when the young men had played a prank on one of their professors by putting a beehive in his room. Amancio's ordination date was approaching, and he lamented that Sebastian would need to repeat the year and not become a priest simultaneously. Sebastian didn't want to burden his friend with the terrible things he had witnessed at Clonmacnoise, so when he described his travels, he mostly told him about Brigantia and the beautiful Cliffs of Moher.

One day, Amancio and Sebastian suddenly happened upon several of their elder classmates who had graduated and had been ordained priests. They huddled around Sebastian, asking questions about his wintry travels. It appears they had received a copy of a printed book which contained the results of his investigation and wanted to learn more. The book was titled *The Malleus Maleficarum—The Witches' Hammer.* They handed him a fresh copy.

Excited to finally see his work in print, Sebastian flipped the pages open to a random section.

The first heading he encountered puzzled him. It was entitled "WHY SUPERSTITION IS CHIEFLY FOUND IN WOMEN." He quickly scanned the text.

> It is adulterous drabs and whores who are chiefly given to witchcraft. But it has been frequently pondered, why are a greater number of witches found in the feminine sex than among men?
>
> It is because there was a defect in the formation of the first woman, since she was formed from a bent rib, that is, a rib of the breast, which is bent as it were in a contrary direction to a man. And since through this defect she is an imperfect animal, she always deceives.
>
> This is indicated by the etymology of the word; for *Femina* comes from *Fe* meaning faith and *Minus* meaning less so. This is apt since she is ever weaker to hold and preserve the faith. Therefore, a woman is by her

nature quicker to waver in her faith, and consequently
quicker to abjure the faith, which is the root of all witchcraft. It is no wonder that the world now suffers through
the malice of women.

What else is a woman but a foe to friendship, an ines-
capable punishment, a necessary evil, a natural temptation, a desirable calamity, a domestic danger, a delectable detriment, an evil of nature, painted with fair colors?
When a woman thinks alone, she is evil.

Sebastian nearly dropped the book. Where did the professors obtain
this bizarre misinformation? It was certainly nowhere to be found in his
research, or any of the source materials he had painstakingly risked his
life to collect and deliver to them. It also seemed irrelevant to the topic.
He kept skimming the book.

Women are intellectually like children and are naturally
more impressionable, and more ready to receive the influence of a disembodied spirit. Therefore, since they are
feebler both in mind and body, it is not surprising that
they should come more under the spell of witchcraft. A
woman is more carnal than a man, as is clear from their
many carnal abominations.

With each sentence, Sebastian's face flushed even more.

There is no head above the head of a serpent: and there
is no wrath above the wrath of a woman. I had rather
dwell with a lion and a dragon than to keep house with
a wicked woman. All wickedness is but little to the wickedness of a woman.

A woman either loves or hates; there is no third grade. And the tears of a woman are a deception, for they may spring from true grief, or they may be a snare.

"What in God's holy name is this nonsense?" he shouted aloud, not caring if his friends heard him.

Others again have propounded reasons why there are more superstitious women found than men. And the first is, that they are more credulous; and since the chief aim of the devil is to corrupt faith, therefore he rather attacks them.

The second reason is that women are naturally more impressionable, and more ready to receive the influence of a disembodied spirit; and that when they use this quality well, they are very good, but when they use it ill, they are very evil.

The third reason is that they have slippery tongues and are unable to conceal from the fellow-women those things which by evil arts they know; and, since they are weak, they find an easy and secret manner of vindicating themselves by witchcraft.

Sebastian could not believe what he was reading. The book expressed abject loathing toward women. He scoured for inclusion of *any* accurate details from his research relating to witchcraft. He could find none. He continued to read.

Many phantastical apparitions occur to persons suffering from a melancholy disease, especially to women, as is shown by their dreams and visions. And the reason for this, as physicians know, is that women's souls are by nature far more easily and lightly impressionable than men's souls.

He shook his head in denial. He turned further into the book, to a section entitled "THE METHODS BY WHICH THE WORKS OF WITCHCRAFT ARE WROUGHT AND DIRECTED," a topic that he felt intimately familiar with from his research. As he feared, the entire book appeared filled with lies and distortions.

No witches do good in the sight of God. All witches raise hailstorms and hurtful tempests and lightning; cause sterility in men and animals; offer to devils, or otherwise kill, the children whom they do not devour. But these are only the children who have not been reborn by baptism at the font, for they cannot devour those who have been baptized. Now the method of profession of allegiance to the Devil is a solemn ceremony, like a solemn vow, and must be made on certain Satanic unholy days, as it were. The most common of these are Walpurgisnacht, or May 1st, or All Hallow's Eve, October 31st, the evening before that holy day in which we honor all the Saints of God.

They stand in ancient stone circles, face the four quarters and worship demons and fallen angels. This evil ceremony is called the Black Mass. It routinely occurs when thirteen witches meet in their unholy conclave on the set day, usually an abandoned church, and a devil appears to them in the smoke of the brazier or in the form of a man, and urges them to keep faith with him, promising them worldly prosperity and length of life. They choose the number twelve to mock the number of apostles who followed Jesus.

They conjure demons, such as Lucifuge Rofocale or Astaroth, and shed innocent blood to placate them. Consequently, all witches must be put to death, as the Holy Book commands.

The Black Mass described was the sorcery and sacrifice at Clonmacnoise that he witnessed, not the beautiful ceremonies of Brigantia at the Cliffs, or the quaint traditions followed by his own mother and family. Even worse, *The Witches' Hammer* contained detailed instructions for conjuring demons and the specific sacrifices demanded by them that were lifted directly from one or more of the grimoires.

This is the evil conjuration that these witches use:

I, do conjure thee, Oh Spirit Astaroth, by the living God, by the true God, by the holy and all-ruling God, who created from nothingness the heaven, the earth, the sea, and all things that are therein, in virtue of the Most Holy Sacrament of the Eucharist, in the name of Jesus Christ, and by the power of this same Almighty Son of God, who for us and for our redemption was crucified, suffered death, and was buried; who rose again on the third day, and is now seated on the right hand of the Creator of the whole world, from whence he will come to judge the living and the dead; as also by the precious love of the Holy Spirit, perfect Trinity. I conjure thee within the circle, accursed one, by thy judgment, who didst dare to tempt God: I exorcise thee, Serpent, and I command thee to appear forthwith under a beautiful and well-favoured human form of soul and body, and to fulfill my behests without any deceit whatsoever, as also without mental reservation of any kind, by the great times of the God of gods and Lord of lords.

I conjure thee, Evil and Accursed Serpent, Astaroth, to appear at my will and pleasure, in this place, before this circle, without tarrying, without companions, without grievance, without noise, deformity, or murmuring. I exorcise thee by the ineffable names of God, to wit, Gog and Magog, which I am unworthy to pronounce; Come hither, Come hither, Come hither. Accomplish my will and desire, without wile or falsehood. Otherwise St. Michael, the invisible Archangel, shall presently blast thee in the utmost depths of hell. Come, then, Astaroth to do my will.

The book contained an encyclopedic collection of the sigils of the 72 demons listed in the *Goetia*.

Andrealphus is a great marquesse, appearing as a peacock, he raises great noises, and in humane shape perfectly teaches geometry. He maketh a man to be a subtle disputer, and cunning in astronomy, and transformeth a man into the likeness of a bird, and there are under him thirty legions.

Glasya Labolas is a Mighty President and Earl, and showeth himself in the form of a Dog with Wings like a Gryphon. He teaches all Arts and Sciences in an instant, and is an Author of Bloodshed and Manslaughter. He teaches all things Past, and to Come. If desired he causes the love both of Friends and of Foes. He can make a Man to go Invisible. And he hath under his command 36 Legions of Spirits.

Why on earth would the Inquisitors want to openly promulgate infernal abomination that had been buried and secured with locks and chains inside crypts and abbeys, thought Sebastian. Surely, this information must remain secret, and should be included in a book that could be read by hundreds of thousands of the faithful. Professor Sprenger had openly agreed to that, Sebastian recalled. He continued to read and learned that the book contained detailed descriptions of spells, herbs, and other baneful magic that he had collected, mixed with falsehoods:

> Rotten sage thrown into running water will arouse most fearful tempests and storms…herbs such as blackthorn, rosemary, thistle, thyme shall prevent conception…valerian root helps one sleep…wormwood, yarrow and mugwort will give your enemies nightmares… vervain, wormwood and dittany of Crete will force a lover to your bidding…cloves will make an evil man faint… nightshade and clubmoss shall cause the death of a newborn child.

> Indeed, all midwives are witches. As soon as the child is born, the midwife, if the mother herself is not a witch, carries it out of the room on the pretext of warming it, raises it up, and offers it to the Prince of Devils, that is Lucifer, and to all the devils. And this is done by the kitchen fire.

He turned back to the first page. In addition to being inscribed with Professor Heinrich Institoris and Professor James Sprenger's signatures, it was signed by several additional faculty members of the University of Cologne and contained the approval of the Pope himself.

But how could this be? This book was precisely the *opposite* of what he had communicated in his journal. He had detailed how there was an enormous difference between benign witchcraft, which had been practiced by his own family and Brigantia, and sorcery, which was the work of devil worshippers and murderers within the Church itself. He continued to read the official approbation from the Pope, astonished.

In the name of our Lord Jesus Christ, Amen. Know all men by these presents, whosoever shall read, see or hear the tenor of this official and public document, that in the year of our Lord, 1487, upon a Saturday, being the nineteenth day of the month of May, at the fifth hour after noon, or thereabouts, in the third year of the Pontificate of our most Holy Father and Lord, the Pope Innocent, by divine providence Pope, the eighth of that name, in the very and actual presence of me, Arnold Kolich, public notary, and in the presence of the witnesses whose names are hereunder written and who were convened and especially summoned for this purpose.

Given at Rome, at St. Peter's, on the 9 December of the Year of the Incarnation of Our Lord one thousand, four hundred and eighty-four, in the first Year of Our Pontificate.

It seemed impossible that the Pope could have approved this book. Furthermore, it had not been completed by 1484 and the notarial signature from 1487 made no sense. Sebastian *knew* that this book could not have been completed by 1484, as he had not yet set out to conduct his field research. And who was Arnold Kolich?

Not a month earlier, Professor Sprenger had agreed that this material was dangerous and should be secured from public knowledge. Why would he have included it?

Sebastian closed the book and exhaled deeply. He knew that he must find out the truth. He thought about approaching Dean Sprenger again, but that seemed treacherous. Perhaps the man had misled him?

Instead, he raced off to show it to Fra Giovanni. He would know the answers.

PENANCE

Sebastian ran at top speed to Fra Giovanni's residence. The room was empty, and the monk was nowhere to be found. Sebastian hurriedly asked two nearby friars and was quickly informed of terrible news.

While Sebastian had been traveling, Fra Giovanni had caught ill and passed away peacefully in his sleep. He left behind no mortal possessions, save a sealed note for Sebastian. Sebastian now regretted that he had not visited the monk when he first returned. Sebastian was handed the note.

My Dear Sebastian.

In the event you are reading this letter, I have gone to meet my Heavenly Father before your safe return. In that case, do not weep for me, as I have found my everlasting salvation in the bosom of Abraham.

But what you must know, and what I could not tell you then, is that the Inquisitor has been using you as a tool to commit more murders. He has declared war on innocent witches because he is a sorcerer. These victims are his sacrifices. Heinrich Institoris is not what he seems. He is not a zealous man of God.

His book serves to disseminate his practices to his followers who are spread throughout the world. I suspected that was true before you left, but I was afraid to warn you and face his wrath. And I take that regret to my grave.

There is only man who has the power to stop this madness: Pope Innocent. It has come to my attention that the Pope's approval of *The Witches' Hammer* was a fraud. In fact, all the signatures of the faculty of the University in *The Witches' Hammer* are forged. Apparently, Heinrich Institoris coerced a Notary named Arnold Kolich to forge the entire document.

Dean Sprenger did not know the full extent of Heinrich's madness, but he does now. When Pope Innocent learns the truth, he will have no choice but to declare the Inquisitor *anathema*—accursed—and cast him in the outer darkness as the heretic and sorcerer that he is.

If you are still alive and reading this, that means that you were fortunate enough to arrive back in Rome while Heinrich is still traveling. If he were in Rome, you would be dead already.

Immediately take this letter to His Holiness Pope Innocent. Let him read it carefully, and pray God, the Holy See will save us all from the Devil's Power. May God forgive us all for the innocent blood that has been spilled.

God bless you, Sebastian.
Fra Giovanni
1487 Anno Domini

Sebastian ran to find Amancio, who quickly read the note aloud.

"We must inform the Pope at once," he said. Sebastian agreed.

They set out hastily on foot to approach the Pope's private residence. They approached the Swiss guards who stood watch over the gates.

They handed the scroll to one of the guards.

"What is this?" the guard asked.

"This is a message from Fra Giovanni that the Holy Father must read," said Amancio.

"Giovanni? I thought he was dead," the guard said.

"Yes, I know," said Sebastian. "Before he died, he left this scroll to be read by the Pope." The guard looked quizzically at it, and said, "Stay here." He then walked off and after he return said, "You're in luck, I just handed it to his assistant. Now, off with you."

Sebastian and Amancio walked back to their dormitory.

"I cannot believe it. I feel sick to my stomach," said Sebastian.

"There is nothing more we can do. We can only pray the Pope reads the note," said Amancio.

The next morning after matin prayers, a seminarian ran into the chapel to find the two men.

"Did you hear the news?" he asked.

"What news?" asked Amancio.

"The Pope is putting the Grand Inquisitor on trial."

"Did you hear where the trial will be?" Amancio asked him.

""It starts now! At Mary and the Martyrs. How perfect for the Grand Inquisitor, who is accused of killing innocents, to profess his own innocence...to Pope Innocent!" guffawed the seminarian, delighted with his own sardonic joke.

Sebastian cringed. The hellish torment he had witnessed at Clonmacnoise Abbey was no laughing matter. However, the irony was that Institoris would be subject to the indignities of a public trial in the very same place where he first approached Sebastian over a year earlier. Sebastian wondered who had made the decision to conduct the trial there, and why. They raced out of the chapel to the Pantheon for the trial.

INNOCENTS

"Is this what the Coliseum looked like with gladiators?" said Amancio.

The Pantheon was buzzing with activity. It was rare that the public would be invited to ecclesiastical matters of such importance. Sebastian thought that Institoris's infamy must be behind the public's apparent interest in the spectacle. Be that as it may, Sebastian desired whatever divine justice the Pope would mete out to Institoris. He was confident that the Pope would address these terrible crimes appropriately.

"He is charged with only two counts," Amancio uttered, looking back down at the scroll in his hand like it was a program for an opera. "Forgery and fraud. But no heresy, blasphemy, witchcraft, or murder," noted Amancio, flipping the scroll to look at the back as though a major charge might be hidden on the reverse of the document. "Is that an oversight?"

"May I look at it?" Sebastian asked and Amancio handed him the scroll. "This is wrong. I mean, you are right, fraud is here, but not murder or heresy—"

Interrupting Sebastian was a multitude of trumpets bellowing, announcing the entrance of the Holy Father Pope Innocent into the great round building. Everyone stood, many in the crowd of onlookers cheering. Priests, monks, and seminarians bowed their head in respect, removing their hoods.

The Pope sauntered slowly down the main aisle of the Church, blessing onlookers with the sign of the cross with two of the fingers on his right hand and leaning on his gold crosier in his left like a walking stick. At least two dozen Cardinals and Archbishops flanked him. They were not dressed in their usual resplendent garments for a Mass. Rather, they were wearing simple unadorned white albs and black stoles that would typically be worn at funerals of the laity. Sebastian did not recognize one cleric walking in the back as Georg Golser, the Bishop of Brixen.

"*Dominus vobiscum*," the Pope began. "The Lord be with all of you."

"*Et cum spiritu tuo*," the crowd responded in unison, "And also with you."

"We are gathered here today to lay to rest the charges against the man that you now know were first brought to my attention on the 7th day of July in the Year of Our Lord 1487. Guards, you may now bring in the man."

Onlookers craned their heads to view the antechamber. Heinrich Institoris was brought into the center of the Church in shackles, like a common brigand. The crowd gasped audibly as he was dragged beneath the same Great Eye in the Dome in the center of the Church where he had first met Sebastian.

A guard removed his shackles. He looked odd without his imposing robes, vestments, or long hood. He was dressed in a white frock with no stole. The crowd had known that Institoris was going to be put on trial. What they did not fully expect was the spectacle of seeing the tall imposing Inquisitor in manacles.

The Pope and several Archbishops hung their heads. Several Cardinals covered their eyes. Through it all, though, Heinrich Institoris never flinched or demonstrated any emotion. Sebastian could have sworn that a few times, he saw Institoris muttering to himself, but he could not be sure from his vantage point, Sebastian was also mindful to try to hide behind townspeople to avoid being seen by Institoris. But it was to no avail.

After a few moments of scanning the crowd, the Inquisitor found and focused his gaze on Sebastian. Sebastian could have sworn that he even saw a hint of a smirk from the priest upon recognizing him, but he could not be certain. Amancio didn't seem to notice.

The aged Pope took his seat on a decadently adorned golden throne flanked by smaller thrones occupied by Cardinals on each side. A short Dominican priest walked over and handed the Pope a black folio that seemed to contain scripted handwritten text.

"Ahem," the Pope cleared his throat. "Father Heinrich Kramer Institoris, of the Order of Preachers, you are hereby charged by the written instrument now before you."

Another Dominican priest handed a document to Institoris, who never looked away from Sebastian. The Pope continued, "Priest and Preacher of the Gospel of the Lord Jesus Christ, be prepared to be subject to the strict examinations and interrogatories of the faithful servant of God, Professor and Dean Jacobus Sprenger."

The crowd gasped as Dean Sprenger emerged from marble stairs behind the pulpit. Until now, no one knew who would publicly question the Inquisitor. Sprenger was witness to the fraud and forgery. For Sprenger to be the authority interrogating Institoris made this spectacle one for the ages. As if on cue, dozens of additional seminarians and villagers pressed in against the crowd, attempting to witness the salacious activities.

Sprenger spryly ascended to the pulpit, and stood at the lectern, opening a weighty book. This time, Sprenger was wearing the distinctive robes and hood of an Inquisitor himself.

The Pope continued. "Priest and Preacher of Jesus Christ, do you swear before God Almighty, before the Throne of Saint Peter, and on His Holy Saints and Martyrs, that you will bear only true witness?"

Institoris did not answer. He was still glaring at Sebastian.

"The written record shall reflect that the Witness Father Heinrich Institoris has refused to bear true witness before Almighty God and His Saints. Let the charges be amended to include additional obstructions," announced Sprenger.

"Duly noted," a seated Chancellor's Notary seated near the Pope acknowledged, scribbling on parchment.

"Your Holiness," Sprenger turned toward the Pope and continued, bowing his head slightly. "Father Institoris stands accused of diverse acts of fraud and forgery. Most notably, Your Holiness, Father Institoris has abused the position of Inquisitor and pretended that the Holy See had blessed this…book." Sprenger held up a tattered copy of *The Malleus Maleficarum*, and dropped it onto the floor with a clatter. "According to divine and canon law, the punishment of such a forgery is death—"

"I admit nothing," interrupted Institoris. "Only God may judge me." He looked up at the overcast sky through the Eye in the Dome.

The crowd gasped at his first utterance. Hearing his hoarse voice made Sebastian tremble. Sebastian remembered first hearing that same echoing voice in this very spot a year earlier.

Dean Sprenger continued to address the Pope, "In the event that he remains silent, I respectfully request that the Throne of Saint Peter accept his silence as admission of his own guilt and amend the charges and punishments accordingly."

Sprenger opened a smaller book and began to read aloud. "The first charge. On or about Saturday, the 19th of May in the Year of Our Lord 1487, Father Institoris did suborn and aid willful forgery and intentional fraud by inducing one Arnold Kolich, Public Notary, to affixing the signatures of at least seven members of the Faculty of the University of Cologne to *The Witches' Hammer* and in doing so, intentionally and with malice, intend to confuse and deceive the faithful."

"The second charge," Sprenger continued after turning a page, "is that he deliberately affixed the Holy Father's Papal Bull of the 9th of December in the Year of Our Lord 1484 to *The Witches' Hammer*, giving rise to the false inference to the faithful that His Holiness Pope Innocent VIII gave his full appropriation and Imprimatur to the contents therein. How do you respond to these charges?"

Institoris looked up and pointed at the book on the floor. "These charges against *The Hammer* themselves constitute heresy. To not believe in witchcraft is the greatest of heresies."

"Yes, in fact, you pleaded that very same statement on the very title page of *The Witches' Hammer*, did you not, Father Institoris?" asked Sprenger, in the same Socratic tone familiar to all his students, several of whom chuckled in the audience.

"The book speaks for itself. You should know, James. You wrote it," said Institoris. The crowd hushed.

Sprenger's name was sprinkled throughout the book. For that very reason, the fact that Sprenger was questioning Institoris about it made the interrogation even more dramatic and personal. Sebastian waited intently to see what Sprenger's reaction would be to the accusation.

"Let the charges be amended to add willful perjury," said Sprenger to the notarial scribe, without excitement.

Institoris snickered at Sprenger's tepid response. Institoris then spoke loudly. "The Divine Law commands that witches are to be put to death. Suffer not a witch to live! God would not impose the extreme penalty of this kind if witches did not really and truly make a compact with devils in order to bring about real and true hearts and harms."

Sprenger retorted. "But the question before us, Father, is first and foremost whether you did, in fact commit *fraud*. The question before us is not whether witches exist or should be punished according to Divine Law." The Pope gave a quick nod.

Institoris responded indignantly. "If Divine Law teaches that the death of the body and soul is the proper recompense for witchcraft, then Divine Law would also countenance all necessary means to combat that heresy."

Sprenger turned to the scribe again. "Let the written record reflect that Father Institoris has now admitted that he committed fraud in the first instance. The accused is attempting to avert his liability for his crimes by virtue of flawed logic," Sprenger retorted, turning back to the witness.

"On the second charge of misinforming and deceiving the public," Sprenger continued, "Father Institoris, what is your response? On 9 December of the Year of the Incarnation of Our Lord, one thousand four hundred and eighty-four in the first Year of the Pontificate of His Holiness Pope Innocent VIII, did you receive the Papal Bull?"

"I did," Institoris said with a nod.

"And did you indeed affix it to *The Hammer*, which was not written or submitted until 1486?"

"I did."

"And in doing so, you intended to give the false impression that His Holiness had read and approved your work?"

"You would know, James—syou read and approved my work," responded Institoris, accusing the accuser of being complicit once again.

"Ah, but now you have contradicted yourself, Father Institoris. First you accused me of writing the book, now you accuse me of only reviewing and approving it after *you* wrote it. Which is true, Father Institoris?"

Institoris had been caught in his own lies, and he knew it. Sebastian smiled at Sprenger's successful interrogation, which had been done without any threats or torture, merely simple logic.

"We will arrive at the charge of perjury again. But for now," Sprenger continued, "the question is only your intention. Did you intend to give the false impression to the faithful reader of the book that His Holiness had read and approved your work?"

Institoris was again silent. He knew that had been his intention all along but deemed it imprudent to admit it now.

"Well, again, Father, your silence is your tacit admission of the same. Let the record reflect that Father Institoris has again indicated his guilt by silence—"

"I possessed all the right and dignity of my office to do so, James, and you know it," interrupted Institoris.

Sprenger returned to his notes and repeated the question to the witness more forcefully.

"Father Institoris, did you not affix to *The Witches' Hammer* a document that stated, in relevant part, 'know by all men by these presents, whosoever shall read, see or hear the tenor of this official and public document, that in the year of our Lord, 1487, upon a Saturday, being the nineteenth day of the month of May, at the fifth hour after noon, or thereabouts, in the third year of the Pontificate of our most Holy Father and Lord, the lord that Innocent, by divine providence Pope, the eighth of that name, in the very and actual presence of me, Arnold Kolich, public notary, and in the presence of the witnesses whose names are hereunder written and who were convened and especially summoned for this purpose, a document which is whole, entire, untouched, and in no way lacerated or impaired, in fine whose integrity is above any suspicion."

"I did," responded Institoris.

"And indeed, this statement was false the very day that it was affixed."

Institoris was silent again.

"Your Holiness." Sprenger turned toward the Pope again. "We have witnesses, including one Arnold Kolich, public notary, and others who are prepared to swear and testify under the most stringent penalties of perjury, that Father Institoris's written statement was indeed false and forged the very day that it was affixed."

Institoris scanned the crowd, now looking for Arnold Kolich's face. Instead, he saw Abigail, standing in front of the crowd, grinning at him. She had a massive scar across her face where the Inquisitor had enjoyed cutting her repeatedly in the dungeon.

He pointed at her.

"These witnesses are all heretics," Institoris said accusingly. "Abigail Kolich admitted under oath that she consorted with all manner of incubi and succubi and engaged in illicit sexual acts under their persuasion. I spared her life, but she must be put to death!"

"But again, that is not the question before us, Father," responded Sprenger. And indeed, the witness we have here sworn is *not* Abigail Kolich, Father Institoris. It is the very Notary himself."

Institoris strained but could not see Arnold's face in the crowd. He wondered if Sprenger was bluffing. If he was not and Arnold was indeed prepared to testify, the case against him was sealed. Institoris chose to go silent.

"Further, Your Holiness, we have here present in our midst all the faculty members of the University of Cologne. Namely, we have Professors Lambertus de Monte, Jacobus de Stralen, Master Thomas de Scotia, John Vorde of Mechelin and the sworn Professor Bedel. Each one is an honorable Christian man who is prepared to testify that the Accused conspired with the disgraced Notary Arnold Kolich to falsely endorse their names and approbation of this book."

"I did so, and would do it again and again and again," blurted out Institoris. "I did what needed to be done."

"The case is thus charged and can be wholly proven, in the presence of God and His Holiness Pope Innocent VIII," Sprenger concluded and stepped down off the pulpit. The crowd continued to remain silent as they awaited the punishment that would inevitably be meted out. Certainly, Sprenger had convinced the crowd in attendance that Institoris was guilty on both counts, and his confession sealed it.

The Pope, exasperated, stood up slowly from the chair.

"These charges are indeed proven and admitted, Professor Sprenger. Thank you for your service to the Throne of Saint Peter." Sprenger stepped down quietly and disappeared behind the pulpit.

The Pope continued. "Dean Sprenger has convinced me that there is no doubt as to whether Father Institoris committed these grievous offenses. However, I also note that many persons of both sexes, unmindful of their own salvation and straying from the Catholic Faith, have abandoned themselves to devils, incubi and succubi," the Pope continued, seemingly reading from a prepared scroll now.

"By their incantations, spells, conjurations, and other accursed charms and crafts, enormities and horrid offences, these persons have slain infants yet in the mother's womb, as also the offspring of cattle, have blasted the produce of the earth, the grapes of the vine, the fruits of the trees, nay, men and women, beasts of burthen, herd-beasts, as well as animals of other kinds, vineyards, orchards, meadows, pasture-land, corn, wheat, and all other cereals; these wretches furthermore afflict and torment men and women, beasts of burthen, herd-beasts, as well as animals of other kinds, with terrible and piteous pains and sore diseases, both internal and external; they hinder men from performing the sexual act and women from conceiving.

"They blasphemously renounce that Faith, which is theirs by the Sacrament of Baptism, and at the instigation of the Enemy of Mankind they do not shrink from committing and perpetrating the foulest abominations and filthiest excesses to the deadly peril of their own souls. The abominations and enormities in question remain unpunished not without open danger to the souls of many and peril of eternal damnation."

"*But*," the Pope emphasized, "no matter how serious the threat of witchcraft remains, it is a grievous mortal sin to have forged my approval and the approval of the good professors. Such a crime can never be allowed, or else the rule of law will be abrogated and the authority of my Throne, the Throne of Saint Peter himself, be defiled forever. The authority of the Pope is sacred. I am the bridge between man on God on earth. Let no man render that asunder.

"Furthermore, I have been warned repeatedly, by the Honorable Bishop Georg Golser, by the Honorable Excellency Archduke Sigismund and the Holy Roman Emperor Maximilian himself, that you have indeed done terrible things in their districts. You have maligned and slandered the Emperor, conducted false trials and caused scandal to the Church."

Hearing this, Amancio leaned over and whispered to Sebastian, "There is no way Heinrich will escape a death sentence now!" Sebastian nodded and held his breath.

"Father Heinrich Kramer Institoris of the Order of Preachers, you are hereby exiled. You may never set foot in the City of God again, and you will spend all the remaining days of your life in disgrace and far from the Church's graces. May Almighty God have mercy on your soul."

The Pope made a dramatic sign of the cross over Father Institoris, who exhibited no emotion. Sebastian exhaled and shot a glance at Amancio. This was not the result they expected.

Four guards roughly seized the Inquisitor and placed iron shackles on his hands and feet. Weighed down by the heavy metal braces, the Inquisitor was forced to trudge down the center aisle of the Church toward the rear. The crowd was silent and averted their eyes as he passed by. He stopped and turned to look at Sebastian. He slipped him a crumpled and torn piece of parchment as he stepped out of the building and into the piazza where he was thrown onto a waiting wagon and hauled off like a common thief. Sebastian looked down at the scrawled note. On it was inscribed a symbol that he had not seen before.

I enjoyed putting the hot poker through your mother's pretty little feet. Your father bragged he was in bed with a witch, so I hunted her down.

When you arrived here, I found you too.

The Witches' Hammer will live forever. The pupils will learn the secrets of sorcery <u>you</u> collected for us.

Brigantia and her coven are your sacrifice. Thank you for identifying when and where we can find them. I would taste her ashes if I could.

RACE

Sebastian was shocked to his core at the display of pure evil. He realized that the symbol could be understood by reading the letters clockwise. "L-U-C-I-F-E...." He stopped himself. When Sebastian looked up, the Inquisitor was gone.

The horrifying puzzle of Sebastian's family history came together in a horrifying way. His mother Diana had told Sebastian that his father Leone had been tasked with designing the new St. Peter's Basilica by the previous Pope before Sebastian was even born. His father must have inadvertently informed Institoris about his mother's occult practices, which Institoris would have viewed as the ultimate heresy to be hunted down and punished. Institoris had sought her out in La Spezia and crippled her.

His mother had then sent Sebastian away, so that Institoris would never find him, and he would be spared. But somehow, all these years later, Heinrich had found her and killed her. Then, he found Sebastian and played him like a musical instrument. The fact that Sebastian had unknowingly empowered the very Inquisition that crippled and killed his mother and that would now seek out and murder Brigantia and her coven made him physically ill.

Speechless, he handed the note to Amancio.

Amancio was the first to speak after they had both read it. "Lord Jesus, what will we do now?" he asked anxiously.

"I cannot allow Brigantia to be slaughtered by madmen," Sebastian said, standing back up and wiping his mouth.

"I will join you!" pronounced Amancio.

"No, you will not." He put his hand on Amancio's shoulder. "You cannot go with me."

While he hated the truth, Amancio knew that if both men committed the ultimate insubordination by leaving Rome now, the Inquisition would not only kill them but would hunt down Amancio's father, mother, brothers, and sisters and slaughter them. As an orphan, only Sebastian possessed the freedom to risk what needed to be done.

"What if Valentino assists with your passage back?" asked Amancio.

"That would be a help, but I cannot risk your safety and that of your family any longer. But thank you." The men hugged tightly, knowing that they would never see each other again.

Sebastian hastily headed to the harbor of Civitavecchia. A brew of rage and fear stewed in his heart. Without the help and resources of the Inquisition, journeying all the way back to Brigantia may be nearly impossible. Just last year, it had taken him weeks to travel to Galloway from Cherbourg, time he could not afford now—not to mention the real cost of paying captains with freshly struck gold coins to let him board their ships. He also knew that this trip would take him through the Straits of Gibraltar and through the Celtic Sea at an inopportune time of year.

Once he departed, he would never return. Years spent working and studying toward his ordination would evaporate, as even tolerant Bishops would not favor Sebastian's decision to mutiny. He knew that the Inquisition might eventually find him and kill him no matter what he did, so there was no choice but to embark upon a new—and unknown—life totally outside the graces of the Church.

Upon arriving at the first dock, Sebastian was welcomed by spiteful stares. The ships' captains seem to recognize his face, and refused to allow him to board their ship, presumably under the strict orders of the Inquisition. He walked down the full length of each long pier, seeking out rogue captains that may not be squarely under the Inquisition's thumb. This task proved harder as the hours went by, and he was beginning to run out of prospective captains—and options.

Sebastian continued to plead with mariners of lesser vessels, hoping just one would accept him onboard a route to Hibernia, even if circuitously. He began lowering his standards and conceded to them that he would agree to sail on any type of ship that would take him in the general direction through the straits of Gibraltar. He found none.

Sebastian heard a whistle coming from an alleyway adjacent to the last pier. A hooded man gestured for him to come hither. Fearing similar figures from the past but growing desperate, Sebastian warily approached the dimly lit alley, only to be cornered by four bearded ruffians lying in wait.

They manhandled Sebastian, looking through his pockets for coins. Sebastian resisted and held his own, but they made off with all his remaining wealth. Sebastian was lying on the ground hopelessly as the men continued to roughly kick him.

The violent engagement abruptly ended at the sight of six shielded men with a bright Red Cross embroidered on the long white garments they wore. Sebastian immediately recognized them as the mysterious Knights Templar. The brigands ran off upon seeing them.

In Rome over a year earlier, Institoris had mentioned that their Order had been in hiding but Sebastian did not know whether to believe it then. He knew that the Order had represented the most successful and richest monastic institution the world had ever seen. Ever since their founding to fight in the Crusades and save Jerusalem from Turks, they had recognized no authority other than the Roman Pope himself. However, as their military power and untold wealth and spoils from the Holy Land and beyond began to rival Rome itself, the Pope had not only disbanded them; he declared the Order *anathema*—accursed. He had ordered their simultaneous execution as heretics on a Friday the 13th. Nonetheless, even centuries later, Sebastian had heard only whispers and rumors that the Knights Templar remained encamped throughout Christendom, no longer loyal to the Holy See but rather safeguarding esoteric knowledge and incalculable treasure.

"Declare yourself," demanded a Knight with blonde hair and blue eyes, much taller than the other five, who flanked him closely with their swords out of their scabbards. "Why is a man of the cloth seeking safe passage to Hibernia without the blessing of his own Church?" The tall Knight was imposing and spoke with authority.

Sebastian described his original work for the Inquisition and how Institoris betrayed him. He explained how he happened upon Brigantia, whom the Inquisitor had now pledged to burn alive once *The Witches' Hammer* text reached the area. Once the book would reach those who live in her County, she would be in great peril, as the book specifically identified her by name as a Satanic witch. He then explained that Institoris and his minions believed that they were serving Lucifer, and were murdering innocent victims as some form of perverted sacrifice.

Moved with sympathy, as well as their solemn vow to help those in need, the tallest Knight introduced himself as Brother Luke, the Grand Master of the Knights Templar.

"We cannot permit such evil. We are duty bound to combat it. We will assist you with your voyage, but it will need to wait for weeks or months. We are waiting out the waters ourselves before resuming travels away from Rome to familiar ports of call," the Grand Master said. He explained that unbeknownst to Rome, the Knights Templar had retained control over many of their own harbor facilities in certain ports, mostly those required for the surreptitious movement of personnel and equipment. These days, they were not as involved in mainstream commercial enterprises which might be discovered by the secular or ecclesiastical authorities. Therefore, they mostly plied the waters of the North Sea, around the coasts of Britain, down the western seaboards of Europe, across the Mediterranean, the Aegean, and the Black Sea. Templar preceptories located at ports such as Bristol and La Rochelle allowed them to manage their own profitable cargoes out of sight. But Hibernia was not on their trade route and was dangerous for many reasons. Most of the county chiefs there were fiercely loyal to the Church in Rome and viewed the Knights as an anachronistic heresy and ongoing threat to the peace.

But Sebastian remained adamant about his need to rescue Brigantia immediately and pleaded with them to take him to Hibernia that very night. He also explained that Finan O'Brien in western County Clare was an ally who could be trusted.

"Sebastian," Luke said, "we have our navigational maps from Bartolomeo Perestrello. Do you know him?"

"Yes, I am familiar with him. He was originally from Lombardy, but I believe is now in Portugal. He worked for Prince Henry the Navigator before he died," replied Sebastian.

"Well, he was the son of King John and was our former Grand Master," Luke explained. "His maps allow for us to travel safely as far as Hibernia. We also have maps from Columbo. But they all warn that late autumn is not the right time to embark on a trip across the Celtic Sea. Indeed, those shipping that book will wait autumn out before those waters are calm enough to sail upon, so there is no urgency."

"With all due respect, Sir, that book will already be well on its way to Hibernia, regardless of the weather. Will you be able to rest with many innocent lives at stake?"

The Knights conferred among themselves.

"Very well," said Luke. "We will do all we readily can to ensure a safe trip back to Hibernia and even help rescue Brigantia and her coven from these madmen. But while we can promise safe passage, we cannot promise that it will be timely enough to save those you seek to protect."

"I understand completely," said a relieved Sebastian.

Luke pointed to a fleet anchored off the coast. "There is small number of guarded ships that should be able to deliver our men safely with enough space to transport the coven away to safety if need be. However, we will not have a large force of arms once we arrive; just a contingent to get safely ashore there. Is that understood? We will take a dinghy to the fleet and depart by nightfall."

Sebastian agreed and offered to make the rounds at the small marketplace near the dock, purchasing dull-colored robes for the Knights to wear over their white garments, thus disguising them from wandering eyes. Sebastian did not understand why Pope Innocent was hunting them down, but he was nonetheless certain in his heart that these men could have done no moral wrong.

Set to sail that night, a dozen Knights gathered with their Grand Master Luke in the dark alleyway, and knelt, drawing short swords out of their scabbards. They said a prayer before boarding their ships, which would all head west and northwest towards Hibernia through Gibraltar. Not all of the Knights were to depart on the trek though, as many remained to continue the various missions Brother Luke has assigned. The men hugged and kissed each other in brotherly embraces, wishing safety and blessings upon each other; for those heading on the journey, and for those staying within reach of the Pope and the dangerous Inquisition.

As the ships left the port, all the men on board said another prayer, this time for good weather. Sebastian joined in. As they pushed out to the Mediterranean, the waters were calm. For the first time in a long while, Sebastian smiled as a cool sea breeze washed over him. He was now more determined than ever to see Brigantia safe, knowing he was accompanied by strong men who traveled with him.

STORM

As Sebastian stood on the deck of the ship, the moon lit up the night; nothing but the coos of the night birds could be heard in earshot. Sebastian believed that it was a privilege and an honor to uphold the beliefs of these Knights, unknown as they were to him, as they clearly took pride in their selfless, newfound, and dangerous mission without any expectation of financial recompense.

After dark, the men started to settle in. It did not take long before Sebastian became well acquainted with a few Knights over a rowdy supper. Sebastian and the Knights shared a love of morality as well as bravery. A mutual respect formed in the hearts of the Knights for Sebastian, and he for them.

Sebastian particularly befriended two brothers, Pierre and Hugues, who had recently devoted themselves to the Order after a gruesome attack on their village near Trieste. Their town was near the Adriatic Sea, and had been attacked by the Inquisition's loyal soldiers, taking the lives of both their sisters and mother. Pierre and Hugues had then sworn themselves to chastity and honor before God. This was difficult, especially for Pierre who also lost the love of his life in the village attack. Hugues explains that his birth name was Richard. He has declared his Knight's name as Hugues in honor of the First Grand Master and founder of the Order of the Temple, one of the original nine Knights Templar.

Both brothers were tall, with broad shoulders and mud-colored hair. They were handsome and even their scruffy appearance couldn't mask their good looks. The brothers left their beards to grow into a thick brown bush, but it didn't prevent their teeth from piercing through whenever they smiled. Pierre was older and taller than Hugues. Both men were in very good shape, with big muscles but Pierre was slimmer in size. Pierre explained that the reason for his slender frame was love, as love will always drain a man, which made Sebastian laugh.

Sebastian was briefly transported back to his youth, where he spent much time with men such as these on the fishing ships in Saint Malo. The brothers built a bond with Sebastian, eventually confiding in him the truth behind the Pope's warrant against Luke, their leader. The Pope and the Inquisition wished to permanently break the stronghold of the Knights Templar, rendering them extinct, by murdering their leader. The Inquisition was only the latest enemy of the Knights. Sebastian knew that Institoris detested humility and spent his time only with those that would placate his murderous intentions. Sebastian now realized that the Pope was no different.

The brothers explained to him that the lifestyle that the Knights Templar swore to live was just and true, which the Pope saw as a threat to his supremacy. Thus, the new Pope has issued another bounty on the heads of the Knights, sending them into permanent hiding. Sebastian realized that he now shared a permanent curse with the Knights, never able to return to the good graces of the Church that raised them.

On the first night aboard the ship, after supper, Luke sat down next to Sebastian.

"Welcome, Sebastian. You will soon consider joining our ranks, I believe!" He explained that because of the ongoing threats from the Church, they had yet to replenish military ranks to his satisfaction. They would not yet dare to challenge the powers of the Pope and Inquisition now, so they had to split up and meet in secret to discuss their plans for ongoing safety. So far it had been going well enough, but the Knights did not wish to separate from their loyal companions on shore for too extended a period.

After a week at sea, the Knights' ships arrived at the straits of Gibraltar and passed through safely. Two weeks more passed without incident but there was no end to the trip in sight. Sebastian has given up counting the days and spent his time working, praying, singing, fishing, and dining with the men. Fortunately, due to the common people's love for the Knights, food was never an issue. There was enough tack and salted meats to last a year's worth of travels. Plus, they were never far from the coastline if they needed to dock for provisions. However, given the nature and urgency of their mission, they agreed that it would be best to stay on course.

One night at dinner, while the ships passed through the Bay of Biscay, Sebastian tore apart a loaf of bread, hardened by its partial staleness and dipped it into a stew thickened with water and dried beans. He smiled and invited the other men to join his "feast." Suddenly, a strong wind sent the ship off balance.

Several men fell, and Sebastian's meal poured over onto the floor of the hold. As they stood and tried to steady themselves while the ship rocked, the captain yelled for the men to head to the deck.

Sebastian and several Knights scurried on deck, trying to ensure that the ship was balanced and leveled. A thick, dark cloud formed overhead, and the approaching waters appeared very unstable. Deafening thunder bellowed above them. The sky took a sudden turn from blue to ash as the waters roared in anger. Some of the men complained that they should never have embarked on a trip during this time of the year, while others tried to remain calm, assuring the doubtful that all would be well once the storm subsided.

But it was only a matter of time before the ship drifted directly under a cloud as dark as the alleyway in which Sebastian encountered the ruffians a few weeks earlier. A heavy rain suddenly descended from heaven. The downpour of rain sent the men into another panic as the ships began to move on their own, rendering their captains useless. The captain maintained his hold of the ship's wheel regardless, as he attempted to steady it in the squall.

Crackles of lightning with loud thunder returned. The flashes were repeated in several other locations, brightening up the ship in short bursts of light. Several of the Knights panicked, worrying that the storm might be the end of them. As wave after wave of salty water poured inside the ship, two men slipped and fell in terror as the waves crashed upon them and flooded into the ship's hold.

Sebastian glimpsed the others on the accompanying ships, all in an equal panic.

"Brothers! Remember the story of Jonah! He was saved by God at sea! Pierre! God will not let anything happen to us on their sacred quest!" They saw Sebastian and nodded.

Both Pierre and Hugues were at the stern of the ship now and remained confident and steady, at least as far as Sebastian could tell. The squall must have been nothing compared to the gruesome attack that they witnessed on their beloved village, he thought to himself. The brothers advised the captain to move towards the eye of the storm, as that was where calm would begin.

The captain also nodded. He had his men beckon to the other ships behind to follow closely. The Knights' ships, now all headed towards the eye of the storm, formed a bold line, though still rocked by the harsh waves.

Slowly, the waves began to recede, and the heavy rain made way for lighter droplets of water. As all of the men were completely drenched, the change in weather made no difference to their appearance. Hugues happily told the men to look yonder, an order barked through the entire fleet.

Following Hugues's direction, Sebastian's eyes were led to the small opening of a cloud, revealing the sun. As the ships drifted onward, the light became brighter and stronger. The men let out loud shouts of happiness, mighty enough to wake the dead. As the rainclouds made way for the sun, the men continued to roar, grateful that not a single life had been lost. Pierre and Hugues wrapped each other in a tight, brotherly embrace, their bodies soaked in hours' worth of rain, their beards dripping.

The ship was also thoroughly soaked, but there were no signs of serious damage, and no leaks. The strong ships had endured the powerful currents and remained unharmed. Sebastian said a grateful prayer before being joined by the brothers. The men spent the next few hours unloading pools of water from the ship while heartily singing songs. Sebastian was now very hungry as the storm had robbed him of his meal. He called upon the brothers to help him catch some fresh fish, as he announced that he had no appetite remaining for the preserved salted fish in storage.

Soon, it was nighttime again, and the men had caught plenty of fresh fish and began to roast them atop a small fire, singing songs from earlier with a newfound satisfaction and joy evident on their faces. Each man aboard the ship took turns telling the others about his life before joining the Knights Templar, recounting stories of battles.

Sebastian was filled with awe at some of the stories he heard. Many of the men had left noble titles and fame and fortune for the sake of the Order. Sebastian told the men that he deeply respected them and wished he could join them, but his heart burned for Brigantia. The men laughed and cheered him on, teasing him but also encouraging him to follow his true passions.

Sebastian began to tear up as he described his life with Fra Giovanni and how he was unable to see him before his untimely passing, as well as the note that he was left, warning him about Institoris's misdeeds. He did not tell them, however, of his mother and father.

As several of the men chatted until dawn, they continued to learn more about each other, discovering new things, some even after years together as Knights. They thanked Sebastian once more for the opportunity to embark on such an adventure and said that they hoped that they would not be too late to save Brigantia.

Sebastian excused himself from the group and found a tight space by the edge of the ship to sleep. As he drifted into a deep slumber, he heard the voice of his beloved Brigantia calling out to him, saying to him that she could not wait to see him again, and that her heart ached for the moment they would reunite, something she has prayed for. She began to sing softly for Sebastian, and he smiled softly at the woman he had set out to be with forever, her voice like a summer bird whistling on a warm day. She took her hand and lifted Sebastian's face to hers. As the two locked eyes on one other, Sebastian moved closer to embrace her.

Sunlight, the smell of roasted fish and the boisterous laughter of the men woke Sebastian from his slumber. Recovering from the pain and struggle of the last few hours proved easier than expected. Sebastian leaned over the ship and stared down at the mighty, uncontrollable water, which was reckless just hours ago, but now was calm and still, gently caressing the ships in playful twists and turns as the reflection of the sun caused the waters to sparkle.

Sebastian was ready to fight. He had come to this decision in Rome, even before departing for Hibernia. His mind was set on his love for Brigantia and he was aware that it might come down to physically protecting her.

The men informed Sebastian that in the next few days they would be approaching Galloway Bay in western Hibernia and they hoped that he would soon be reunited with Brigantia. His heart raced in anticipation, recounting his dream to the men, who smiled in adoration of his sheepish grins and the way he spoke so fondly of her. They told Sebastian that they would need all the rest they could get, as the moment drew near when they may have to battle with their enemies: The Inquisition's loyal troops.

The Knights brought out a heavy gold-plated chest and placed it in the center of the ship's deck. All of the men gathered around it, and Sebastian also moved closer. Pierre opened the chest, revealing branded longswords inside of it. Sebastian was shocked that he had never asked the contents of the closed chest, having been so many weeks aboard the ship.

Each Knight took up a sword, and from the ones left over Pierre picked one and handed it to Sebastian, who took hold of it.

"We do not know whether the Inquisition's men are already at Hibernia," Pierre said, "but we should be prepared for a fight, if they are. It is in our best interests."

The men, now proudly adorned in their white and red garments again, prepared to dock close to the Green Road where they could easily access Poulnabrone Dolmen, where Brigantia was hopefully near.

"Thank you, Brothers," said Sebastian. "God will be the reward of good deeds that will never be forgotten."

Pierre held Sebastian by his shoulders. "We are grateful to you for giving us a sense of purpose, as the months spent in hiding before our encounter have been particularly difficult."

As the ships began to dock one by one, soon, the men began their second journey and main mission: to rescue Brigantia and her coven from the dark forces of the Inquisition.

DOLMEN

"**D**ry land," said a wobbly Sebastian to Hugues. Shakily, the knights each stepped off the ships in Lahinch, slowly regaining their balance. After a month of endless rocking by the intense waves, the men remained woozy. Several sat on the ground.

The shore in western Clare was rocky, but there was more than enough flat land for the men to set up camp near the stony beach, despite how icy it was. Scraggly trees lined crude roads, with bushes of various sizes and mountains off in the distance. North of Lisdoonvarna, the Burren Way joined a boreen between the townlands of Ballinalacken and Formoyle, crossing the plateau above the Caher Valley below Slieve Elva Mountain. It was a difficult trail, so the area attracted few visitors. Lahinch was also quiet, which was not unusual for such a rocky shoreline that time of year.

The men noticed no large ships on the crude docks save theirs, which lifted their spirits as they believed they had arrived before Institoris's men. Still, they maintained caution, as rogues could be lurking anywhere. Given the wide view that the plains gave them, though, they were confident that they could not be stalked without detection.

"Wonderful place to settle," Hugues said sarcastically, tapping the rocky meadow beneath him with his boot. Only a few flowers and plants crept through the rocks. Some of the Knights laughed in agreement.

"Aye, like my own Scottish shores," said another knight. "That is where my love waits for me." He put his gloved hand over his heart.

"We cannot camp," Sebastian ordered, trying to lead the men

forward. He was the only one familiar with Brigantia's location and the route there, and he knew that they must arrive there as soon as possible.

"He is right," said Hugues to the weary knights. One of the men offered to walk to the nearby stable and purchase two dozen horses with a bag of gold coins.

Soon, the over forty knights were on horseback in an all-out gallop, hooves clacking against the stony surface of the Burren Way. The mares seemed to detect the urgency by the length and force of their stride. Leading the way, Sebastian patted his mare's soft neck to reassure her that her efforts were appreciated.

The searing, icy wind bit their faces and misty rain pierced their skin with countless tiny needles. But Sebastian could not feel anything other than the profound nausea of dread welling up deep in the pit of his stomach. He remembered the trepidation with which he had first approached Brigantia, and how he had accused her of bewitching him. That she had done, but now he realized it was entirely without magic. But only now did he realize how far he had come in his understanding of the nature of good and evil in the space of less than a year's time. He feared that this understanding would have to come at the price of even more innocent blood.

He now knew that the Inquisitor's countless legions had lost all trace of reason and had moved into the dark realm of the netherworld, where nothing except malice and madness reigned. The realization that he was dealing with evil so profound that it would cross continents to murder the upright unnerved him to his core. As they rode on, he reflected to himself, lost in his thoughts.

There have been enough blameless lives forfeited to satisfy a thousand demons. The damned Inquisitors should have already sated their ghastly desires. They did not need their malevolent forces to come all the way here to this exquisite countryside, and mock God's glory by committing more murders in His name.

As Sebastian led the way, the Knights followed closely behind, one hand on their swords in case they should need to attack or defend swiftly. Their horses' hooves created a drum-like pattern, one after the other in a quick rhythm. The road was long and wide, each side surrounded by rocky meadows, leading up to Poulnabrone Dolmen. They pulled their horses to a trot as they neared the knoll where Sebastian indicated the stone dolmen stood.

As they dismounted and inched closer to the foot of the monument on foot, the zeal and fervor the Knights had was beginning to wear off as the men noticed a foul smell in the air. The closer they approached, the stronger the stench grew.

"Lord, please do not let it be," Sebastian muttered under his breath, as terrible thoughts began to fill his mind.

"Smells like death!" one of the Knights said loudly, before being hushed by his comrades.

At the foot of the stalwart pillars lay more than a dozen half-burnt corpses. They were frozen in awkward positions with arms and legs tangled, jaws gaping, glazed eyes staring into space. Human blood was pooling into puddles and seeping into the earth, leaving a crimson ring on the ground. Torn garments were violently flapping against the eerie forms in the raw wind.

Sebastian ran pell-mell up the hill toward them, his eyes hurriedly scanning the pale faces of the dead. He recognized all of them.

Cara's lifeless eyes stared up at the sky. Aife's gray hair fluttered in the wind, as her body lay face down.

He dashed frantically around their corpses, looking for Brigantia among them. Not finding her the first time, he inspected the bloodless faces again and again, fearing his mind was defying him by refusing to accept that one of these was hers. But still he could not find her among them.

It was clear that loyal troops sent by the Inquisition had not only arrived but had fulfilled their mission. Their blood was still fresh, meaning they must have arrived not long before Sebastian and the Knights Templar. The bodies had been stacked side by side and on top of one another like cordwood. Immediately, flashes of the scene at Clonmacnoise appeared in Sebastian's head.

When he saw the small body of the child named Orla next to her mother Roisin, he lost control and dropped to his knees on the damp earth, weeping bitterly and biting his palms. He had held this child when she was just an infant. Now, at a little less than two, she had been brutally slain. Her mother's legs had been broken, recalling the story Diana had told him about his very own mother when she was accused of witchcraft.

He demanded to know why these fine women who had honored nature and loved their enemies in the true manner of Christ, but who had been persecuted in His name, should be murdered by his own Church. The courageous women whom Sebastian had come to admire had met their end here, under the time-honored megalith of their pagan forefathers. One thing was certain—these women had not fought back. They were all weaponless, clothed in long, flowy, beautifully embroidered gowns made with different textures and comprising several patterns and designs, all now burned with the splatters of blood across them. They had been killed without mercy. Deep hoofprints were still visible in the bloody mud. From their deep head and chest wounds, he knew that a large band of the Inquisition's troops had slain them mercilessly using swords and clubs.

The knights would need to bury the women's bodies in proper graves beneath the dolmen. He remembered a strange quote from the Gospel, *let the dead bury their own dead*, and realized that his sole purpose now was to find Brigantia.

Minutes passed before any of the knights moved. They had been left in shock, some down on their knees with their hands either on their heads or shielding their eyes and mouths. They had never witnessed a sight so gruesome, even as members of the Knights Templar having been in many hard-fought battles.

"We should have arrived sooner," Sebastian cried. "They killed these innocents. I knew them all."

"There is nothing we could have done," Pierre replied. "The book must have come via a better sea route or overland after the Channels. I am sorry." He hung his head.

"She is not among them," he told Pierre, wiping a tear from his cloudy eyes.

"Are you sure?" Pierre asked and looked up.

"Of course I am! I have looked at every single one. She is not here."

Sebastian departed for Brigantia's shack. Some of the men ran after him, while some remained behind to remain with the bodies, offering prayers up for the deceased.

As Sebastian and several of the accompanying Knights reached where the cottage once stood, they saw that it had been burned to the ground. Nothing remained except rubble and fine ash. Sebastian did not see any bones or teeth in the ashes.

"Maybe she escaped," Hugues insisted, trying to offer some sort of comfort to his brothers as they used their longswords to sift through the ash piles.

Despite these gruesome surroundings, Sebastian unexpectedly felt a satisfying and overwhelming sensation. A profound and unwavering hope that everything was going to be fine welled up inside of him and took over.

"I must find her," Sebastian declared. "She is alive, I know it."

"Let us follow you at least!" Pierre exclaimed, hoping Sebastian would agree.

"No, this is something I have to do on my own, my brother. Wait for me here. I promise I will be back."

The only person who would now know the whereabouts of his beloved Brigantia would be none other than the feudal lord of western County Clare, Finan O'Brien. Sebastian claimed his horse and began the trek to Leamanaugh Castle. The horse was fast, but Epona had been faster.

ARAN

As he spotted Leamanaugh Castle from the distance, Sebastian kicked the mare's side, urging her to gallop faster. His heart started to flutter with a little hope.

Perhaps she sought refuge with Finan, he thought to himself.

But as he reached Finan's castle, he was met with an even greater disaster. Villagers were digging trenches filled with soldiers' bodies. Blood stained the ground everywhere.

Suddenly, Sebastian was seized by a few guards and brought to the presence of the feudal lord.

Foaming at the mouth, Finan yelled, "You! You did this! You caused this! Your damned book caused this! My men! My people! Those innocents! How could you, Sebastian?!" Finan screamed, with tears rolling down his eyes, recounting the brutal deaths many men in his force had faced.

"Please, hear me, Brother Finan—"

"Do not call me that! You have no right," Finan screamed. The stress of his sorrows coupled with his anger had caused the obese lord to develop a cough. He had to catch his breath before speaking again. Finan breathlessly explained the events of recent weeks.

Apparently, word had gotten to Finan that atrocities were occurring at the foot of Poulnabrone Dolmen. He had sent forty knights and three dozen infantrymen to help ward off the rogues that the Inquisition had sent to murder the women of the coven. But the contingent was too small. Eventually, Finan received word that the Inquisition was prepared to attack his castle.

By morning, all the military forces at Finan's disposal had arrived to fight the intruders. Due to the generosity Finan had exhibited towards the people of Clare, there was no shortage of men who were ready to protect him. As the rogues approached Leamanaugh Castle at midday, Finan's men were prepared to fight. Finan's guards ultimately succeeded in defeating all of the Inquisition's troops, but hundreds of his own men were lost in battle.

"He tricked me," Sebastian began, his voice low, but still commanding and audible. "The Inquisitor. I swear, he tricked me. I had no hand in this, Lord Finan. He crippled my mother. When I was a boy. I am an orphan because of him—"

He began to weep again, cutting his own words short. Summoning courage, he resumed his speech.

"You must believe me. I love her!" His voice gradually increased in volume. "You entrusted me to go to Poulnabrone on my own and I promised you I would never harm her. You know me—I would never hurt her."

As Sebastian moved closer, the guards stopped him, but with a wave of Finan's hand they stayed back.

"'Tis that damned book," Finan said. "Came in crate after crate. Every parish has more copies of it than the Scriptures themselves. Christians that couldn't read or write paid monks to speak it for 'em. Whole countryside is up in arms. The book said Brigantia was killin' and eatin' babies. 'Destroy the witches!' they said. The same people who once bought trinkets from them…"

"Where is she?" Sebastian asked. "I searched all the bodies and counted twelve plus the child, and I did not see her face. Is she the one who survived?" His voice was achingly louder than before.

Finan nodded.

"Please, Lord Finan!" Sebastian said, falling onto his knees. "Where is she? Take me to her, please. I will be forever in your debt!"

Finan let out a sigh.

"'Twas as if she knew they were comin' for her," Finan muttered. "She came up to Leamanaugh on her own, without a hint of fear about 'er."

Sebastian did not doubt it. Brigantia was the most confident person he had ever met. And she wore her confidence comfortably, not arrogantly like the Inquisitor, but peacefully, sure of herself and the powers on her side. He had never felt such an aura of strength like when he was around her.

"I protected 'er," Finan spoke on. "Sent her to the Aran Islands." He pointed toward the islands that could be seen as outlines against the sky in the distance, but Sebastian's gaze never left Finan, holding on to his every word.

"I sent my men to protect her coven. I gave 'er my word, but I failed 'er." He bowed his head. "She'll be safe where she is. She's protected behind the fort of Dun Aengus."

"Dun Aengus?" Sebastian asked.

He remembered how the Aran Islands weren't on any of his maps, and when he asked about it, he was told that the impenetrable prehistoric fort of Dun Aengus was a powerful citadel on the islands that housed a buoyant military contingent. Sebastian vaguely remembered that Brigantia had said that her mother and father had gone there when they were threatened.

"Then she is safe!" Sebastian exclaimed. "Please take me there. Let me see her," he begged Finan.

"Aye, but ye may never leave once ye go," said Finan.

It was true. Sebastian knew that he would need to spend the rest of his days as a resident of the island, contributing to the welfare of the contingent. Brigantia had told him that if a man were of good stature and strength, he would train with the troops, to defend the fort. New skills and indeed a whole new language would need to be taught to him, from baking and carpentry, to blacksmithing and sewing, and all other trades.

She had said that the art of healing through medicinal herbs was also taught. The only requirement was that no man or woman could leave and then return. For someone to head to the Aran Islands, there must be a dire need for protection or safety from death, and once one was saved, he or she must repay such a favor forever.

The only true family Sebastian knew was no more. Amancio was being ordained a priest, and Fra Giovanni was gone. He could finally be with Brigantia, abandoning all further duties to Rome and the damned Inquisition.

"I will go. I will give my next life if it means being with her," Sebastian declared, without a hint of doubt. "Since the moment I set my eyes on her, she has dwelled in my heart, Finan. I think of her every day. I am ready. This world holds nothing more for me."

Finan could tell that he meant every word.

"Remember, Sebastian—"

"I know. I will never leave her. Do not worry—our God will be with us. But there is something I need to do before I leave," Sebastian said.

CONCLUSION

I t had been a few hours since Sebastian had left the Knights Templar at the bloody dolmen. The Knights had buried the bodies, saying prayers for each woman. Not long after, from the distance, Pierre noticed men on horses approaching them.

"On guard!" he yelled, pointing toward the incoming men on horses. The Knights, expecting a battle, unsheathed their longswords, surrounded the stone dolmen and prepared to engage before they heard a familiar voice.

"Settle down, brothers. It is I!"

Sebastian's words sent a wave of instant calm upon the men, who put down their weapons.

"I bring gifts, courtesy of Lord Finan, who is thankful for your bravery, and for traveling all this way to help me."

Finan and a dozen of his men came down from their horses with crates of drinks and enough food to last even a long winter. If there was one thing Finan was good for, it was food and drink. A young girl holding a basket of soda cakes approached Pierre, assuming him to be the leader of the knights, and handed him the token.

"I want you all to have a comfortable journey home, or wherever you wish to travel from here. And for those who wish to stay, let it be known that Western County Clare welcomes the Knights Templar," Finan's Chief Knight Louis declared. Louis walked over to Luke and offered him three sacks of golden coins. Luke bowed, thanking him and handing them to Pierre.

"Sebastian?" Pierre asked, "is she alive?"

"Brigantia is safe," said Sebastian as he stepped off the horse he was riding. "She is safe on the Aran Islands, at Dun Angus. I will be heading there to be with her soon."

"But if she is there, that means—"

"Yes." Sebastian cut off Pierre before he could finish his sentence.

"And if you are going to her, then…"

"Yes. I will never return," Sebastian said gravely.

Pierre walked up to him and gave him a hearty embrace. He looked Sebastian in the eyes and spoke words of Scripture.

"Remember, Sebastian, love is patient and kind. It does not envy, it does not boast, it is not proud. It does not dishonor others, it is not self-seeking, it is not easily angered, it keeps no record of wrongs. Love does not delight in evil but rejoices with the truth. It always protects, always trusts, always hopes, always perseveres. It never fails. It has been an honor knowing you and traveling with you these months. You have become a brother, a true Knight of the Temple," Pierre said. "As someone who has loved and lost before, I say chase her, because love can be taken from you at any time. We will surely miss you, brother. I will miss you."

Sebastian embraced him tightly, kissing him on the cheeks one by one, as their eyes welled with tears.

"You chose to fight for a stranger you had never met before and you brought me here safely," said Sebastian. "I am eternally grateful. It would have been the greatest honor of my life to join the Knights Templar. Know that my heart will follow you all on your journeys. I will miss you all so dearly—but I must go to her now."

Sebastian then turned to Finan O'Brien and asked, "When can I depart?"

Afterword

Some scholars believe that over one million women were burned alive because of the popularity of Heinrich Institoris' book *The Witches' Hammer*. The book even influenced the witch trials in Salem, Massachusetts centuries after his death.

Letter from the Author

Until now, Heinrich Institoris escaped notice as perhaps the most prolific serial killer in human history. Most recent estimates put his death toll at 60,000 to 100,000, although some authors prefer much higher numbers, perhaps reaching into the *millions*.[1]

The term "serial killer" is a modern invention. According to the standard definition, a serial killer murders three or more people, usually in service of some abnormal psychological gratification, with the murders taking place over more than a month and often including a significant period between them.[2] The Federal Bureau of Investigation defines serial killing as a series of two or more murders, committed as separate events, usually, but not always, by one offender acting alone.[3] Over the last century and a half, those who have studied serial killers observe that they are typically Caucasian with an average age of 30 and 97% of the time, they are male.[4]

We can only prove that Institoris himself took two lives directly: Anna of Mindelheim and Agnes the Bathkeeper. However, he proudly proclaimed that he had personally killed over 200 more. We may never know the exact number, but Institoris' personal torture manual became a handbook influencing official judges after his death. It even

[1] Thurston, Robert W. *Witch, Wicce, Mother Goose: The Rise and Fall of the Witch Hunts in Europe and North America.* Pearson, 2001 at 93-101.

[2] *Segen's Medical Dictionary*, 2012.

[3] Robert Kastenbaum (ed.). *Macmillan Encyclopedia of Death and Dying*, 2002.

[4] *McGraw-Hill Concise Dictionary of Modern Medicine*, 2006.

contributed to judges in Massachusetts hanging a dozen more innocent women, centuries after his death.[5]

Like most serial killers, the German-born man began to manifest proclivities toward sexual violence and religious fanaticism by his early 30s. By that age, he was well on his way toward collecting dozens of the perfect targets for his rage: young and middle-aged women. This group would remain the focus of his obsession for the rest of his life. As his political power grew, he began seeking his ultimate trophies: Women of status like Helena Scheuberin, who he viewed as a witch and the enemy. We have his own written words to give insight into why he chose these targets as the most suitable.[6]

In *The Pope's Butcher*, several characters were intended to be somewhat faithful to known historical figures, including Georg Golser, and much of what we know and suspect about Institoris himself. However, we do not know if Sebastian or Brigantia ever truly existed. Many people like them most certainly did.

While Heinrich was pulling the strings in the shadows to try to kill witches in creative ways, countless intrepid souls were working to stop his rampage. For example, it is documented that Bishop Georg Golser tried to stop Heinrich from murdering more innocent victims, even at personal and political cost to himself.

While Georg succeeded by at least having Heinrich's efforts halted in Innsbruck, like so many serial killers, Institoris moved on to find greener pastures where his mission could continue unobstructed. His true body count remains unknown to this day. In 1878, the president of Cornell University, Andrew Dickson White, showed a copy of *The Witches' Hammer* to his class. He announced that this book had "caused

---

[5] In Boston in 1684, Increase Mather's essay on those living in the Colonies and in league with the Devil, "Remarkable Providences," cites the *Malleus Maleficarum* with approval.

[6] MacKay, Christopher S. *The Hammer of Witches: A Complete Translation of the Malleus Maleficarum.* Cambridge Univ. Press, 2009 at Part I, Question 6.

more suffering than any other written by human pen."[7] Others have said the book "rivals Mein Kampf as one of the most infamous and despised of books."[8] It has been called "a malign bequest to posterity" and "both the wickedest" and "most insane and accordingly most disastrous book in world literature."[9]

The undeniable fact that Heinrich repeatedly risked his own reputation and life as a high-ranking cleric, solely to disseminate a manual of effectively torturing women, demonstrates the lengths to which he was committed to the values he held in his psyche.

In fact, it is clear from the way he was repeatedly abjured by various Catholic authorities throughout his life that Institoris developed contempt for the ecclesiastical regime he found himself operating within as an Inquisitor. It was only his savvy use of political espionage that apparently allowed him to dodge scandal after scandal and elevated him to a powerful position of authority in the Inquisition to permit more murders.

For example, the chapter "Cats" is based entirely on a story recounted by Heinrich himself in *The Witches' Hammer*.[10] He bragged about successfully using a ridiculous explanation to justify his gruesome torture of three women who were the original *victims* of an assault.

In hindsight, it can be disputed whether he was afflicted with various serious pathological mental illnesses. But to dismiss Institoris as insane and personally misogynistic is to excuse the violent milieu within which he was operating.

For example, "koro" is a little-known but documented psychological disorder in which a man experiences the delusion of the loss of his penis. When a powerful man such as he would sincerely accuse a woman of

[7] Rosell Hope Robbins, Introduction, in Witchcraft: Catalogue of the Witchcraft Collection in Cornell University Library, Millwood, NY: KTO Press (1977).
[8] Smith, Moira. "The Flying Phallus and the Laughing Inquisitor: Penis Theft in the 'Malleus Maleficarum.'" *Journal of Folklore Research*, vol. 39, no. 1, 2002, pp. 85–117. JSTOR, www.jstor.org/stable/3814832. Accessed 24 Feb. 2021.
[9] *Id.*
[10] *Malleus*, at Part II, Qn. 1, Ch 9.

stealing his penis, a literal witch hunt would ensue. On the other hand, Institoris may have been joking, given how bizarre his own descriptions were. Again, his own written words may indict him.[11]

In *The Pope's Butcher*, I took the literary license of expanding on his expressed intentions and methods by proposing that he was fiendish to the point of intentionally disseminating Satanic information to his followers.

While clearly a work of fiction, this prospect is not entirely impossible: *The Witches' Hammer* contains a shocking amount of detailed information for its readers to learn about the details of how to *perform* witchcraft. It has always seemed very odd that the handbook ostensibly designed to stamp out the occult could become the cookbook for effectively practicing it.

By way of just a few examples, *The Witches' Hammer* gives out details of how to perform spells, make potions and concoctions, curse your enemies, and conjure specific demons by name. If one were truly committed to stamping this conduct out as blasphemous heresy, why dignify and communicate details to hundreds of thousands of people? Certainly, Helena Scheuberin wondered that exact question aloud, earning Institoris' wrath.

And it is indeed true that many apocryphal occult books originated in the Renaissance by unknown authors within the Church itself. These books demonstrate more than a passing familiarity with doctrine and methods and may have been written by wayward priests and monks, who were the ones in society most literate in Hebrew, Greek and Latin as well as Church rituals.

But ultimately, because he died over five hundred years ago, there remain questions than we may never completely answer about Institoris himself.

How much did Pope Innocent know about Heinrich's book? Why did the Church formally ban the book in 1490, only 6 years after supposedly

---

[11] *See* Smith, Moira, id.

approving it?[12] Who even wrote it? How did Heinrich become the Papal Nuncio to the new Pope in 1500, essentially becoming Pope Alexander's right-hand man, after being censured by previous Popes? And how did he find a way to harness the newly invented printing press by Johan Gutenberg to export his bloodlust across the sea to America, even centuries after his own death? A bibliography is included for intrepid researchers who want to investigate this matter further.

The Pope's Butcher contains a variety of medieval and Renaissance terms that may not be familiar to the reader. For that reason, a glossary is included.

Finally, every single one of the locations described in this book is real, although the names have evolved over the last five centuries. I enjoyed visiting virtually every location and encourage my readers to do the same. The Cliffs of Moher are indescribably beautiful, and the real Mont-St-Michel is particularly memorable. A new bridge constructed in 2018 made the surrounding tidal flats a bit easier to navigate without a ferryman. I recommend taking a tour bus instead of walking. To this day, pilgrims still drown when the tide roars in like a galloping horse.

---

[12] The Catholic Church formally banned the book in 1490, placing it on the *Index Librorum Prohibitorum* ("List of Prohibited Books").

Glossary

Abbot: an ecclesiastical title given to the male head of a monastery in various western religious traditions, including Christianity and Catholicism. The office may also be given as an honorary title to a clergyman who is not the head of a monastery. The female equivalent is abbess.

Breviary: a book containing prayers and the Mass for each day, to be silently recited by those in religious orders in the Roman Catholic Church, usually monks and priests.

Cappa: a cape, especially as part of ecclesiastical or academic garb.

Chancellor: title of various official positions in the governments of many nations.

Clavicula Solomonis ("Key of Solomon"): Latin name for a grimoire attributed to King Solomon. It probably dates back to the 14th or 15th century Italian Renaissance. It presents a typical example of Renaissance black magic.

Diocese: a geographic district under the pastoral care of a specific Bishop in the Catholic Church. The Bishop of a Diocese is sometimes called an "Ordinary."

Dolmen: a megalithic tomb with a large flat stone laid on upright ones, found chiefly in Britain, Hibernia and France.

Dominican Order: formally known as the Order of Preachers, the Dominican Order is a mendicant order of the Catholic Church founded in Toulouse, France, by the Spanish priest Saint Dominic. It was approved by Pope Honorius III via the Papal bull Religiosam vitam on 22 December 1216.

Fortnight: unit of time equal to fourteen calendar days.

Florin: a standard Florentine coin struck from 1252 to 1533 with no significant change in its design or metal content during that time.

Franciscan Order: The Franciscans are a group of related mendicant Christian religious orders, primarily within the Catholic Church. Founded in 1209 by Saint Francis of Assisi, these orders include the Order of Friars Minor, the Order of Saint Clare, and the Third Order of Saint Francis.

Goetia: *The Lesser Key of Solomon*, also known as *Salomonis Regis* or *Lemegeton*, is an anonymous grimoire on demonology. It is divided into five books—the *Ars Goetia, Ars Theurgia-Goetia, Ars Paulina, Ars Almadel*, and *Ars Notoria*.

Grimoire: a grimoire (or "grammar") is a textbook of magic, typically including instructions on how to create magical objects like talismans and amulets, how to perform magical spells, charms and divination, and how to summon or invoke supernatural entities such as angels, spirits, deities and demons.

Gulden: the historical German and Dutch term for gold coin.

Heresy: a belief or theory that is strongly and fundamentally at variance with established beliefs or customs, in particular the accepted beliefs of a church or religious organization such as the Roman Catholic faith. Examples of heretics to the Catholic Church included Cathars, Albigensians, and the Knights Templar.

Holy Father: another name for the Pope.

Holy See: also called the See of Rome, the jurisdiction of the Bishop of Rome, known as the pope, which includes the apostolic episcopal see of the Diocese of Rome with universal ecclesiastical jurisdiction of the worldwide Catholic Church, as well as a sovereign entity of international law, governing the Vatican City.

Indulgence: in the teaching of the Catholic Church, an indulgence is a way to reduce the amount of punishment one has to undergo for sins. A "plenary" indulgence is a complete indulgence for all sins.

Inquisitor: an official in an Inquisition

Inquisition: an organization or program intended to eliminate heresy and other things contrary to the doctrine or teachings of the Catholic faith. Literally, an Inquisitor is one who "searches out" or "inquires."

Jubilee: a special anniversary of an event, especially one celebrating twenty-five or fifty years of a reign or activity.

Malleus Maleficarum: Latin name for *The Hammer of Witches* or *The Witches' Hammer*, the book written by Heinrich Institoris and Jacob Sprenger and published in 1486.

Magistrate: term used in a variety of systems of governments and laws to refer to a civilian officer who administers the law, as opposed to a permanently appointed Judge. In ancient Rome, a magistratus was one of the highest-ranking government officers, and possessed both judicial and executive powers.

Matins: a service forming part of the traditional Divine Office of the Western Christian Church, originally said (or chanted) at or after midnight, but historically often held with lauds on the previous evening.

Notary: a person authorized to perform certain legal formalities, especially to draw up or certify contracts, deeds, and other documents for use in other jurisdictions.

Ordinary: An ordinary (from Latin *ordinarius*) is an officer of a church or civic authority who by reason of office has ordinary power to execute laws. For example, diocesan bishops are ordinaries in the Roman Catholic Church.

Papal Nuncio: An apostolic or papal nuncio is an ecclesiastical diplomat, serving as an envoy or a permanent diplomatic representative of the Holy See to a state or to an international organization.

Portcullis: a heavy vertically closing gate typically found in Medieval fortifications, consisting of a latticed grille made of wood, metal, or a combination of the two, which slides down grooves inset within each jamb of the gateway.

Prior: an ecclesiastical title for a superior, usually lower in rank than an abbot or abbess. Its earlier generic usage referred to any monastic superior. The word is derived from the Latin for "earlier" or "first."

Sacristan: an officer charged with care of the sacristy, the tabernacle, the inner part of a church, and its sacred contents.

Scriptorium: literally "a place for writing" in Latin, is commonly used to refer to a room in medieval European monasteries devoted to the writing, copying and illuminating of manuscripts commonly handled by monastic scribes. Lay scribes and illuminators from outside the monastery also assisted the clerical scribes.

Seminary/Seminarian: a seminary, school of theology, theological seminary, or divinity school is an institution for educating students ("seminarians") in scripture and theology, generally to prepare them for ordination to serve as clergy, in academia, or in Christian ministry.

Sigil: an inscribed or painted symbol considered to have magical power.

Strega/Stregeria: *Stregheria* is a form of Witchcraft with Southern European roots but also includes Italian American witchcraft. *Stregheria* is sometimes referred to as *La Vecchia Religione*. The word *stregheria* is an archaic Italian word for "witchcraft", with the most used and modern Italian word being *stregoneria*. A *strega* is a practitioner of *Stregheria*.

Vespers: a service of evening prayer in the Divine Office of the Western Christian Church (sometimes said earlier in the day).

Bibliography

Behringer, Wolfgang. *Hexen. Glaube, Verfolgung, Vermarktung [Witches. Belief, Persecution, Marketing]* (German). C.H. Beck, 1998.

Bishop, Morris. *The Middle Ages.* Houghton Mifflin Co., 2001.

Broedel, Hans Peter. *The "Malleus Maleficarum" and the Construction of Witchcraft: Theology and Popular Belief.* Manchester University Press, 2003.

Broedel, Hans Peter. "Fifteenth Century Witch Beliefs," in Brian Levack, ed., *The Oxford University Press Handbook of Witchcraft in Early Modern Europe and Colonial America.* Oxford: Oxford University Press, 2013.

Bussagli, Marco, ed. *Rome: Art & Architecture.* Könemann, 1999.

Butler, Alan. *The Knights Templar.* Shelter Harbor Press, 2011.

Cabinet of Catholic Information. Murphy & McCarthy, 1904.

Campbell, Colin D. *Of the Arte Goetia.* Teitan Press, 2015.

Cawthorne, Nigel. *Witch Hunt: History of a Persecution.* Chartwell Books, 2004.

Cosman, Madeleine Pelmer. *Medieval Wordbook: More than 4,000 Terms and Expressions from Medieval Culture.* Fall River Press, 1996.

Danet, Amand. *Le Marteau Des Sorcières [The Hammer of Witches]*. Jérôme Millon, 1993.

D'Orazio, Federica. *Rome Then and Now*. Thunder Bay Press, 2004.

Dell, Christopher. *The Occult, Witchcraft & Magic: An Illustrated History*. Thames & Hudson, 2016.

Farrar, Janet and Stewart. *A Witches' Bible: The Complete Witches' Handbook*. Phoenix Publishing Co., 1984.

Foer, Joshua, Thuras, Dylan & Morton, Ella. *Atlas Obscura: An Explorer's Guide to the World's Hidden Wonders*. Workman Publishing, 2016.

Gies, Frances & Joseph. *Daily Life in Medieval Times*. Harper Collins, 1990.

Hansen, Joseph. *Quellen und Unterschuchungen zur Geschichte des Hexenwahns und der Hexenverfolgung im Mittelalter [Sources and Examinations of the History of Witchmania and the Witchhunts of the Middle Ages]*. Bonn: Carl Georgi Universitats-Buchdruckerei, 1901.

Jones, Prudence and Pennick, Nigel. *A History of Pagan Europe*. Barnes & Noble, 1995.

Kastenbaum, Robert (ed.). *Macmillan Encyclopedia of Death and Dying*, 2002.

Klaasen, Frank. *The Transformations of Magic: Illicit Learned Magic in the Later Middle Ages and Renaissance*. Penn State Press, 2013.

Kors, Alan C. and Peters, Edward. *Witchcraft in Europe 1100-1700: A Documentary History*. Univ. of Pennsylvania Press, 1972.

Institoris, Heinrich and Sprenger, Jacob. *Malleus Maleficarum* ("The Witches' Hammer"), 1486. Translated into English with

Introductions by Rev. Montague Summers, Dover Publications, New York, 1928, 1971 (reprinted).

Kunze, Michael. *Highroad to the Stake: A Tale of Witchcraft.* Univ. of Chicago Press, 1987.

Lea, Henry Charles. *A History of the Inquisition (Vols. I-III).* Harper & Bros., 1888.

Liberati, Anna Maria & Bourbon, Fabio. *Ancient Rome: History of a Civilization that Ruled the World.* Stewart, Tabori & Chang, 1996.

MacKay, Christopher S. *An Unusual Inquisition: Translated Documents from Heinrich Institoris Witch Hunts in Ravensburg and Innsbruck, English & Latin Ed.* Brill, 2020.

MacKay, Christopher S. *The Hammer of Witches: A Complete Translation of the Malleus Maleficarum.* Cambridge Univ. Press, 2009.

Man, John. *Gutenberg: How One Man Remade the World with Words.* MJF Books, 2002.

Mather, Increase. *Remarkable Providences: Illustrative of the Earlier Days of American Colonisation.* Boston, 1684.

McCall, Andrew. *The Medieval Underworld.* Barnes & Noble, 1993.

McGraw-Hill Concise Dictionary of Modern Medicine, 2006.

McGregor Mathers, S. Liddell. *Key of Solomon the King (Clavicula Solomonis).* Samuel Wiser, Inc., 1989.

McGregor Mathers, S. Liddell. *Lesser Key of Solomon the King (Clavicula Solomonis Regis).* Samuel Wiser, Inc., 1955.

McNally, Kenneth. *Standing Stones and Other Monuments of Early Hibernia.* Appletree Press, 1988.

Moriarity, Catherine, ed. *The Voice of the Middle Ages in Personal Letters 1100-1500*. Peter Bedrick Books, 1989.

Mortimer, Ian. *The Time Traveller's Guide to Medieval England: A Handbook for Visitors to the Fourteenth Century*. Random House, 2008.

O'Brien, Jacqueline & Harbison, Peter. *Ancient Hibernia: From Prehistory to the Middle Ages*. Weidenfeld & Nicolson, 1996.

Panati, Charles. *Sacred Origins of Profound Things: The Stories Behind the Rites and Rituals of the World's Religions*. Penguin, 1996.

Pergola, Philippe. *Guide with Reconstructions of Roman Catacombs and the Vatican Necropolis*. Vision, 1989.

Portella, Ivana Della. *Subterranean Rome*. Könemann, 1999.

Poynder, Michael. *Pi in the Sky: A Revelation of the Ancient Celtic Wisdom Tradition*. Collins Press, 1999.

Quetif, Jacques and Jacobus Echard. *Scriptores ordines praedicatorum recensiti*. 1719-1723, reprint 1960 (microfilm).

Rowling, Marjorie. *Life in Medieval Times*. Perigee, 1968.

Russell, Jeffrey Burton. *The Devil: Perceptions of Evil from Antiquity to Primitive Christianity*. Cornell University Press, 1977.

Schmauder, Andreas. *Frühe Hexenverfolgung in Ravensburg und am Bodensee. 2. Auflage (Historische Stadt Ravensburg)* (German) Hardcover – 3 April 2017.

Schnyder, Andre. *Malleus maleficarum von Heinrich Institoris (alias Institoris) unter Mithilfe Jakob Sprengers aufgrund der dämonologischen Tradition zusammengestellt: ... 1487* (Hain 9238) (Litterae) (German Edition) (German) Paperback – January 1, 1993.

Segen, J. *The Dictionary of Modern Medicine*. CRC Press, 1992.

Segl, Peter, ed. *Der Hexenhamer, Entstehung und Umfeld des Malleus maleficarum von 1487 [The Hammer of Witches, Origin and Environment of the Malleus maleficarum of 1487]*. Bayreuth Historical Colloquium. Köln: Böhlau Verlag, 1988.

Segl, Peter. Heinrich Institoris: *Personichkeit und literarisches Werk [Personality and Literary Work]* in Segl, ed., *Der Hexenhammer*.

Simmonet, Nicolas. *Mont-St-Michel*. Bonechi, 2004.

Smith, Moira. "The Flying Phallus and the Laughing Inquisitor: Penis Theft in the 'Malleus Maleficarum.'" *Journal of Folklore Research*, vol. 39, no. 1, 2002, pp. 85–117. JSTOR, www.jstor.org/stable/3814832. Accessed 24 Feb. 2021.

Summers, Montague. *The History of Witchcraft & Demonology*. Castle Books, 1992.

Thurston, Robert W. *Witch, Wicce, Mother Goose: The Rise and Fall of the Witch Hunts in Europe and North America*. Pearson, 2001.

Wilson, Colin. *The Occult: A History*. Barnes & Noble, 1971.

About the Author

Joe Gioconda spent several years as a Catholic seminarian, which preceded his further career development in the secular world. He earned his law degree from the prestigious Yale Law School and is now a trial lawyer. He lives in Newtown Pennsylvania with his wife (a fellow author) and his son Luke and daughter Morgan. This is his first novel.